# SHAR DEA, EMPRESS OF PEACE

a novel by

## Robert Vincent Gerard

Copyright 1986, 1988 by Robert Vincent Gerard
Library of Congress Catalog Card No: 87-71722
ISBN: 916383-40-7

**AEGINA PRESS**
**59 Oak Lane, Spring Valley**
**Huntington, West Virginia 25704**

**Cover by Cindy Schubert**

# Contents

# Acknowledgments

The author thanks the following writers and organizations for their contributions to *Shar Dea, Empress of Peace:*

Beyond War Foundation: Palo Alto, California

Carl Sagan Productions, Inc.: Excerpts from *Cosmos* by Carl Sagan. Copyright 1980 by Carl Sagan Productions, Inc.

Harper and Row Publishers, Inc.: Excerpts from *Think On These Things* by J. Krishnamurti, Copyright 1964 by K&R Foundation, Inc. Reprinted by Permission of Harper and Row, Publishers, Inc.

Masterworks, Inc. Publishers: Excerpts from *Voyage to the New World* by Ramtha and Douglas Mahr. Copyright 1985 by Masterworks, Inc. Publishers. Reprinted by permission of Masterworks, Inc., Publishers.

Partnerships in Peace, Inc.: Quote from Andrea Kay Smith. President. Used by permission of Partnerships in Peace, Inc., Atlanta, Georgia.

*Tulanian Magazine:* Excerpts from "Back to Nature," by Michael Zimmerman. Reprinted with permission from *Tulanian Magazine*, Vol. 56, No. 4, Winter, 1985.

The author would also like to extend his gratefulness to a few individuals who encouraged and guided him with this work: Cliff Biggers, Lynn Haynes, Louise Bruch, Jaqueline LaValle, and of course, his beautiful wife, Anita.

## Dedication

To my wife, Anita, the Empress of Peace in my life,

whose influence and inspiration has brought me to this point.

# INVOCATION

IT WAS NOT TOO LONG AGO THAT A VISION
CAME TO THIS EARTH. NOW WE SEE HIM MANY
TIMES A DAY: NOT TO RECOGNIZE HIS BEAUTY,
BUT TO BE REMINDED ONLY OF HIS PAST.

SO IF OUR MINDS DON'T COME TO AN
AGREEMENT, OUR VISIONS GET BEHIND THE
FUTURE, WHERE IT IS NOT OURS TO DECIDE.
WE KNOW SO LITTLE, YET LEAD OTHERS TO
DESPAIR. ISN'T IT TIME WE STOPPED?

ANOTHER VOICE WILL COME ONCE AGAIN ONLY
TO LEAVE. WHAT MESSAGE SHALL SHE BRING?
IN YOUR HEARTS, FIND SIGHT OF LOVE, AND
IN YOUR SEED, THE CHILDREN OF LOVE. FOR
MAN AND WOMAN MUST FIND UNITY—THAT'S
THE AGREEMENT?

MIRACLES ARE OURS. THEY ARE AT OUR
COMMAND, THOUGH OFFER THEMSELVES ONLY
OUT OF LOVE.

WE SAIL ALONG THE COLORS OF CLOUDS, HELD
CAPTURED IN THE SKY. AND IF BY CHANCE WE
STOP IN THE WONDER OF WHAT IT 'IS', THEN
IT'S OURS TO DESIRE WHAT WE SEE, AND GIVE
IT LOVE.

# PREFACE

*Miracles are made in love. They trans-*
*cend through us in the moment of perfect love.*
*Only then can we see the relationship between*
*the maker and the receiver, the yin and the*
*yang, and become one.*
*—Shar Dea*

The power of the human mind is still not understood. As the civilized individual becomes more knowledgeable and content, the natural powers of his mind become unusable and extinct. Man has permitted himself to seek existence as an objective rather than the dream. He pursues the comforts of earth, and sacrifices the ecstasies of the heavens. Over time, his dreams are exhausted, and he finds himself influenced by the minds of others.

Countless numbers of sages and prophets, and tyrants and warriors have all demonstrated the ability to move the masses, bring hope to the world, or destroy the mind. From the beginning of history's journals, thousands of great leaders have walked the lands. The majority were unfortunately aggressive, self-centered and, simply barbarians. Others were great architects and builders of cities—the poets and philosophers, the scientists and the writers. The reality of the warriors and barbarians was destruction and deterioration of the cultures. The reality of the philosophers and humanists was hope for mankind.

For whatever reason, each and every one of us chooses his or her own destinies. The laws of the universe, whether seen or unseen, spiritual or physical, are consistent and absolute in their fulfillment. In the same sense, the destiny of each civilization is determined by the spawn of its own collective self-consciousness. This is true for civilizations existing on the planet or outside the known universe. The manifestation of the peaceful or the pugnacious character of a civilization is destined by the orientation of its mental self-conscious faculties. The foundations of a civilization stem from the process of individual thought which builds upon:

We are what we think.
We are who we are.
We are here because we chose to be here.
We are a global society which is destined to our own collective ends.

Love is the energy life force of the spiritual universe. It is the blood and source of all mental and physical life. In our Solar System, the Planet Earth functions as the heart—the center for love and emotion. Earth is where all living souls migrate in order to learn and gain experience of the Great Dichotomy. As told by Earth's First Speaker, Ara E Hum:

"On one side it can be seen as well as touched. But on the other, it cannot be seen nor touched. Therefore, believe it 'IS' and never dare to possess 'IT'. Love all now. Don't regret or hold on to the past. Don't fear or hold on to the future. If the children of this planet take advantage of the simple mystery, the miracle of life is unfolded."

Peace and understanding of all humanity could then be realized. However, if the cancer of greed, selfishness, and power over others is kindled and permitted to flourish, then the inevitable deterioration of the Earth's purpose will be realized, and she will be doomed.

It is at these times, when the superior forces of the earth's consciousness evokes voices from within, which serve as warnings to her children. They are the WORDS of peace and hope, and are clearly given over time. However, if not believed, then someday soon, when the hour is no longer, mother earth will once again be cleansed.

Unbeknown to mankind, the laws of the universe had been evoked, and the evolution of life unfolded. It was about twelve thousand years ago, when a great asteroid fell from the heavens. It crashed into the southwest waters of the North Atlantic Ocean. The fireball roared in its own flames and illuminated the surrounding vaporescence, which crystallized in the air. Its appearance captured the breath of every creature who dared to watch its path just moments before the eventful collision with Earth.

The asteroid's impact upon the earth was traumatic. The earth trembled. Momentarily it was shaken off its rotating axis, and it wobbled to and fro. Massive flames rose hundreds of miles into the atmosphere. With majestic reverence and with roars of fierce beasts, gigantic tidal waves, some hundreds of feet in height, spread their wrath across the North and South Atlantic Oceans. They traveled at tremendous speeds, some possibly up to six hundred miles per hour.

The impact of the crashing asteroid was too great for the earth's mantle to bear. Volcanic eruptions and electrical storms began to appear in a state of frenzy all over the world. Earthquakes, with comparable magnitudes as high as twelve on the Richter scale could generate thirty to forty foot waves of rolling land mass, leveled cities and even mountains, and mercilessly consumed most of its creatures, including humans. Then, in its aftermath, the Great Deluge began, and washed the disease and misery from the lands.

Several years later, only a few inhabitants of the world survived. Most of the islands of the North Atlantic seas disappeared, sinking below without warning to the islanders. Along the shores, millions of people had been literally swept away, never to return. These were the killing forces, unleashed by the planet, and sponsored by the Heavens.

The Earth was cleansed, and began anew.

\* \* \*

About ten thousand years later, the universal love for life and hope for humanity had been given another chance. The wisdom of the Heavens delivered yet another miraculous Soul to the children of earth. One of the greatest voices had evolved from this most beautiful planet. In this voice, the petition for peace and hope for humanity was echoed. Over time, the WORD was spoken through the gentleness of a great leader, who led His people to the promised land.

Once again the WORD was brought forward. However, few of the children of earth understood the WORD. Behind this ignorance, the world responded with partiality and disrespect. It had returned to a state of uncleanliness, turmoil, and hopelessness.

The virgin lands of the North American continent were discovered by the Europeans nearly 11,500 years after the dreadful asteroid fell. This discovery should not be looked upon as a coincidence or quirk of fate, but the essence of a miracle bestowed upon mankind in the name of hope. It was, in fact, a fleeting moment in the collective consciousness of the countless multitude of Europeans, who felt the temporal pangs of hope, freedom, and inspiration. Despite its purpose, many Europeans celebrated the arrival of new wealth, power, and expansion.

During these early discoveries, the high cultural order of the native North and South American civilizations was destroyed. Its ancient and mysterious artifacts disappeared, and sacred resources were raped and stripped away. These lands were put aflame and left in ruins. Most of this was masterminded by unprincipled and ruthless European leaders, who were the competitive and cunning patriarchs of new lands. Many of these inhuman barbaric acts were supported under the myopic-minded sanctuary of religious pompous greed. Guised in human causes, they repudiated the very essence and purpose of the most valuable miracle of contemporary times.

One of the greatest sins of modern civilization is the outright neglect of the miracle granted the world—the discovery of the Americas, the last great frontier of hope for mankind.

\* \* \*

Twelve thousand years have passed since mother earth cleansed her body with fire and water. Today, we bear witness to the chaos and pains which resound across the poverty-stricken lands. And in its wretched midst, we are witness to the comfort and selfishness which settle in the lands of hope. Let us be reminded of the forgotten miracle which we still have, and rekindle the hope and bring peace to this planet.

Unless mankind can rectify its selfishness, singlemindedness, and greed, the miracle will be retracted.

This is the process of balance and the essence of karma: the natural phenomena of returning back to the beginning all lessons of life which were abandoned by man or mankind. If humanity does not sow the seeds of hope, peaceful coexistence, and prosperity, then humanity cannot reap or experience these attributes. Instead, mankind will be justifiably destroyed in order that these attributes be recreated and mastered by others.

Time is moving faster and the hour is becoming shorter. Hope is being replaced by permissiveness and the comforts of security. Soon, hope will disappear. If we lose sight of the individual's journey for peace, then we will lose our foundations for life, hope, and love. The basis and purpose of that most sacred miracle which was given to us over five hundred years ago -- the discovery of the Americas will be doomed forever.

There were many great prophets who spoke of purity and love. Their WORDS which were petitioning forgiveness and salvation for mankind have disintegrated. And, instead of peace, have only lead to senseless wars amongst its own kind throughout the world.

Almost without exception, it has been through the words of a male that the voices from God were revealed. MAN differs from WOMAN. He serves the planet from the exterior, while the woman serves from the interior. Man has always been considered the hunter and gatherer; the woman has been considered the bearer and the homemaker. It's the male who plants the seed; it's the female who nurtures the seed. Over time, man has unsuccessfully planted the seed of peace and hope for humanity. This time, however, it will be the WOMAN who will bear the miracle of peace and joy for humanity.

As witnessed, the land of hope is rapidly becoming uncleansed. Mother Planet Earth, as a celestial parent, must therefore fend for herself, within her own consciousness. She will have no choice other than to protect her own destiny. Under the laws of balance of this vast universe, it must be done—whether through love or punishment. She must enact her discipline by expressions of her own nature—on her terms, not ours.

Will the miracle of life subconsciously deteriorate into oblivion? Will it happen again? Is this our fate? In Revelations it says "If you will not awake, I will come like a thief, and you will not know what hour I will come upon you."

\* \* \*

And so it was. From within the depths of the outer universe, the Supernova, Aetaneus, burst into existence. Simultaneously, in the form of a silver and blue light, the last voice of Planet Earth was conceived and the soul of a WOMAN was born. The supreme miracle was given its final earthly destiny.

# CHAPTER 1
# THE MESSAGE

*". . . miracles cannot be taken for granted. Mankind is not the maker of miracles, though he may be the medium or the channel from which miracles arrive . . ."*
—Bene Dea

She could be seen sitting on a gray volcanic rock dressed in white. Her head rested gently in the palm of her hands while her knees supported her arms. Her cotton gown was softly flowing by her sides, yet there was no wind to be seen nor sounds to be heard. There was absolutely no movement or expression radiating from her as she totally immersed herself in contemplation.

A quarter of a million miles away, the living blue planet Earth majestically turned, yielding on its darkest side speckles of brilliant lights, unknown to ancient minds. Above and beyond, 93 million miles in the distant void of space, the Sun pulsated relentlessly. With the mind of a wise old sage and the heart of the true celestial spirit, she looked outwards towards the Mother Planet Heart that we call Earth.

As she looked, she saw all, even into the unseen world. While staring at the blue and white planet she knew of the past, and could experience the present. This time, however, she was looking into the future. As she sat on the barren rock of the moon, she knew of her time and place.

She was a loving soul and mother of an ancient civilization. She traveled far into the future in order to seek an answer to her daughter's destiny. In her heart she was moved by the awareness of how innocent children lose the sacred knowledge of simultaneous time, and inevitably exchange it for fear. Generation after generation, the children of her society were becoming more fearful of the laws of the spirit. She understood well that more sorrow would come than joy.

Her name was Bene Dea, an ancient traveler. Her ability to travel freely, into the future, was seldom used. However, her reasons were justifiable, for the fate of her daughter and mankind rested upon her.

Bene Dea turned her head slightly towards the paternal star, the Earth's Sun. She began to hear the sounds emanating from its surface. These sonic radiations and cosmic vibrations of the Sun

1

foretold the ecological activities of the planet. Knowing this, Bene Dea, was able to interpret them and intuitively complement this information with the collective consciousness of all civilizations on Earth.

She suddenly rose, as she looked angrily towards the blue planet. With a stiffened and erect body, she raised her hands into the dark blackened space, and prayed outwardly into the heavens:

"Ara E Hum, my Lord. I see too much fear on the Mother Planet. She is distraught by her inhabitants—her children. They are wearied about their inability to survive as a global civilization.

Her supreme entity is cognizant of their doubts and fears for survival. She is becoming alarmed as to her own fate, should they falter.

The planet irks with disturbance, tension, and fear. If she interprets these civilizations as hazardous to her celestial body, she will destroy them first. The children of this planet are the essence of her own living consciousness. She seeks not fear, rather, life.

Ara E Hum, my Lord, she grows impatient. I see vast amounts of planetary changes in the horizon.

Is it time for Shar Dea?"

The ancient traveler stood still as she was surrounded by solitude. Under her feet she felt a sense of fright echoing from within the Moon, Mother Earth's only celestial offspring. Above her, she felt tugs from the infinite. These were her only forms of consolation in this space-time continuum of the metaphysical universe. In the wisdom of her mind she recapitulated one of the secrets of life:

". . . how difficult it is for souls to realize the two primal and opposing forces of the spiritual universe. One is the ascending love toward Eternal Peace—*being*. The other is the descending love towards cosmic matter and physical substance—*having*. Both are beautiful and good. Both are infinite in knowledge.

Once the soul takes on human form, it almost invariably seeks the love and comforts of the earth. It eventually loses sight of the heavens which hold the way of peace. The soul's whole purpose is to experience the manifestations of earthly matter, while never losing the visions and dreams of eternal peace.

Why is this, my Lord? Over generations, fears collect in the subconscious minds of the planet's total population. This major distortion plagues civilized MAN. It strengthens MAN's inability to reconcile with depths of HIS subconscious fears. Lord, this is outright spiritual deterioration—a form of hopelessness."

2

Bene Dea penetrated her sights upon the beautiful blue globe. In her astral visions she saw many souls migrating back to the planet. The souls were old and wise, and had suffered many times before. She knew quite well that this massive undertaking, by these souls was done in hope for a new and peaceful civilization. She envisioned humans evolving from this soul migration. They were extraordinary: brighter, highly scientific, extremely adventurous, and most importantly, peace loving. "Who are they? Where did they come from?" she asked, realizing that 'time' was not a dimension of this migration. Most of the souls she saw were mature and knowledgeable. One fact was certain to her: it was happening. And Bene Dea knew it would continue until a new civilization was formed and existed prosperously on the planet.

She saw three levels of souls migrating, most of whom would once again experience the fascination of birth and all the joys associated with that most glorious process.

The more mature souls would readily and lovingly emerge with their soul mates already on the planet. Fewer in number, these more experienced souls would be identified as the positive minded, artistically talented personalities.

The most elite that she saw were the ordained souls, the highest soul mates who were awaiting the moment of Divine Covenant: the agreement between man and woman. These special few would be the speakers and the aspirants of a new peace-loving leadership. Their destinies would be to teach the leaders of the new arrivals and inspire the survivors of the old civilization. For these speakers, their earthly and physical entities would soon end. Then they shall experience the final rapture with Ara E Hum.

Bene Dea's love for the planet and her children was profound. She had traveled clairvoyantly and saw the world's future. She accomplished her mission, and was at rest with her visions and newly gained knowledge. Now she must return to her land and her own physical reality.

Then, as would mist vaporize into the heavens, Bene Dea disappeared.

* * *

It was an early Spring day and the warm breezes of the Gulfstream currents blew gently across the lands of Atlantis. Bene Dea was standing in the gardens of the Atlentium Dea, who was her husband and the Spiritual Pontifex of the Atlanteans. There she saw her children playing and singing near the fountains. Knowing that she must never reveal her astral visions

3

and knowledge to Shar Dea, her daughter, Bene Dea began preparing for her daughter's destiny.

Slowly she walked over to the children. She kindly requested that her son seek his father for play. Then she wrapped her arms around Shar Dea and said, "My little Empress, let's walk together for a while." Cuddled side by side, they walked along the pathway which overlooked the ocean and the ragged cliffs beneath them. They came upon a large flat rock and sat down. The rock was warm from the rays of the sun and offered them comfort.

"My dear child, for our lesson today, I would like to talk to you about miracles! Do you recall what miracles are?"

"Yes, mother. They are gifts from Ara E Hum and are granted only to humans who cannot attain higher laws of nature for themselves," replied the innocent young girl.

"Good," complimented Bene Dea. Then she pointed to a small rock on the other side of the walkway, saying, "Shar Dea, let's see you move that rock with your mind and bring it to our feet."

"Yes, mother." Soon the rock rose about two feet off the ground and began moving towards their feet.

"Now was that a miracle?"

Shar Dea looked up at her mother and moved her head back and forth sideways suggesting a definite "No." "Miracles are not made by man; they are given to him," explained Bene Dea. "The only recipients of miracles are humans. And, when miracles do come, it's because of a joint inner communication between 'ALL THAT EXISTS' and one's total self. It's as if there was a simultaneous and perfectly balanced agreement between them." The little girl questioned her mother with a curious overtone, "Well, what if you don't want them or do not use them, mother?"

"Regardless, miracles cannot be taken for granted. These mysterious events occur many times, in many places, for many reasons. However, mankind is not the maker of miracles, though he may be the medium or the channel from which miracles arrive," informed her mother.

Bene Dea thought that little Shar Dea would better comprehend some of these principles if explained in a short story. "Let me tell you a story about how Ara E Hum granted a miracle to a troubled civilization called, Luroppus. The people of Luroppus had been ruled by evil emperors. Eventually, these people became sad and strickened with poverty. For hundreds of years these people envisioned peace and freedom from these emperors.

"Then, on a cold and dreary night, the beautiful Princess Milorha had a dream. In that dream she envisioned that she left

4

those evil lands and sailed across the sea to a new land. The land was beautiful and peaceful. The empress went back to tell all the people. One day the dream came true. Soon many of the people came to settle on this new land of hope.

"Milorha became the ruler and Empress. The new land was called Amergin. The people were happy and free. They built a great and beautiful city, with gardens, and many fountains. They tilled the ground and produced enough food for all to eat. They prayed and thanked Ara E Hum for his goodness.

"Several hundred years had passed and the people of Amergin became lazy, too relaxed. The older males began to debate and rationalize. They no longer sought work as a form of contribution and discipline. They became dependent on others, especially on the women and younger men, for food and shelter. This created an unbalanced state of existence.

"Eventually, younger men took after the the elder men. This put more strain on the women, and even the children. The stronger and more aggressive males challenged the Empress, and forced Milorha to leave. Things became very unbalanced. Over a period of time, the people of Amergin became just like the people of Luroppus. This was very displeasing to Ara E Hum.

"Things got worse—there was less food and plenty of sorrow. The lands were no longer beautiful and clean. The visions and dreams of the spirit of life were no longer present. Day after day, the lands began to tremble, the soil became more arid, and many building structures crumbled. Annihilation of a once beautiful vision and land was inevitable. Then, on a clear day, the earth shook violently and opened up. Towers of fire came out from under the ground and rose to the sky. The emperor could not stop the planet, and he died with his sword raised up to the sky." Bene Dea paused for effect. "All the people and the land disappeared into the sea."

"But mother," cried out Shar Dea, "What about the Empress Milorha?" Bene Dea looked at her daughter's saddened face, took a deep breath, and said, "Milorha will always live. She left when her dream was erased by the emperors.

"You see my child, what really happened was that the people no longer believed in the Empress's principles of balance and peace. Instead they sought power and the leadership of their aggressive emperors, and started worshipping them. Even worse, the emperors began to worship themselves, instead of Ara E Hum. The people of the land eventually forgot why the miracle was granted them. The purpose of the new land no longer lived in the hearts of the people.

"So the moral of this story is that whenever you forget to thank Ara E Hum for a miracle, the miracle retracts. You're then back where you started from."

5

They began to walk slowly along the well-laid stone pathway. Tears came tumbling down Shar Dea's innocent face. She grabbed her mother around the legs as tight as possible. Bene Dea was taken aback by Shar Dea's actions and knelt beside her troubled daughter. "Why are you crying so deeply my dear little one?" she asked.

Quickly, with a mark of fright in her eyes, Shar Dea looked into her mother's eyes, and said "Can fire come out of the ground and eat me up, too? I'm scared."

A sense of relief hit Bene Dea as she realized that the child's imagination took advantage of her fears. She picked up the frightened child, and assuredly said, "You know that this planet is just as alive as you and me. She listens to Ara E Hum too! We have had many lessons about that before. When the Mother Planet Heart wants to change something on its surface, it does so by quakes, rain, wind, or fire. Those are her ways of expressing her feelings and making the necessary changes. Shar Dea, don't look at the evil in it. It serves her well, and we live here based on her rules, not ours."

Bene Dea kissed Shar Dea and put her down. As she did she felt that the simple message was safely embedded in her memories, in preparation for the future events to come.

# CHAPTER 2
# BIRTH

*"Life exists as a gigantic incomp-
rehensible phenomenon. It does not give life to
you. Instead, you give live to it. You are its
maker—ask the butterfly!"*
—*Shar Dea*

Somewhere on the shores of the South Carolina's coast, not far from the place where the great ancient asteroid fell, the final legacy of a young woman's life finds its beginning. Her purpose is to remind us of our purpose and the world we live in. This is the last transcendence of supreme life for the people of planet Earth.

The night breeze was static and quite stuffy. In the distance, an offshore electrical storm put on a magnificent show. Each flash of its electrical might reflected the glory and power of nature. It's just one of her many ways of keeping balance, expressing her beauty, and reminding mankind that she, the EARTH, was indeed a living organism.

The distant storm grew more intense as it moved ever so slowly towards the coast. The faint sounds of thunder began to dominate the air and brought words of caution to all that heard it. Protected by the wisdom of their senses, birds and neighboring wildlife prepared to shelter themselves from the storm. Along the beaches, lovers and mesmerized storm gazers gathered together, all focusing their sights upon the spectacular color arrangements within the transparent clouds of the approaching storm.

The earth began to occasionally tremble from the might of the thunder. The salty winds grew more turbulent, sweeping with them the static, moist air which was preceding the storm. The voice of the storm became louder and louder. Rods of power escaped from the clouds and into the sea, each lighting up the waters below, as if the gods of the electrical universe pointed their staves to the sea.

Now all began to take shelter, for the might of this awesome storm brought warning to those who challenged its path and its purpose. The moisture in the air grew thicker. Gale winds solidified by the cold and tremendous downpours of rain, captured the coastal areas. Fierce electrical jolts and echoing crashes of thunder penetrated into the veins of every creature and every soul. The storm's conscious purpose brought a cleansing purity to the earth and cleared the way for an event which would not be seen by anyone.

Along the deserted and storm drenched beach staggered a wayward young woman. She was fatigued by her desperate attempt to free her mind from the morbid reality of her life. Lonely, and without cause, she welcomed the fierce storm to aid in her departure. She sought an end to her strife, and cared no more about her life.

Exhausted, disheveled and disillusioned she fell onto the cool wet sand. Her face was distraught and her eyes petrified. Curled up in a fetal position, she awaited the surge of electrocution. The young girl hoped that its quickness would offer freedom in exchange for a point of balance.

The eye of the storm was upon her. Her heart was riddled with fear; she trembled and cried. Her final thoughts were of peace and a place to rest her ailing heart. She needed comfort and love, but that was not for her in this life.

Suddenly there was a deafening crackling sound. Then there was a brilliant white light, within which was a evolving circular silver and blue coil of pulsating light. The young woman was touched. Her eyes were captured by its brilliance. The thrashing thunder echoed throughout her entire body, penetrating deep into her mind and into her soul.

Fatally crippled by the awe of nature, she felt herself drawn into the pulsating coil of light. In her sight she moved upwards, higher and higher, knowing that this was indeed the moment of departure. The young woman realized that it was through her heart that she saw new visions.

Steadily she rose. Her eyes were swept clean by the crisp breezes caressing her face. The echoing sounds of thunder departed only to form an orchestrated melody of hope. Her heart felt joy, and in her mind, she reunited with the life forces of pure thought. She felt her body enlarging and becoming healthier and stronger. She sensed oneness with nature. She was all that she was. And for the first time, she was one with All That Exists.

She began to saunter in her journey into the electrical heavens. As she approached the end of the silver and blue coils of pulsating brilliance she saw an image. Time became still, as the young woman in absolute awe saw her face.

# CHAPTER 3
# AWAKENING

"... the force born of truth and love—'Satyagraha' ..."
—Gandhi

The morning light was approaching as the faint hues of pink and blue broke high above the shadow of the horizon in the sky. The misty morning breeze of fresh salt water air eased itself over the sand where the transient young girl lay. Her body was damp from the moist sand and drenching rain. Slight chills moved throughout her body as the breeze keep its invisible fingers moving over her soft skin. She would soon awake into a new reality, a world of life and peace.

\* \* \*

Long ago, just before the great cataclysm of Atlantis, the Princess Shar Dea mysteriously disappeared from the continent. She was to be the next ruler of the land, the Empress of Peace. At that time, her disappearance was surmised to be the work of the evil-minded emperor, King Lur Atol. He was frightened by his adversary, and petitioned the people to pray for her death. He prophesied that she was so pure and morally prejudiced that she spoke only for the elite, and not on behalf of the common people.

She was never to be heard from or seen by any one, during the era of Atlantis.

Folklore has its roots safely hidden within the minds of the high priests of the islands who spoke of Shar Dea's departure as being of sacred and divine nature. Some priests spoke of Shar Dea as the ruler who would one day return and rid the continent of the evil, the decadence, and war. The continent of Atlantis, to this day, remains a mystery to the world. But, in the hearts of all those souls who carry with them the secrets of this once sacred and God blessed land, there is still the knowledge of hope. The quest is to love and live in peace, as was once a living truth on this great planet of the heart.

\* \* \*

The orange-yellow sunburst broke the Eastern horizon. Its brilliance gave birth to the colors of the day and made the ocean florescent with greens and blues. The radiating sounds transmitted the morning message of renewed life to all that spoke of it. The calm waters of the Atlantic caused not a wave or a ripple on the beach. The sea was quiet. The gentleness of the breeze holding the seagulls and sandpipers over the sleeping young girl was all to be seen.

Then there was movement. Her fingers twitched. A moment later, her head twitched. She was alive! Within a few minutes, her body rallied to signal the local inhabitants of the sand and breeze that she had returned. Her arms and legs stretched out. Her head turned toward the sky and she yawned. The young woman sat up straight. She raised her legs inward and bent her knees toward her chest. She rested her forearms on her knees and continued to enjoy the sunrise. In her mind she remembered her last conversation with her brother, Dah Etro Dea, who was telling her about the magnificent electrical storm that was approaching the island.

The young woman stood up, looked around, and said to herself, "Dah Etro was right! It was a fabulous and most electrifying storm. Such a storm is the creation of Ara E Hum, Our Great Lord, who's shares His nature for all to see."

Her mind was sharp and clear. There was a lot of hard work to be done. She needed to speak to her brother right away. Her quest was to confront King Lur Atol, and bring peace back to the land. This was her birthright and her destiny.

# CHAPTER 4
## TWO WORLDS

*"Satyagraha is not merely resistance to evil. It is the positive action of doing good. . . . Satyagraha is force; if it became universal would revolutionize social ideals, and do away with despotism and . . . militarism . . ."*
—*Gandhi*

The young wayward girl turned around and headed up to the beachfront area. There she stood, on top of the dune, with her torn, shredded clothing draped on her body.

Then the shock of her reality took place. First, she pondered in her mind, "Where is my silk and satin gown?" Then she screamed, "My rubies? My pearls? My Necklace? What has happened to me? Why am I like this?"

Horrified by her losses, she began to run along the beach in desperation. Then she saw something frightening approaching. She immediately jumped into the water and swam out in order to avoid being attacked. There were two strange beasts galloping along the beach. The pounding sounds emanating from the creatures caused her to be terrified. Then, unbelievable to her eyes, she saw children riding on top of these strange long legged giants. As they passed the young frightened observer, she noticed that the children were laughing. She was confused and exasperated.

Cautiously, she walked out of the water and proceeded straight up to the top of the most pronounced dune. There, she saw a road. However, she felt at odds with the way it was constructed. Leaning over, she touched the black surface and inquisitively nodded, saying to herself, "What an unusual type of stone?"

Unfamiliar with its composition, she began to walk along the blackened path, steadily looking down at it as a precautionary tactic. In the distant background, she began to hear a rumbling sound. Moments later, she heard another frightening noise approaching. Not wishing to be seen, she stepped back off the road and squatted behind some seashore bramble. The noise grew intense. What was soon to pass proved awesome to her eyes and most profound to her thoughts. As it passed in front of her she screamed, and became paralyzed by its sound.

11

The driver of the red Mustang saw the freakish stance of the horrified girl and pulled over. He stopped as fast as he could in order to rescue the young woman from her fears. He shut the engine off and jumped out of the car. At first he thought she was being attacked. Or maybe, it was a rattlesnake. He was unaware of his fate in this discovery.

As he approached the panic-stricken lady his thoughts began to wander. From the very first sight of her eyes, the unaware young man found himself totally magnetized by her presence. In a slight, spellbound manner he offered the first words. "Are you okay?"

Initially perplexed by the foreign and hostile loud noises which emanated from the red cart, the young lady regained her composure.

"Are you OK?" repeated the driver.

The young woman instantly interpreted his vocal sounds by comparing them to his mental sounds and images. She had the inherent ability to understand any language spoken by any person or creature.

With a bit of frustration, the handsome driver repeated his question. "Hey lady, are you OK?"

"Yes, I am alright," she said.

Then with a curious gesture and voice Shar Dea said, "I have never heard such horrible and terrifying sounds in my life. They frightened me when I first heard them."

Relieved by the fact that she could speak, he let his survival instincts relax, shrugged his shoulders and said, "Oh. That's just a bad muffler."

The young lady, not knowing what a muffler was, ignored the meaning and commented, "I see that you have a good understanding of the powerful forces of nature and Ara E Hum."

The young man let that statement go right over his head, and responded, "Thanks lady, but that's a Mustang!"

"A Mustang?" she repeated with doubt.

"Where am I?" she said.

"What do you mean, where am I?" he replied. "You're on the beach, not too far away from Charleston."

"Where?"

"Charleston, South Carolina. You know. Right!" he mumbled sarcastically.

With a little bit of annoyance, she said, "I'm not from there."

"Well then, where are you from?" he replied in haste.

"Atlantis!" she exclaimed with pride.

"Oh! Atlanta! I've been there many times, it's a great place. Don't you agree?" he responded awkwardly.

She was very relieved about his positive exclamation of

Atlantis and voiced her approval "Thank the good Ara E Hum. I fear the evil gods of darkness, for the Emperor Lur Atol wishes sole power of our beautiful land, and final death of my everlasting soul." Then she asked the young patriot, "Were you sent to help me?"

"Listen lady, you've got me a little mixed up and confused. Let's get you some dry clothes and some food," he said.

"That sounds fine."

As they began to walk to the Mustang, the new friend of the lost lady found himself more immersed into a mystery that would take him beyond the life which brought him comfort and confidence.

He politely asked, "What's your name?"

"Shar Dea!"

"Shar Dea? That's a beautiful name. Are you in college or in high school?" asked the young man.

"What?"

"Here we go again," annoyingly murmured the young man.

"Where did you go to school in Atlanta?"

"Oh! You mean "Who taught me the great Words of Ara E Hum," replied Shar Dea.

"No, Shar Dea! Where did you learn to read and write?"

"My father, Atlentium Dea, was my great teacher. My mother, Bene Dea, taught me the cultures."

"What do mean by the cultures, Shar Dea?"

"Don't you know? You told me that you lived in Atlantis, so you should know about all these things. Why do you ask me silly questions? Isn't it time we go to . . . ." She paused.

Reality struck the young woman for the first time. Something peculiar had taken place in her life and she had just grasped the fact that maybe she needed to find some precise answers as to what had happened to her.

In an investigative manner, she began a probing conversation. "We speak the same tongue, yet your words are so detailed. They prohibit the telepathic mind from exchanging accurate meanings of truth between us. Your language attempts to make sense, but it loses its meaning in the end. Where I went to school tells you nothing in regards to where I am going. Shouldn't that be of your first concerns? Am I of good or of evil? Do I seek peace and love or do I seek to destroy in order to rid me of my fears? Are my powers of the heart worthy of my parents' love for me? Do I live to further life or terminate it?"

She momentarily came to a halt. Then she asked the young man "Who are you and why did you come to me?"

The young man was petrified. He was silent only because he could not comprehend Shar Dea's motives. In his thoughts he pondered "Did she escape from the local insane asylum . . . or, is she just acting out the character in some play she's been studying for?"

Shar Dea spoke out with confidence. "Who are you? Please offer me your parents name."

"Michael!"

"There's no such family in Atlantis with the name of Michael!"

"What's this crap about Atlantis?" The young man loudly exclaimed.

Immediately Shar Dea turned to the young man, looked through his eyes and paralyzed his thoughts. He stood next to her helplessly. She looked about to find some familiar sights, but to no avail. Shar Dea ran back down towards the beach to see if she could find the castle of her family, but it was not to be found. She knew exactly where it was located, but her senses could not register its existence. Shar Dea grew frightened once again.

She felt hopeless and truly lost, a feeling she had never experienced before this day. In the land of Atlantis, she was heir to the throne, and soon to be Empress of the people. She slowly walked toward Michael and with an inner sense of wisdom she said to him, "Open your eyes young man. We need to speak of life, . . . of time, . . . of place."

# CHAPTER 5

# FRIENDSHIP

*"You are what you are. I respect you for*
*what you are. If you don't know who you are,*
*that's your problem, but I care."*
—Shar Dea

"Michael? What does Michael mean?"

"That's my first name. My full name is Michael McClure. So my family name is McClure. My great great grandparents came from Ireland."

She interrupted and questioned him "What's Ireland?"

"Ireland is an island about four thousand miles across the North Atlantic Ocean," explained Michael.

"Are these the waters which you call Atlantic," asked Shar Dea.

"Yes they are."

Shar Dea informed Michael of a little tidbit of history. "Did you know that these great waters of earth were named after my father's family?

"No."

Nodding her head she said knowingly, "I guess the name remains. At least I know I'm on the right planet."

"Michael, does a strange land lie thirty sunsets away from these shores?"

"Do you mean thirty days traveling time by boat, or by plane?"

The word 'plane' caught her thoughts and quickly halted her mental process. She puckered her lips and then said, "A boat I understand, but what's a plane?

"You mean you don't know what a plane is?"

"Correct."

"Ah! It's a flying machine. And, it makes a lot of noise," he replied jubilantly.

"I think I understand. Does it take thirty days to travel also?"

"Only several hours or so."

She was still not clear as to what in fact constituted the meaning of a plane, but was more concerned about the lands to the West. "My father told me that should the Great Ara E Hum make the heavens fall with fire, then we must journey into the

15

sunset thirty times and settle on the new lands, the land of new hope."

"Europe? Africa? They are both across the ocean. However, that's to the East. Which one?"

"There are two promised lands?" she replied.

"Don't worry. They are not what you would call the 'Land of Hope' anyway," explained Michael.

"But they are there."

"Yea, they are there, but get your directions straight, Shar Dea. There isn't any ocean to our West, just land."

Shar Dea was confused. She took a deep breath and said, "Ara E Hum walked on the Mother Planet Heart a thousands of years before my journey to the planet. He brought us all a beautiful vision. Slowly, empress after empress, emperor after emperor, did our ability to retain the vision diminish. According to Atlentium Dea, Ara E Hum has little tolerance, and will soon cleanse the lands and the waters of fear and shame."

Michael interrupted her, and said, "I'm sorry Shar Dea, there's no such land."

Hum, Michael said to himself. I think this time I've got to take the initiative, and get this little lost girl back to some form of reality. "Come on!" he said. "Let me take you to my beach house. We've got a lot to straighten out and catch up on."

She gave him a cold stare. Deep within her heart she trembled with confusion and lost pride. Something was missing or interfering with her pursuit to rid Atlantis from the evil emperor, Lur Atol. But she sensed that Michael was of good heart, and accepted his offerings of comfort and shelter.

16

# CHAPTER 6
# HOME BY THE SEA

*"A new consciousness is developing which recognizes that we are one species. Our loyalties are to the species and the planet. Our obligation to survive is owed not just to ourselves, but also to that cosmos, ancient and vast, from which we spring."*
—*Carl Sagan*

The ride along the coastal parkway was an adventure for Shar Dea. Never in her physical state did she move so swiftly in any form of vehicle. Within a short time she grew accustomed to the speed and the noisy sounds. Each turn further convinced Shar Dea to trust in the driver's ability to handle such a newfangled creature. Michael was becoming her new friend and guide.

The markings and symbolisms of a different kind of civilization were registered along the roadsides. At one point, Shar Dea assumed that the people on the billboards were captured in stillness because of some wrong deed. "Michael," she asked, "why do they smile in such an imprisoned state?"

"Shar Dea! that's a picture. It's not real. See, here comes another sign advertising about the city Charleston."

"Michael, by the word 'picture' do you mean image?"

"Yes, you pick up things fast, don't you."

"Reading your mind helps, too," she muttered.

Soon they neared the outskirts of the quaint historic southern city. A Chamber of Commerce welcome sign read "Enjoy Charleston's historic seaport. . . ."

"How far back into the past do you mean by historic? A million years?"

"No, no little lady. A million years is considered prehistoric. That's when the earth was full of dinosaurs and maybe a few cave men. Historic to Charleston is about four hundred years ago."

"That's nothing in my lifetime. You mean that people don't live a couple of hundred years or so?"

"What? How old are you Shar Dea?"

"Six hundred and sixty five moons, including the blue moons which appear in honor of the Child God of the Sky."

"What was that mathematical gibberish?" grumbled Michael.

17

"Michael, all it means is that I am fifty five years of physical earthly life."

"Physical earthly life! Oh boy! Can't you just say that you're fifty five years old?

"Feathers! I am not old!"

Shar Dea showed signs of frustration when he teased her about her age. In defense of her vanity, she took a good chestful of air and said "See! Look at my breasts, my hair, my teeth, my thighs, my voice, my eyes. In my land, Atlantis, I will come upon the Great Separation when I celebrate the day of the seven hundred and twentieth full moon."

"Need I ask? What's the Great Separation?"

"It's the moment when my soul transcends my Embryotic Spirit and unites with my Physical Spirit.

"The Great Separation, the Embryotic Spirit, how tacky. How about the Great Gildersleave?" grunted Michael.

"Sometimes, my friend, you are a fool. The Great Separation is when a boy becomes a Godsend, and a girl becomes the Chalice of life. The Embryotic Spirit is the Child Spirit from which we descend from the God of the Sky, Ara E Hum. This is done in order to journey where we choose and to learn about our part in the ALL THAT EXISTS."

In order to regain some sense of self-esteem, Michael asked, "What about . . . ?"

Shar Dea instantly replied, "The Physical Spirit is but one of thousands of which we are a part and seek to understand. We must be prepared to leave the physical plane without hesitation, and we must never forget our destiny, as so many of us do."

The ride and the exhausting conversations placed a heavy burden on Shar Dea. As they approach Michael's beach house, Michael noticed that Shar Dea had slipped down in the comfortable bucket seat and had fallen fast asleep. Michael turned the motor off and sighed in relief. The view of the ocean was just beyond the windshield. He began to contemplate. "Here I am with a beautiful stranger who appears to be from a distant civilized land. I'm sitting next to someone who claims that she is preparing to overthrow the villain emperor of her deteriorating and troubled promised land. She is definitely beautiful, but who is she?"

While looking out across the ocean, he captured all the illuminating sparkles reflecting off its surface. He felt mesmerized by this scene and felt a strong urge to protect this mysterious woman, who considered herself to be a child of heart. He thought, "Suppose she is for real. Maybe she is an empress from a lost land, misplaced by a freak black hole time warp screw-up. Is she magical? Or, maybe she's a witch looking to roast a young naive boy."

Michael was a little scared.

"Why me, Lord? Why me? What did I do to get this two time zoned beauty in my car?" lamented Michael.

He opened the sports car door slowly. Bending over, he gently positioned his hands under Shar Dea's knees and behind her back. As he lifted her up, he was surprised by her very light weight. At first, he thought she was at least 110 pounds, but at most she could not have weighed more than seventy pounds.

Michael held Shar Dea comfortably in his arms. She was deeply asleep, totally limp, and radiating the most gentle and delicate air of love and kindness. Each step towards the beach house with this bundle of mystery in his arms brought Michael's thoughts into a frenzy of changes. His first thought was of making love to her. Her body was a work of art. But then he was thinking that he could easily fall in love with this stranger. Jumping to conclusions, he now thought that if he did make love to her, he might possibly get electrocuted or something. One moment she was the greatest lady to ever enter his life, the next moment he was downright scared of her.

Using his foot Michael pushed opened the guest bedroom door. The bed was surrounded by an arrangement of exotic Chinese ming trees. All the light needed to guide a pretentious bull into the sacred cow was provided by the elaborate thirty foot bay window which overlooked the ocean front. This was one of Michael's architectural innovations designed to impress and arouse the fantasies of his lovers.

With a gentle macho consideration, Shar Dea was given title to the spacious bed, without consent. Her rest would last until dawn of the next day. Michael demonstrated his concern for her comfort by checking on his new princess religiously every half hour. Throughout the night he found himself a nervous wreck. He mixed coffee with scotch, and even milk with sugar substitute, which proved sickening to his stomach. Michael's everyday survival patterns were out of synch.

Awakening in the guest room of Michael's beachfront hidden paradise, the eyes of the distant traveler slowly readied for the sunrise. Outside, the sky displayed its first might. Its powers echoed into the dreams of Shar Dea's changing consciousness, and the sounds of a new day arrived. The rising mind is partially dependent on the scroll of the wind, as if already known, but not just quite understood.

Shar Dea slowly opened her eyes and focused on the ceiling, which was mistaken for snow. She then caught a glimpse of the sky's blue and pinkish tint. Affixing herself in this reality, Shar Dea came to her senses, though still somewhat bewildered by her place in the space-time continuum.

Shar Dea was slightly off kilter. She tried to figure out why she felt so apprehensive and thought maybe my spirit is diffused? then hesitated, maybe I am . . . feathers! I'm lost!

As she walked about the bedroom, her big blue eyes caught sight of herself in the corner chestnut framed mirror. Shar Dea captured a quick glimpse of her attitude. She stepped back a few inches and pondered, tilted her head and looked closely into the mirror. Staring seriously into her face she saw someone new.

Curious and intrigued by this face, she focused on it. Her lips began to quiver and she saw how it looked. Her face became taut and she saw how it looked. Then her face became serene and she saw how it looked. She realized that the only force in her life that could change her was herself. Shar Dea moved very close to the mirror, about six inches from the surface, far enough away not to cloud it up with her own breath. Very intensely she focused on her lips. Then she slowly lifted her eyes upward from her lips to her eyes. Her face changed once again. She looked deeper and deeper into her eyes. Which one am I? she cried inwardly. She rapidly shut her eyes and felt her heart palpitating. She took a deep breath, opened her eyes and focused into the mirror, concentrating on the mystic blues of her eyes. It was then that she was able to capture a moment in time, and communicate with her other self: her inner being, her aspect soul.

Knowing two entities, but one communicant of one's self is a tremendous achievement. It is a sensation restricted to only those few who are willing to sojourn a step beyond themselves in order to feel part of their own completeness. Her mind began to race. She fantasized on one thought and pitied herself on the next thought. Tension mounted and anxiety surged as she entered into a state of limbo. Shar Dea plopped herself onto the side of her bed. Instantly, the waterbed returned a complementary thrust of force upwards and jolted her back to her senses. Within a few seconds the wavy motion of the waterbed ceased and Shar Dea felt more relaxed.

Shar Dea needed to regain some control. She desired insight as to her situation. With her hands lying on her lap, palms facing upwards, she entered into a meditative mode and sought wholeness. After five minutes of prayer and mental stillness, she subconsciously uttered, Ara E Hum, my Lord, where are my roots? Why am I here?

Unknown to her eyes, the room began to glow white. Brighter and brighter it became. She heard a faint but definite sound, somewhat similar to an electric crackle. Inwardly, she saw a silver and blue light pulsating slowly towards her and she began to concentrate on its movements. She felt her body getting warmer and dryer. Then it began to feel weightless. Out of the light she heard the sounds of the wind and felt herself moving into the silver and blue spiraling light. Then all sensations stopped. All bodily senses disappeared. All sounds, all visions, all movements were gone and nonexistent. Her mind became silent as thoughts no longer arrived. She was traveling somewhere in the space-time continuum and was mystical.

It was then, while in this absolute state of awe, she heard a voice, which surrounded her entire being, and said:

"You are the last Messenger—an Empress.
You are the new WORD.
No one will follow you.
You are a reflection of time, but not of time.
Give steadfastly through love and truth.
You are finally that of a woman.

You are here to tell mankind that the Earth is alive!
They must seek peace!
Time has returned to you for only a star moment.
Sleep and find the chord of your existence.
Awake into your new reality."

# CHAPTER 7
## TWO DREAMS

*"Not by might, but by love and the power of love can you survive. It's the only truth that you need to know."*
—*Amerii Kai*

It was close to 4:00 P.M. that same afternoon. Michael was downstairs in the living room reading a book about the ascent of man. He wanted to find out more about ancient civilizations. About the only thing that made sense from his research came from Plato's famous "Republic." Michael, however, couldn't decipher whether Plato's great works were a myth or a historical reality.

He heard the taps of light footsteps and moved his eyes upwards over the edge of the book. He saw that his new friend was coming down to visit.

"Hi there, young lady. Are you feeling better?" he asked.

"Yes, thank you."

"Would you like something to drink or maybe something to eat?" Michael offered hospitably.

"Something hot to drink would be nice."

"How about some hot tea?"

"What is tea?"

"It's little dried leaves which came from plants. Some are spicy and aromatic."

"That sounds good. I'll try it," said Shar Dea.

Michael made her some spicy apple cinnamon herbal tea. He served it with some good old fashion Lorna Doone cookies. They sat together and spoke about Michael's beach house.

"Actually," said Michael, "my father and mother had built this house in the early thirties. Then, in the fifties, they actually moved it by boat from Cape Cod, Massachusetts."

"Move a house by boat? That takes a lot of love."

"I actually consider this beach house to be part of my family. Many of the artifacts and fine reading materials left in the library were my Dad's. They offer me a great amount of sentimental value."

"What do you mean by 'dads'?"

Michael chuckled a bit, and said, "That's a more relaxed way of saying 'father'."

Shar Dea grew very interested in Michael's family history.

22

"Your parents must have been a great couple."

"Yea, you got that right. They were journalists in Boston. They were enthusiasts of nature, connoisseurs of history, and wrote obsessively about mankind's struggles with survival."

"Well, I'm proud to know that you come from good minds. I see it in your eyes and feel it within your heart."

They spent a few hours talking about his family life and his dreams of tomorrow. Shar Dea was well versed on the subject of dreams and their possible meanings. That interested Michael because he had been having a rough time sleeping at night, primarily because of too many dreams. The deep conversations made Shar Dea sleepy. She excused herself so that she could take a nap. Michael carefully watched her go upstairs and into the bedroom.

She stretched herself out on the bed and took a few deep breaths to help ease her way into a good sleep. On each side of her head, she placed a fluffy pillow. She then slid her hands underneath each pillow to make her feel secure with her environment.

Sparked by the conversations with Michael concerning dream states, Shar Dea's mind embarked on an adventure of taking on two dreams simultaneously. The first one took her back to the time she lived in Atlantis. She saw herself walking through the gardens of her father's castle which overlooked the palisades on the western shores of the continent.

Her father, Atlentium Dea, was about to join her. In so doing they would discuss the teachings which he had prepared for that day. It was their custom to learn lessons of life while walking in the corridors of nature. Atlentium Dea only spoke of spiritual and natural realities. The words were not written, for it was believed and practiced that all good knowledge must be remembered and forever seeded within the minds of those who sought oneness with ALL THAT EXISTS. Except for the various forms of art drawings, written language was nonexistent. Communication was translated verbally and telepathically. To the inhabitants of the continent, each person spoke in the present tense with their deepest emotions, in accordance with their minds.

Atlentium Dea's message for Shar Dea concerned a mystic traveler, Amerii Kai, who mysteriously arrived on the island continent from the Eastern Sea. He departed two years later, to the day, at precisely noon, on a small sailboat that he personally hand crafted. Atlentium Dea, pointed to area where this traveler left land and was never to be seen nor heard of again. His fingers pointed only a short distance away, adjacent to where his castle stood.

"Shar Dea," said Atlentium Dea, "Amerii Kai spoke to

all—no matter who they might be. He spoke 'eye-to-eye' with the high priest and young men, but gently to the woman and the children. Amerii Kai kept within his heart many secrets of wisdom, and offered many words on love and on warning. Of love he said, "Love's beginning comes from within our hearts. It does not come from above. Love is our birthright, and our greatest power. When people gather in love so do their surroundings. The more the love, the greater the power and the longer we live to see our childrens' children live." On the other hand, he said, "with no love, the less our power to keep our lands free from war."

"Oh, Shar Dea," said her father, "Amerii Kai never slept. He was totally occupied with people. He was always talking and reminding our brethren of their forgotten purpose and destiny. He came here to tell the people of this land: 'Not by might, but by love and power of love can you survive. It's the only truth that you need to know. It's the greatest power in the entire universe, yet least known'."

Shar Dea's reaction at this point was joyfully expressed when she said, "So Amerii Kai was a visiting God?"

Atlentium Dea cheered her response, but gestured that she was close, though, incorrect. Then he said to her: "He was a Speaker."

"That's like a God, Father, but . . . doesn't he see 'eye-to-eye' to whomever he speaks," commented Shar Dea.

"Better!" he commented. "Generally, a Speaker brings forth critically important WORDS of wisdom to a civilization. From these WORDS, people must decipher the importance of the meaning, and act upon it."

"And if they don't!" Shar Dea retorted.

"Well . . . the laws of nature decide your destiny," declared Atlentium Dea.

"Nature isn't evil, father!" exclaimed Shar Dea.

"My dear daughter, let me explain," said Atlentium Dea. "LIFE and NATURE are ONE. They are in perfect balance with each other. LIFE is the consciousness of NATURE, and NATURE is the BODY of LIFE. The entire Universe is built on this principle. Therefore, mankind and the nature which supports them are all one and the same."

Shar Dea was slightly confused and said to her father, "So what does all that have to do with the Speakers?"

"Aha! My dear one, that's the issue you are pursuing. Consider the Speaker a form of a miracle, sent personally by Ara E Hum to remind all of humanity of the relationship between LIFE and NATURE."

"So father, what is the message?" demanded Shar Dea.

"All creatures operate in perfect harmony with the laws of

NATURE. Mankind has one option, the freedom of CHOICE. That is what separates humanity from the rest of nature. Should humanity evolve into a state of existence which brings harm to the Planet's Balance of NATURE, then LIFE is threatened. LIFE, Shar Dea, IS ABSOLUTELY EVERYWHERE.

It cannot be destroyed because humanity has chosen wrong," lamented Atlentium Dea.

"So Speakers are aspect Gods, and we are here to learn how to create LIFE, not destroy it," commented Shar Dea.

"True," said Atlentium Dea. "Nature does not destroy itself, unless for good. That's the cycle of life we must appreciate and learn to accept.

"I'm beginning to understand, father."

"Remember, Shar Dea," he said, "only man interferes with this law, sometimes to the point where the Planet Earth assumes the responsibility to rid itself of an infectious society."

The tall, serene master of thought smiled at Shar Dea, and in his heart he said to her, "I feel your love ever so deeply within me." He gently began to fade away into her inner visions, until there was calm.

Then Shar Dea's mind began racing away. The scenario was changing rapidly. White whirlwinds were clamoring and making horrible sounds. She began to hear echoing within her head. She twisted and turned. Then there was complete blackness—total silence. She did not know where she was.

Slowly a bright light engulfed her. Then she saw the rich blue sky above open wide with puffs of clouds playfully dancing about. She was on her back, relaxed and feeling totally supported by the earth. She was in euphoria. Under her was a lifting force of security, pushing her higher and higher into the beautiful sky.

Suddenly, a man in a dark blue uniform, wearing a black brim patent leather hat, peeked into her vision. His face was angered and showed disgust and disrespect. In his eyes were screams of another person, his nose rough from the weather: bleached white and red. His untidy beard showed signs of careless grooming, and frustrated mannerisms. His hat was trimed with meaningless ornaments and was frightening to her. Above all, his voice was harsh and cruel.

Shar Dea's heart was shattered by his thoughts. The euphoric mysteries of the sky were rudely interrupted by his pitiful looks.

"Ok you poor thing, get your stupid ass up . . . drugged out again . . . Ugh! . . . Well this time you're finished." He dragged her painfully to her feet. With a smile and a tear she turned her numb head only to see hundreds of unconcerned city dwellers mocking her and whispering vulgarisms about her as they passed by. Shocked, hurting from the policeman's clawing hands, and overwrought by paranoia, she fell to her side. Her eyes closed and her spirit abandoned her.

Shar Dea's mind was racing. Then there was silence. When she woke up, she found herself strapped in a hospital bed. She couldn't move. The emergency ward was cold and noisy. It seemed as if everyone in the world was talking about her. The door swung opened and a short, fat nurse came up to her. She looked down at Shar Dea and took her pulse. The nurse nodded and said, "Listen Miss. In a couple of days you'll be out of here. Most likely back in the streets."

The nurse bent over and felt maternal as she cared for her patient. As she put her hands on Shar Dea's forehead, she said, "Sherrie! If I can be of any help to . . ."

Shar Dea immediately interjected, and said, "Who did you call me?"

The nurse was taken by her mental strength and ability to speak so clearly. She replied "Sherrie, Sherrie Dailey. That's what your I.D. states."

Then it all came out, Shar Dea realized that she was in the body of someone else. But whose body? In her dream state she sensed being the personality of a wayward girl, who desperately sought freedom in the euphoric high of heroin. Her name was Sherrie Dailey. She was twenty-three, homeless, parentless, loveless, and obviously penniless.

Shar Dea's dream was a reality in another space-time continuum. All that she saw in her dreams existed in the dimension of Sherrie Dailey. Shar Dea's eyes saw Sherrie running away along a beach. Sherrie was at arms reach, directly in front of Shar Dea, and was crying aloud, hysterically as she ran. Her dirty tangled hair was flowing in the wind behind her. Shar Dea screamed: "Sherrie! Stop! Please stop! I can help you!" But she didn't. Shar Dea tried to grab her, but couldn't quite catch up to her. Sherrie kept on running faster and was pulling away from Shar Dea. As she did, she was yelling the words "Kill me God! Kill me now! Please kill me!" Shar Dea felt that she had to touch Sherrie or else Sherrie's soul would die. Shar Dea felt tremendous pain and guilt. She was unsuccessful, and was losing Sherrie. In desperation, Shar Dea began to scream hysterically. Her dreams converged back and forth from one ancient scene in her father's garden to the horrid cries of a woman lost in a lost world. Louder and louder she screamed.

"Shar Dea! Shar Dea!" cried out Michael, as he came running into the guest room. He quickly embraced her with his might and his love. She was shivering, in a cold sweat, crying and moaning. She sobbed for five minutes before letting go of Michael's compassionate embrace.

"I'm frightened, Michael, I'm frightened."

# CHAPTER 8
## AURORA BOREALIS

*"I now see peace and friendship in you. Is*
*your God mine, too? Are we becoming one?"*
*—Shar Dea*

The sun was out of the east about shoulder high off the horizon and rising in the sky. The sea was calm and chilled enough to remind you of its awesome power and hidden treasures of the past. The distant melodies of the ocean chanted in the background. Along a stretch of the shore near the beach house, Michael and Shar Dea walked side by side and spoke about the nature of things.

"Michael, do you believe that every tree has a shadow?" asked Shar Dea.

"Sure! Why not?" he replied sarcastically.

"Be serious, Michael."

"Well then, ask me a serious question next time," said Michael jokingly.

"Ok. Is the origin of the planet Earth well documented?"

Michael's face lit up, as he said, "Now that's a probing question."

"But don't answer it!" Shar Dea immediately insisted.

"Ugh?"

"Try this one instead," she humorously pleaded as she walked backwards in front of him. "Where are the supreme laws of nature and the history of the evolutionary process documented?"

Michael hesitated for a moment, and replied, "At the library: in the Science and Philosophy departments."

Shar Dea crossed examined him with, "Then we could find out about the great city of Aquilo, who's founder was the Great Protector of the Constellation Aquila?"

"Aquilo? I never heard of such a city. What country is it in?"

"That's the city were I grew up as a child."

Michael caught his breath as he said, "You mean in Atlantis?"

"Precisely. I want to know were I can read about its history and destiny," commented Shar Dea.

"You're joking me," laughed Michael. "Atlantis is a myth to

most intelligent people."

Shar Dea's face was saddened at what she had just heard. With reluctance, she asked, "If I heard you correctly, Michael, what you are saying is that the beautiful lands and civilization of Atlantis are not part of your history or heritage?"

Michael now looked at her with total remorse as if he committed a crime. His expression revealed guilt and neglect. Then he said, "That's the truth, my friend."

Shar Dea's heart fell. Her cheeks flattened, her shoulders drooped and she felt dejected. Michael sensed a need for acceptance coming from Shar Dea. He quickly caught up to her, embraced her tightly, and said, "I believe you."

As they walked along the beach, splashing their feet childishly in the water, Shar Dea became more relaxed. Somehow, Michael transmitted a comforting and secure feeling to Shar Dea, and this made her feel grateful and closer to him.

Michael took the palm of her hands and made an interesting comment. "Shar Dea," he said, "are these beautiful hands really ancient?"

Shar Dea stopped moving, turned face-to-face towards Michael, and gently kissed him. As soon as she released her soft lips from his, she looked into his big blue eyes, and said, "And so are these lips."

Naturally Michael's knees buckled, his heartbeat zoomed, and his macho mind went astray. However, in Shar Dea's mind, she knew that Michael was growing closer to her by the second. Furthermore, she knew that they both needed to do a lot of homework and find out what was really happening to them. She thought about her presence in the 'here and now' as a possibility of a space-time continuum mishap. Or, maybe it was a lesson to be learned about her destiny. As far as Michael was concerned, she had no idea of his purpose or involvement.

"Michael," she commented, "do you believe that the heritage of plants and animals is forever unfolding?"

"Sure."

"Do you believe that the history of mankind and societies is also unfolding?"

"Sure."

"Michael, then is it permissible to say that the laws of nature provide answers to the mysteries of life?"

Michael didn't listen to her last question, but instead prepared a question for her. "That depends," he said, "on how many times in one given moment a man, such as I, is taken in awe by your sweet kisses."

Shar Dea realized that her new companion was not interested in historical explanations of life and responded favorably to him saying, "In just two short days Michael, you have grown very dear to me. I feel your heart to be humble and caring. Sometimes, though I feel your body is thirsting for romance."

"Well," he humbly admitted.

"It's true, Michael. You have desired me several times since we met. Some day soon I'll experience you—that is, if you don't mind."

"Well, not really."

Michael was flabbergasted by Shar Dea's candidness. His sexual attraction for Shar Dea was quite obvious and uncontrollable.

"Shar Dea, do you feel attracted towards me like I am towards you?"

"Michael, are you hinting to the idea that we have children, and become one forever in this physical plane?"

"Yow! Ah I'm not quite ready for that, at least not now," he exclaimed.

"Good, for a moment I thought you wanted to use my feminine body to satisfy your phallic gratification."

"Wait just a moment, Shar Dea! Where do you get off being so protective and defensive after coaxing me to getting it on with you?"

"Getting it on what, Michael?" she innocently questioned.

"Shar Dea you're driving me bananas!"

"Feathers, to you Michael!" she shouted out angrily.

Shar Dea started to run ahead of Michael.

Michael felt stupid for upsetting Shar Dea. "Hey, wait a minute. I'm sorry! Stop!"

She kept on running and he followed her as best as he could. Just as he got close enough to grab her, she sped up. He turned on his masculine pride and mentally said, I'll show that little half-pint who's faster.

Unfortunately for Michael, she read his mind instantly. Her pace quickened. Soon, her angelic body exerted itself beyond his imagination and easily set a new four minute mile record. Needless to say, Mr. Macho's stance suffered its second major defeat. Within a few minutes, her barely clothed body was out of his sight.

Michael's eyes were searching for his companion. Then he spotted her sitting on top of a large rock by the water. The waves were splashing and beating on the giant rock's sides, spraying mist into the air, causing faint rainbows to flicker in and out.

Shar Dea knew of his presence and of his mind, but did not turn to greet him. Mad and confused about the way Michael thought and spoke, she sought relief and comfort in the sounds of the sea. She knew him as a friend, but was not ready for him as a lover. It was not her time to share the Sacred Chalice, of which her mother, Bene Dea, often spoke.

He put his hands on her shoulder. Leaning over, he gently kissed her cheek, and said lovingly to her, "For whatever reason you came to me, God only knows, but I'll serve and protect you forever, as long as I shall live."

Responding to Michael's touch, Shar Dea placed her hands over his. Then she slowly turned until her eyes captured his, and said, "I now see peace and friendship in you. Is your God mine, too? Are we becoming one?"

This was truly the first time that Michael's soul revealed its identity to Shar Dea. Their first communication was solidified. The constructs of eternal bonding and friendship were again present between these two children of Life.

Tears were in her eyes. The waters and mist of the sea cleansed the air surrounding the giant rock which supported the reunited friends. Silence ushered itself in and the sea could not be heard and the breeze became still. There was a mystical void surrounding these two souls. And then, a voice entered into their minds. It was spiritually intimate in meaning and said:

"Look up into the auras that surround you,
read and learn from them in quickened spirit.
Tell the people of the world what the auras
foretell. Tell them what they must do, for
this is the very last time they shall inherit
the earth."

The breeze and the sounds of the sea returned, and the stillness that begot them dispersed.

Shar Dea and Michael sat quietly on the rock for several minutes. Then Shar Dea said, "Michael, since yesterday morning, I've heard that same voice speak to me. Each time it becomes more meaningful and persuasive."

"What did the voice mean by 'Look up into the auras?'" asked Michael.

"My father, Atlentium Dea, used to speak of the electromagnetic fields that surround the earth. Just as each of us has an aura, so does the earth. As a matter of fact, every existing animal, plant, rock, planet, and galaxy has an aura. Knowing and reading auras is the way a higher order soul interprets the composition and personality of an entity. To bring it down to meaningful terms, our own subconscious minds read auras all of the time, offering us information about others as to whether we should be cautious or accepting."

The sun was at high noon, as Shar Dea and Michael continued their long walk on the beach. As time passed, Shar Dea became the dominant member of the newly formed duo.

Michael's temperament had relaxed, but his curiosity quickened. He began to ask many questions, as does a child when probing for answers about Life's many mysteries. The bombardment of questions shattered Shar Dea's ears. Nonetheless, there was a balance between the teacher and the student. In return, Michael, through his questioning served to provoke new thoughts and compassionate wisdom in Shar Dea.

"How much do you know about auras?"

"I was trained as a child how to read auras. There are many different levels and colors in the aura. Generally, red indicates anger, extreme heat, and often disease, while white informs us of compassion and love, coolness, cleanliness and purity."

"Ok, so they're color coded, but what really are they made of?"

"It all boils down to this, Michael. The universe is composed of electro-chemical energy. Their density, color, and sound are determined by the electro-chemical frequency existing for that entity."

"Go ahead, I'm following you," encouraged Michael.

Shar Dea continued, "Find a rock."

The task was easy. There was a small rock near his foot.

"That's a good one," she claimed. "Now what's your opinion of its electro-chemical composition?

Michael held the rock in his hands, and looked at it from all sides, pondering over it as if he was a anthropologist. Then he proclaimed, "It's solid as a rock!"

Shar Dea sarcastically commented, "Right, Michael."

"I mean that it is really dense," he said defensively.

"Do you think it is a slow or fast electro-chemical entity?"

"Very slow."

"Actually," she said, it's extremely slow. It's not dead, but almost slow enough to be taken for granted as lifeless."

Shar Dea took the rock from Michael and held it out at arms length while concentrating on it. "Michael, this little rock is quite active and alive, that is, molecularly speaking. Its aura remains in a consistent state of browns. Now watch me change its aura to red. Watch closely, as its molecular activity intensifies."

"Wow!" said Michael, "it's smoking."

As the rock cooled down, parts of its crumbled. Then Shar Dea gently placed the altered rock back on the sand, and they continued their walk.

About a half an hour later, another lesson occurred.

"Michael, do you see that little boy over there playing in the sand?"

"Yeah."

"Let's get closer to him, but we'll walk slowly, because I have something interesting to share with you."

"Fine with me," he agreed.

"OK! Now! Is the boy's electro-chemical field moving slow or fast?"

"Fast."

"Nope! It's moving very fast and his aura is extremely fast, too" stated Shar Dea.

Michael looked bewildered, and said, "You mean the kid's got two electro-chemical entities?"

"No, not quite that. Actually, his physical body, what you and I see is only part of a total electro-chemical being. The aura is the outer, finer and faster aspect of his electro-chemical being. The outer aura relates exactly to its inner counter part, but doesn't appear to physically exist, as you currently comprehend it. However, it reveals every minute detail of the inner part's functional process and state of existence."

"Oops, you lost me," Michael said hopelessly.

"What I want to show you is that this little boy recently burnt his left arm, near his elbow. It wasn't a bad burn, though. His aura has a mixture of red, blues, and greens in fashion that indicate a healing of a wound caused by a burn."

"Let's ask," suggested Michael.

Shar Dea's face lit up with excitement. She now knew that Michael was definitely interested in learning about auras.

"Hi there! Are you the mother of that beautiful boy?" Shar Dea politely asked the lady who was sitting in a beach chair next to the happy child.

"Yes, his name is Ryan," the woman replied.

"May I ask you a question about him?"

"Sure."

"Did Ryan have a minor accident last night, and slightly burn his arm near his elbow?"

"Why yes he did. And I promised him I would take him to the beach to see a mermaid, if he would stop crying."

Shar Dea swiftly turned to Michael and said, "Did you hear that, Michael?"

The woman looked perplexed and responded, "How did you know what happened?"

With the facial expression of a mischievous child, Shar Dea said, "I'm the mermaid!"

Little Ryan, with a shovel in his hand, came over to Shar Dea. She picked up the little boy and gave him a big hug and a kiss. Ryan's big brown eyes looked at Shar Dea, and he wished her love and peace with his innocent smile. Shar Dea gave the child a kiss on his nose, then put him down. Ryan's mother remained in awe as the couple walked away, talking about the lesson presented to Michael. To no ones' knowledge, except maybe for Ryan's subconscious mind, his sore was completely healed, and his aura painted light yellow—a sign of emotional peace.

The conversations between Michael and Shar Dea grew intense. Lesson after lesson was presented to Michael. It was getting close to supper time. The sun was on its descent and preparing for a spectacular celestial display on the western horizon.

As the sun gently slipped away behind the curtain of distant pink and grey clouds, Michael and Shar Dea finally found their way back to the beach house. Just before Michael put his foot on the wooden steps leading to the back door, he stopped, turned around and put his hands gently on Shar Dea's shoulders. "Shar Dea," he said, "we have learned a great deal about the nature of things today. I want to thank you for your patience, your honesty, and your knowledge."

Shar Dea sighed and she returned a thank you to him. They embraced, then went up the stairs. As Michael was unlocking the door, he paused, and said, "I've got a good analogy of an aura."

"What's that, Michael?"

"Above the Alaskan skies is one of the greatest wonders of the world, the Aurora Borealis. It is a gaseous and very colorful cluster of nature's splendors. Think, for a moment, that the Aurora Borealis rapidly contracted into a single mass, forming a body of some sort and keeping its colors shining brightly in the sky. Then it would have the most magnificent aura in the whole world."

Shar Dea pinched his bottom, and said, "You've had enough for one day, my friend. Now please open the door!"

Even though they were completely exhausted, hungry, and somewhat sunburnt, their night had only just begun.

# CHAPTER 9
# CATCHING UP WITH TIME

*"If just once per day, . . . we humans took the time to appreciate our true place in the universe, maybe then we would all be at peace."*
— Shar Dea

"I've learned a lot today, Michael. Especially about you and your desire for lust," said Shar Dea with a bold, extruding face.

"Shar Dea, you promised me that you would not harass me about that."

"You're right! I'm sorry."

"Remember, you promised," he reaffirmed.

"Well, I guess it's time for body cleaning and some cooling down. I'm going to take a nice shower."

The hot water was a treat for Shar Dea and she easily acclimated herself to a new found luxury. She began to sing and feel a sense of comfort in her tunes.

Michael overheard her and picked up on her mood. He felt confident and successful about his day's work, too. He locked his thoughts into a scenario of a delicious dinner. His specialty was vegetables with an oriental flare. Just thinking about it made his pallet imagine an orgasmic episode with food.

"Are you hungry Shar Dea?"

"Yes, very!"

"Good, I'll conjure up something delicious for us to eat."

"That sounds good to me!" she shouted from the bathroom.

To satisfy their appetites, he prepared tamari roasted almonds sliced over an organically grown assortment of fresh garden vegetables, with a side dish of brown rice, red wine, a couple of candles, soft music and a touch of happiness. This banquet paved the way for an exciting evening of conversation and exploration.

After dinner, the couple made their way outside to the deck, which over looked the beach. Sitting on the rocker sofa, which was handcrafted skillfully and painfully by Michael, Shar Dea looked up at the crisp and clear night sky.

"You can see at least five levels deep into the stars," enthusiastically commented Shar Dea. "It's as if we were in the midst of the universe ourselves. Oh what a wonderful feeling!"

"Shar Dea, we are in the midst of the universe. We just don't realize that marvelous feeling enough in our life time."

"You're right, Michael. The more we forget to witness and appreciate the stars and ALL THAT EXISTS, the less chance we have of enjoying the beauties of self-awareness and of the worlds around us."

Michael lamented, "True."

"If just once per day," she proclaimed, "we humans took the time to appreciate our true place in the universe, maybe then we would all be at peace."

That's a fact," asserted Michael. "It's when we forget our place and let our egos take hold of our destinies, do we suffer and cause grief."

Michael placed Shar Dea's left hand in his hand and gently stroked it a few times. "Do you know what special thing you did today, Shar Dea?"

"Oh, the whole day was special."

"Well, that's true too, Shar Dea. But around noon today, you spoke to a person other than me. It was the first time I saw you engage in an artful and tactful dialogue. And, I must admit, when you speak, you really exhibit your thoughts well. You're one special person, and I'm kind of proud to know you."

Shar Dea's was pleased by his sincere words. "Michael, how sweet of you to think such kind thoughts of me. In my heart I feel happy and comfortable about your readiness to learn. I am proud to share my ancient talents and knowledge of the higher order laws which govern this planet. My father always reminded me of that special day when a gentleman friend and I would find unity. Though we have only met, your aura is very much like mine, and soon we shall experience immersion. Our bodies and souls will evolve together in glory and ecstasy, while our minds stay relaxed without thought."

Michael's eyes rolled around and when they stopped, he said, "Whatever you said sounds great to me. But, I must admit, that you just caused my mind to envision making love to you while flying through space. And, one more thing, I don't give a damn about anything else, other than enjoying your presence forever."

"That's quite a realistic vision, Michael. To enjoy another's presence while in the state of immersion is the highest form of sexual aspiration. It's at those moments when two souls become one. There is a boundless exchange of energy, usually culminating with a tremendous surge of colors and sounds. And at the same time, they move at great speeds into distant space, which were never traveled before by any living soul."

"I'm ready," Michael said elatedly.

Shar Dea acknowledged him. "I'd bet on it too."

"Michael, let me tell you a few things that my father and

mother taught me when I was a child."

"Please do. I would appreciate hearing some of the great things that your parents were involved in."

"My father told me that all souls living on this planet are aware of sexual sojourns into ecstasy. Both male and female souls forge constantly through life seeking a soul mate who will share in the sojourn of immersion. But, it only comes through 'TRUE' love. It's like riding on a shooting star. As the horizon absorbs the last particle of the falling stardust, its voyage is complete and her passengers will forever share in their love for creation.

"Beyond this love, begins the evolutionary process of creating a new soul. All the energies of the loving souls echo into the distant spiritual space that surrounds the universe. Here, in this vast void, the genetic ingredients of a new soul are formed, just like the sperm and the egg, but on a higher spiritual level. Once the new soul matures to the mindset of its creators, it formulates its destiny in space and time.

"Wait a minute!" said Michael. How does it even know it's got a destiny? As a matter of fact, Shar Dea, it doesn't even know what destiny means!"

"All new souls pass into oneness with their creators, and eventually, Ara E Hum," said Shar Dea. "This Divine Process will continue forever. Whatever the soul cannot comprehend, it will be destined to learn."

"Shar Dea," said Michael, "it might be easy for you to understand all this stuff, but it's really beyond anything I've heard before."

"Feel it, Michael. Let it make sense with you," instructed Shar Dea.

"Feel what?"

"Feel the Meaning of the words."

Michael looked disturbed. "I'll give it a try," he offered.

"The essence of each and every soul is CHOICE. Since ALL THAT EXISTS is good, each new soul must seek to find its place in eternal PEACE with Ara E Hum. The Soul has no fear of CHOICE, for it knows that all is good. However, the learning process assumes a relationship with the aspect ego, a companion of the Soul. It's within the ego that the unknown exists. Incorporated therein is the creative counterbalance of CHOICE. It is called FEAR. FEAR can be a very traumatic experience; equally so is CHOICE."

Michael showed signs of bewilderment and interrupted Shar Dea. "My dear ancient lady, you've got me sweating again. I need a break! OK?"

Shar Dea heard his request, but her mind was still off in her monologue. "Sure, Michael."

"How about some soft fusion jazz," suggested Michael.

36

"What?"

"Music! My dear ancient one. Music!"

"Michael, there are so many things I need to know and how to make good sense of them. Please be patient with me," petitioned Shar Dea.

Michael apologized: "I sorry for getting rattled, but I couldn't keep up with all that heavy stuff. My mind just fizzled out."

"Well then, maybe this will excite you. How about you and I ascend into the Great Aura tonight. I've been there before to learn of Lemurians and other ancients. But, this time I will learn the about the present and seek to better understand the destiny of this planet, twelve thousands years after my birth."

Michael caught his breath, "Did you say twelve thousand?"

"Yep!"

"Remember when we were on the rock at the beach today, Michael?"

"Yeah."

"Remember the inner voice. Well it was a message to act upon. My father told me that aspects of Ara E Hum constantly reach out to those higher souls living on the planets. As long as these souls remain peaceful and unconditionally loving, messages like the ones we heard can be received. They are the spiritual voices that contain TRUTHS and GUIDANCE. It would be wasteful and even harmful not to heed this guiding grace."

"Here we go again!"

But she didn't listen to him. "So, my friend, tonight, I shall explore the Akashic Records. They are the Great Records of history—the aura of the Planet Earth."

"You know I believe you, but do I really have to go too?" he said hesitantly.

"OK! I'll go first, then I will return for you. Together we shall both experience a new dimension of sounds, colors, the etherics, and above all, as much finite knowledge that our little minds can consume and comprehend. How's that?"

"Scary," he replied as his eyes opened wide with concern.

"Up there, our memory must be precise and our comprehension absolute. If our interpretation is not exact, our lives could be easily destroyed. What we will soon see is the etheric present in an absolute reality. All is truth, for all has happened, for whatever reason, and for whatever destiny."

"Oh boy!" he said. Michael was showing signs of being very nervous.

"Be careful not to see FEAR, for it will surely attempt to consume you," advised Shar Dea.

"This can't be happening to me," he muttered.

"Tonight, when I journey up into the sky, please keep me

warm and protect me while I'm away."

The obliging Michael was awed by his ancient friend. He was also scared! "Damn it, Shar Dea! I can't fly? Just you go and tell me what happened when you get back, ok? Please!"

"Michael, hold me tight, just for a moment."

His willingness to touch Shar Dea was without thought. For as the bodily embrace innocently began, Shar Dea enveloped Michael's mind and senses, and put him into an astral dream-like trance. Soon, without resistence, Michael would partake on a journey beyond imagination—into the Akashic Record with only his soul and his etheric astral body.

# CHAPTER 10
# A SET UP

*Happy is the man that findest wisdom, . . .*
*She is more precious than rubies;*
*And all the things thou canst desire*
*are not to be compared unto her.*
*—Proverbs 3:13-15*

The primary responsibility for the physical body is safety, and Shar Dea knew that well. It was critically important that when voyaging out of their bodies, in an astral dream, they knew how to evade potential dangers.

Michael was doing quite well in his happy-go-lucky trance. He was a harmless creature.

Shar Dea got the beautiful pastel colored quilt, and its matching blanket from the guest room. She placed the quilt on the floor of the deck and gently coerced Michael to lie down on it facing upwards. She laid besides him and covered Michael and herself with the blanket.

Michael did not resist in his state of mental captivity and was acting somewhat childish. Enthused by this, Shar Dea found him even more beautiful as a friend. In her heart she saw him as a very special person, simple, and loving in nature. Leaning over and looking at him with softness, she took her hand and with her fingers touched the tip of his nose. She thought of his courage, openness, and inner willingness to explore. She stared at him for about a minute and then kissed him on his cheek. In her mind she knew that there were more intriguing reasons why they met in this space-time continuum than simple coincidence.

"Are you ready Michael? Let's take a few slow deep breaths, and while doing so, concentrate on that large bright star which is directly above us, Okay! I'll take us there," instructed Shar Dea.

Michael acknowledged, "It's beautiful . . . It's cool . . . I'm relaxed." Michael was ready for his first voyage sooner than Shar Dea might have imagined. In her mind, Shar Dea concentrated on the bright star overhead. She felt tugs from Michael's astral body immediately.

"Put your hands at your sides," she said, "and always keep a slow pace with your breathing . . . Lie flat. Feel your body supported by the entire planet . . . as if it were holding you and only you up . . . feel stretched out . . . and let all your feelings and thoughts drift out of your body, . . . exiting from your hands and feet . . . All feelings and thoughts are leaving and going into the earth around you . . . You are starting to feel lighter . . . more relaxed . . . and wanting to rise . . . Let your body rise . . . It wants to rise . . . Let it rise . . . Slowly think of pulling away towards the star above . . . See yourself moving towards the star . . . Now feel the astral body shifting and escaping from your physical body . . . It's ready to jump out and fly freely away . . . Let your body go . . . It wants to go. Your body is pulling away."

Both Michael and Shar Dea experienced separation at the same time. Slowly their astral bodies were hovering, directly above their physical bodies which were resting safely. They were now about as high as the roof, feeling totally free from any sense of gravity or physical earthly properties. Shar Dea began to tell Michael a few things about the astral dreams.

"Michael," she said, "please remember that the concepts of time and space have different dimensions and laws. Traveling and moving around is based on your thinking. You can travel close to the speed of light should you feel more adventurous. So be somewhat careful that you follow me, and always talk to me to let me know what you're thinking. Okay! Otherwise, zap! You'll be somewhere else, and out of my sight."

"Sure!" said Michael. I'll listen to you. But first, let me know one thing?"

"What's that?"

"Who's inside our friends down there?"

"You mean our physical bodies?"

"Yep!"

"No one! At this very moment they are just living matter, and we are their conscious dreams. We need to be aware of any impending dangers so that we can immediately return into our bodies, wake up and protect ourselves," explained Shar Dea.

"How can we do that?"

"It's simple, Michael. Try this for a moment. Ready?"

"Yep!"

Shar Dea began to narrate a scenario for Michael. "You know that we are both up here, right! So if you return to your body and I stay up here, then you can wake up. It would be like waking up from a great dream. Then you can turn on your side and be right next to my physical body. Do you follow? You can make love to me, Michael, kiss me, touch my breasts, and even get positioned inside me. You are free to make love to me."

There wasn't a response. Michael's astral body disappeared. He was gone right back in his sleeping physical body. Shar Dea remained hovering overhead, watching Michael slowly wake up.

Michael turned over on his side and Shar Dea could hear him saying pretty things to her. He was a true romantic. His hands were caressing her face and his fingers were moving through her hair. He was extremely excited. Shar Dea's body remained at rest. He slowly moved the blanket off her body. Tensing up, his heart was palpitating. Shar Dea heard him say that he loved her and wanted her. She remained overhead, carefully watching and listening. Her body did not move or quiver one iota.

Michael had an erection that spelt danger. He was in his own world, never recalling his miraculous achievement only a few moments ago. He was determined to make love with his lover from an ancient land.

He began to kiss her while untying her cotton beach robe. His blue eyes beheld her virgin breasts—firm and beautiful, soft and provoking. He caressed them gently and could no longer restrain himself from the inevitable. As he touched her perfectly textured thighs, he began to speak to her, while his eyes beheld the sights of her naked body. His palms moved slowly around her hip bones, which excited him tremendously. Then in a swift motion, he passed over her vagina as to formally commit himself to passion.

He began whispering in her ear, "Shar Dea, you know I want you. Tell me you do . . . I'm ready for you."

The ancient soul of Shar Dea was above it all, roof high, and slightly annoyed with her programmable best friend. Here she was, in the midst of teaching him something important and there he was ready to climb inside her. She decided to go back down to her physical body and discuss what he had learned. However, as the universal law of balance prevails, her dear friend Michael was about to teach her something as well.

She opened her eyes and saw Michael looking towards her body. He was touching her legs; his head lay on her belly. She wanted to let go and feel his might, for she enjoyed knowing that he had fallen captive to her. She put her hands through his hair and felt his love for her. She also felt his love for her come more from his bodily needs than from his heart. Nonetheless, she was equally enthralled into temptation and ecstasy. She felt pain in her heart for her body was reciprocating to the gentle persuasiveness of his love making.

Then it happened for the very first time. She felt the urge to have him within her. Her body was moist with love as she began to move in response to his touch. Throughout her entire body, she felt herself yearn for more passion. Then the pangs of ancient wisdom broke through her thoughts. She started to hear multiple voices echoing in her mind, all with impulses of caution. The entrapped Empress entered a reality never experienced, a reality of passion, a reality forbidden to her at this time.

"Michael, we are safely back in our bodies," she confirmed.

But he didn't reply. She repeated herself, " Michael, we are back in our bodies. Do you see how easily you've returned? Michael."

He became suddenly cold and barren. His hands stopped their caressing motion as they lay snuggled between her thighs.

"Michael, we're back. We're back in our bodies," she reaffirmed.

His head still looking over her pulsating body began to shake. Soon his breath grew more intense and then he muttered "No! No! No! I don't believe this. A set up!"

His hands quickly moved off her body and to his side. He was silent.

The stars remained above, while the cool night's air gently danced around their naked bodies and even colder thoughts.

# CHAPTER 11

# HISTORY

*"History is a race between education and catastrophe."*
—*H.G. Wells*

The sun broke the horizon, while its brilliant rays pierced into the awakening eyes of the ancient Empress. She stretched and consumed her first breath of fresh morning air. Her mind began slipping back in time to a similar morning when she was walking in the gardens with her father.

There she saw Atlentium Dea telling her stories about the ambassadors from the Heavens. "Ambassadors are not bound by time or space," he said. "Each of us living on this planet has an overseer, who works through the persons soul. They communicate and offer advise and direction through subconscious thoughts, and generate emotions from within the heart."

"So father, who is my ambassador?"

Atlentium Dea looked perplexed and momentarily puzzled. He then extended his hands towards Shar Dea, tilted his head slightly downwards, and offered her a statement of inspiration. "My dear daughter," he said, "there is a high probability that Ara E Hum has personally assumed that role for you."

Shar Dea's eyes popped out when she heard that. Her face turned instantly red. She felt very special and pleased.

Her father then continued, "You know that these ambassadors are protectors of goodness. They constantly seek to reveal the ailing heart and offer it a way of hope. Their presence provides insight and guidance to the soul. They show us ways to master all learning events, regardless of the pains that might come from them."

Then Shar Dea began to recall the many conversations her father told her about Amerii Kai. "Amerii Kai was a wise young man," said Atlentium Dea. "He had very bright blue eyes, was slender and tall, yet had a grayish beard. Amerii Kai was a black prophet who spoke eloquently of peace. However, he spoke vehemently against fear to the people of Atlantis, a century prior to its mysterious and cataclysmic disappearance."

Shar Dea's dream recalled the time when Atlentium Dea mentioned to her about the time he and Amerii Kai first met. "It was a moonlit evening," he said, "and your mother and I were about to sit down for supper. Bene Dea held you in her womb.

43

While I was pouring the wine, we heard a knock on the door. It was Amerii Kai. We invited him in to join us for supper. He was honored, and we served him food and drink. Then I asked him why did he come to the House of Dea? He replied 'It was my mission to meet you after the third day, under the full moon.' Then he told us that he knew of our family heritage before coming to Atlantis and that we were spiritual descendants of Boi E Hom. What surprised your mother and I was that Amerii Kai came to inform us that the family was destined to give rise to a Speaker."

"Father," interrupted Shar Dea, "who is Boi E Hom?"

His reply was quick and simplistic. "She was the greatest Empress that ever lived."

In Shar Dea's dream-like thoughts, she envisioned her father's delight in telling stories about Amerii Kai. "He was brilliant," said Atlentium Dea. "Each word was a masterpiece of thought and meaning, especially when he spoke of the Lemurians and the hundreds of civilizations prior to that mysterious era of mankind."

The ancient memory of Shar Dea's dreams hastened. She recalled another dialogue in which her father told her about Amerii Kai. "On many occasions," her father said, "Amerii Kai spoke of 'one land and one sea', prior to the era of human life forms on this planet. The planet, at that time, was known throughout the spiritual universe as the 'Essence of Nature', and was called 'Heart'. Every physical life form, whether rock or creature, was genetically evolving in goodness. It was a perfect balance of physical and celestial embodiment. It was on the Planet Heart that all spiritual entities learned the 'ARA'—the Great Principle of Creativity."

Shar Dea attempted to challenge her father when she said to him, "But father, you never told me about the 'ARA'."

"My child," he said, "'ARA' means to repeatedly ascend into the heavens. It's the intention of the spirit to take nothing, not even thought, and manifest it into substance. IT IS THE GREATEST PROCESS OF THE SOUL. Without knowing the depth of your question, dear child, you have exercised the very essence of 'ARA'."

Shar Dea was still confused, but Atlentium Dea offered her little comfort. Instead he continued to explain to her about the spiritual civilizations that sought to learn from the planet's nature.

"Each civilization," he explained, "was a replication of one of the billions of spiritual families which evolved into some sort of physical manifestation. Each group was spiritually powerful, unified, and harmoniously working to fulfill its own destiny. Some families lived in the sea, and took on similar life forms of

44

the aquatic vertebrates of the sea. Others chose the land, and some the air. Each family manifested a higher order of consciousness within those life forms. Their sole purpose was to demonstrate that, through their own creativity, they could elevate the species' life forms from their physical forms into higher consciousness and spirituality."

Shar Dea remembered asking her father which families were the most successful? And he said, "Those that cohabited with the porpoises and the whales were both magnificent. Over time, millions of these sea creatures lived and communicated in harmony. They understood the heavens and the magnetic sounds of the planet extremely well. They played most of their life in the realms of nature until they sought a higher existence."

Shar Dea got excited and said, "That's great!"

However, her father informed her of the less fortunate. "But," he said, "some didn't succeed and they became subjected to the life forms they inhabited, restricting their capability of attaining spirituality."

"So what happened to them?" asked Shar Dea while still living in her dreams.

Her father's reply was convincing, "Actually, they assumed the role of 'God' for the species that they attempted to inspire. Eventually, these bewildered spiritual entities succeeded only establish some form of ego mentality for the species with whom they cohabited."

Shar Dea questioned, "Why didn't they escape?"

He explained that "they were limited in the physical realities of the species and of this planet. They grew frustrated and self-destructive. In order to survive in their chosen physical reality, they permitted the erosion of knowledge of their spiritual past. Their conflicts surmounted and their eventual destruction was imminent."

"What about humans, father?"

"Ah, yes!" replied Atlentium Dea. "We were too good to be true. Many spiritual families found their way into early man's animalistic body. It was very receptive of the spirit and offered the greatest reward for the cohabiting spiritual family. Unfortunately, over a short period of time, many families lost their spiritual purposes and found themselves locked into the inhibitions of the ego. They became competitive and aggressive and sought repetitive intelligence."

Little Shar Dea was becoming more confused and couldn't comprehend why these spiritual families had problems. Atlentium Dea sat on a large rock overlooking the cliffs by the sea. He put Shar Dea on his lap and began to share with his young empress the bigger picture of life.

"Little Empress," he commented, "remember that, at one

time in the spiritual heavens, these souls had the luxuries to travel infinitely at will. Stopping on this planet is part of the destinies of all souls, including yours and mine. Always keep in mind that this planet is the heart of our solar system. Each solar system has a body, just like you and me. The mind of each solar system is the collective consciousness of all souls, whether in spirit or physical form. So be constantly aware of the knowledge of LIFE which tells us: '. . . that there is only one MIND, and we are its POWER'. Ara E Hum, our Great God, is the collective consciousness of all solar systems.

"The Great Principle 'ARA' states: that only through the heart of our physical manifestation can the spirit of the soul learn how to create and survive. Remember, my child, GOOD or Evil can only be created when belief is present, and the villains of mankind know this well. So the laws that serve the soul's fulfillment also serve its destruction. Shar Dea, do you understand?

Atlentium Dea continued, it was the ancients who changed the name of this planet from Heart to Earth, that is, they moved the 'H' behind the 'T'. Should the planet not survive, then nor would the solar system. For without its heart, it could not live."

Shar Dea saw herself in her own dream. She saw her face at the age of ten speaking with her father about the nature of things. In her vision, she watched her lips moving as she asked her father if Amerii Kai was a God.

Atlentium Dea said, "No." He then explained, "Amerii Kai represents the spiritual voice that was forgotten by mankind. On the planet there is a great pulling force which gravitates all physical properties. Thought is a physical property. Therefore, spiritual thinking is subjected to this pulling force. The only way to balance and return into spirituality is through BELIEF. It's not a physical property, but can be channeled as an echo of love from the heart. It will ascend rapidly into the heavens, as do dreams. And my little dear one, Amerii Kai came to Atlantis to remind us all of that law."

"So who is he?" she impatiently asked.

"He's a storyteller," replied her father. "Let me retell a story Amerii Kai told me."

"Please father, do so."

Atlentium Dea began, "One time on a far away island to the East, called Amaraii, there was an Empress. Her name was, Boi E Hom, and she ruled only by thought. She communicated silently and perfectly, and all the people and all of nature obeyed her. She lived for over three thousand years and was always beautiful and young. Every winter solstice she would journey into the heavens for three days to be with Ara E Hum. Her supreme femininity bore no children. However, her motherhood ruled two great civilizations.

The civilization to the North was ruled by the Princess Rega Et Hom. The other civilization to the South was ruled by the Prince Dah Et Hom. On the eve of Boi E Hom's 3,000th year of Perfect Motherhood, she was visited by Dah Et Hom, who had just publicly claimed that he had a sacred meeting with Ara E Hum. She knew he had spoken falsely, but the people believed him and disobeyed her thoughts.

The festivities which preceeded her journey to Ara E Hum were held on a grand scale. However, she never returned to this planet. Eventually all the lands to the South were buried under high mountains of sand."

The little empress, Shar Dea, sat still and gathered her thoughts. Her father then lamented, "Amerii Kai had tears in is eyes when he spoke of the Empress Boi E Hom, for she radiated with love and all that she touched flourished in peace. Then Amerii Kai turned slowly to me and said, 'Atlentium Dea, man is but a servant to woman, if he seeks Peace.'"

Shar Dea suddenly snapped out from her trance and awakened from her many dreams. She felt her destiny at last. As she sat on the edge of Michael's bed, she came to several realizations: Atlantis had perished because of its descent from spirituality; that the land which Amerii Kai had spoken of so reverently to her father was here, right under her feet; and that she was the inherent Empress, and through her heart, the populations of the world would touch upon peace, else, would be buried under depths of sand or sea.

# CHAPTER 12
# ONENESS

*"The imperative, . . . is to see ourselves not apart from and opposed to nature, but as part of and harmonious with it. What's involved is not merely our survival, but gaining a deeper understanding of who we are, . . . if we have arisen out of the universe to become its consciousness, then we must realize that all of the universe has value. Our attitude toward nature must change or there'll be a crisis—not just an ecological crisis, but a moral crisis."*
—Michael Zimmerman

There was plenty of contemplation on the horizon for Shar Dea. She spent most of the day lying on the beach in the sun. The ideal setting permitted the sounds of nature to foster her thoughts and orchestrate their meanings.

Michael ran errands most of the day. This was an opportune time for him to think about his new companion—the ancient Empress.

Unknown to their daily activities was the presence of a neighboring Entity of Peace, Phetar Im. This most ancient spiritual entity had one special mission—to be the Ambassador of Shar Dea's soul. Phetar Im was the living soul of Boi E Hom, and was most wise and powerful, loving and godlike. The complex phenomenon occurring in this space-time continuum was that Phetar Im was simultaneously the Entity of Peace of Michael's soul as well.

Prior to most earthly civilizations, Phetar Im's soul served the cause of peace among neighboring celestial bodies that supported soul development. Phetar Im's first physical body was Boi E Hom, the Empress that Amerii Kai spoke of on the Island Amaraii. Her mission was to journey into the future and re-kindle the love for Eternal Peace. In that pursuit, Phetar Im had prepared a mission for Shar Dea.

\* \* \*

"Michael, tonight I want to share my love with you," requested Shar Dea. "And, I am serious!"

Michael's mind went into a frenzy.

Shar Dea continued, "In order for me to offer myself unto you, I must have the promise of your sacred intentions."

Michael contained himself. "Shar Dea," he said, "I truly sense your sincerity. But, I can't help from getting easily aroused. And, please tell me what you mean by 'sacred intentions'?"

Shar Dea took on a sympathetic look. Her face relaxed. "Remember when I spoke of the Sacred Chalice. What I was referring to is the high act of receiving your child. In the moment of love, you must honor my body as an extension of yours. For your body's sacred waters carry life into my cup." Shar Dea paused to ascertain that Michael was still listening and not yielding to his aggressive mode.

"If you do not see the soul of your child entering into my chalice then the new born child will favor me, not you. The gift of the father to the unborn embryo is the offering of time and destination. It's a calling of spirit."

Michael stood still, mentally split between spirit and sex. "Shar Dea, I've never heard anything like that before."

Shar Dea continued, "Many kings falter because they cannot call the male spirit to their kingdom. It's only because they are selfish and want a boy for the purpose of their kingdom."

Michael could not comprehend, but Shar Dea kept on with her knowledge of spiritual unions. "Many females are created in the absence of the father's ability to call the male spirit to his heart. When this happens, the father must go through a learning process of accepting his shortcomings. Otherwise he begins to dislike females subconsciously and eventually overpowers them through jealous hate." There was about a five second interlude. Michael's mouth was affixed open, and Shar Dea looked directly into his eyes saying, "I do not bear a child for myself, it's not my purpose. I bear it for you. Michael, do you want a child?"

Michael was now numb. He said precisely what he had on his mind. "Well? Ugh! I want you, Shar Dea! No son! No daughter? Just you."

His honesty pleased Shar Dea. "Then we shall do it another way, because I want you, too!"

Michael pulled back a little. "Oh Shar Dea! This is getting too damn frustrating!"

"Please Michael, be patient with me. I have an understanding about love which you don't quite comprehend," she humbly replied.

"Oh, what's that?" he snobbishly challenged.

"Simply this," she said, "when man and woman spiritually immerse, the heart is pure; then physically they unite and all the genital organs go into an erotic frenzy. All the delicate parts of the body swell up with hot rushing blood and are over sensitized. You know the feeling?"

49

Michael was getting very annoyed with her advanced sexuality course. He then exclaimed, "Shar Dea, I hope you can see that?

"Michael, you are . . . sexually aroused and frustrated!" she said defensively.

Without hesitation or remorse, Michael beamed in on Shar Dea's voluptuous breasts, looked through her eyes, and found Shar Dea vulnerable to his love. Silence penetrated Shar Dea momentarily, for she knew that her time of knowledge and intellect could not withstand celibacy another second. She let her breath go, her body sighed, and Michael's hands gently embraced her, as his body became pressed against her's.

Michael's mind went into passionate ecstasy. It withheld no thought of the world beyond the sight of Shar Dea's magnificent contour. Each touch was so sensitive that it echoed silence. Each vision professed her delicacy, as if a droplet of rain majestically sat on the petal of a rose.

Within the universe of Michael's mind, he found brilliant arrays of multi-colored lights, all with sound. Then he began to slip into Shar Dea's vast void of space, deeper and deeper into her love. He was never to care of his place in time and space, but only to journey further and further.

Shar Dea had opened a new door of life for Michael to experience. His heart would be forever changed. His mind would be forever awakened, his breath always of life.

As the morning rose upon them, the rough sounds of the sea echoed in their ears and slowly began to rattle their subconscious minds. They were still embraced in each others' arms, and for the last six hours they were one. Michael's eyes opened slowly and Shar Dea's beautiful serene face, captured all his thoughts. He knew that she stepped beyond her bounds, so he could sample a taste of spiritual love making.

Miracles are not made, they are given. In Michael's eyes was a face of a stranger who opened her love to him. His heart was very joyous of her gift. He would never feel frustrated by Shar Dea again. The beauty of life shined into Michael's eyes as Shar Dea began to open her eyes and see into his. Silence was too loud for them to bear, for through their sight was the vision of oneness—the ecstasy of the soul fulfilled. Never again were they to doubt their bond to Ara E Hum. The milestone of love had sanctioned their purpose on this planet. They were one.

# CHAPTER 13

# JOURNEY INTO KNOWLEDGE

*". . . the Truth is in your Face . . .*
    Peace"

    —*Shar Dea*

Michael made eggs benedict for breakfast. It was the newest day in Michael's life and he wanted to start it off with a special treat for his lady. Outside on the beach deck, he had prepared the table with candles, cloth napkins, and champagne.

Sitting face to face, Michael raised his glass to make a toast to his new friend. "Here we go, a toast to you, Shar Dea."

With a smile, she said, "And to you, my kind gentleman."

The clinging of the glass brought nuance to their eyes. Shar Dea's smile kept widening. Her eyes and cheeks kept bubbling. Then as the beautiful breakfast awaited its offerings of extravagant treats, Shar Dea got up and walked over to Michael. She grabbed his shirt and pulled him away from the table, anxiously and passionately dragging him back to the bedroom.

Exhausted, Michael lay fast asleep, while Shar Dea prepared a snack for lunch. Outside, the eggs benedict lay lonely and frigid on the deck table. Shar Dea glanced at their sad personalities, and mumbled to them, "You poor little eggs, don't worry. Your cook's palate got all the satisfaction it could handle. Consider your mission successful."

As she was returning to the kitchen area, she shouted upstairs, "Michael, wake up! We've a lot of hard work to do."

It didn't really matter at that point because he was ready to come down anyway. "Hi! . . . I'm hungry! . . . Hey, that looks good."

"Michael, after we eat, I need to make plans with you. We must discuss some very important concerns."

Michael was easily excited by her, "Sure," he said, "Let's get to it right away. Here, let me help you with lunch." Before his very next move he exhalted, "Oops! First a little music." He swiftly tracked himself towards the stereo and while chugging he sputtered, "Wait till you hear this guy play the electronic harp."

The soft tunes of the music began to filter throughout the entire house. Michael had rigged each room with a sound system.

Upon entering the kitchen he offered Shar Dea a kiss, and she happily acknowledged the treat.

Michael got down to business and prepared his opening

comment. "So, what's up your sleeve?"

Shar Dea's response was innocent. "Sleeve? . . . My arm? . . . Michael, that's a stupid question."

Michael was taken by her candidness. "Yep! I should have known."

He let out a quick and simple smile, and said, "That's just another way of saying 'What do you have in mind?'"

"Oh, I get it," she affirmed. "You know Michael, words are critically important, but the essence of good communication is making sense of what others are saying."

"Yep!" he said, without giving that a second thought.

"So Shar Dea, what are you going to plan?"

"You mean, 'what we are going to plan'," retorted the cook.

Michael felt instant hunger shoot up and down from his belly. "Let's eat!"

"Michael, I'm not going to be around for a long time. As a matter of fact, a relatively short time," commented Shar Dea.

That caught Michael's attention. "How long is that?"

"Oh maybe eighteen full moons or so."

"What?" he shouted. "You mean we have only twenty moons together?"

"It's not a joke, Michael. I'm serious."

Michael's blood pressure instantly rose. "Stop right here. What do you mean by that?" he said firmly.

"Last night, I opened myself up to you. For the first time in my life did a man enter into my total self: mental or physical, that is, my entire consciousness. It was my first journey into ALL THAT EXISTS as a fulfilled soul."

"Fulfilled soul? Explain that for me please."

"Last night you really loved me beyond any doubt or experience of love you had in your entire life. Isn't that true?"

"Yes, very much indeed," replied Michael.

"So how have you changed?"

Michael looked at Shar Dea and said, "I feel taller, see better, feel stronger, and . . . Shar Dea, I love you and am at peace with myself."

"Are we one?"

"Yes, we are one," said Michael in the most holistic manner possible.

"Well, Michael, where I go, you go. And, if I know where I am going, I might as well tell my man where he's going too!"

"Ok, tell me!"

"There. Up there," pointed Shar Dea.

"Wow! Starfighter, Michael. I'm no space cadet," replied Michael, mercifully.

"I'll teach you right this time," offered Shar Dea. Then with a positive voice, she continued, "After lunch, we'll . . ." She paused for a moment. ". . . Hey, you're right! That music is beautiful."

Michael felt successful and honored by his selection of music. "That's Andreas Vollenweider—a man of peace."

"Hum! Let's make it louder," suggested Shar Dea.

Michael jumped to his feet and exclaimed, "Okee dokee!" as he sprinted towards the stereo.

"Okee dokee! What?" mumbled Shar Dea.

"So, what's on the agenda for us today?" asked Michael as he rubbed his hands together in eagerness.

Shar Dea's face immediately took on a serious form. "First, I must reach my soul and touch upon my mission more clearly. Then . . ."

Michael interjected, "Shar Dea, what do you mean by "'touch upon my mission more clearly'?"

"Remember when we were on the giant rock by the beach?" she asked.

"Aha."

"Remember the voice we both heard?"

"Yes!" replied Michael while shaking his head up and down.

Shar Dea spoke softly, but firmly. "It was a message that spoke of my destiny, which you now share. The voice told me that my destiny was to free the people from their decaying beliefs. My mission was to restore the unifying force of peace on the planet so that the people are once again linked to Ara E Hum. But Atlantis is gone and I am here. My destiny must be fulfilled, though, I'm not quite sure where and how."

"Where do I fit into the picture?" asked Michael anxiously.

"I don't really know Michael, but I think your masculinity is the missing link in my soul development. As of last night, my power to comprehend the 'Great Planetary Record', what the people of today call the 'Akashic Record' was magnified a hundred times greater."

Michael shook his head and confirmed, "I've heard that name mentioned several times before."

Shar Dea didn't pause. "During our immersion, I found myself traveling at will, faster than light. I was catching up to the front of light beams. I never saw such brilliance in colors before. At one time, I caught up to a cluster of light vibrations emanating from the sun. As I passed them and looked back into the center of the cluster, I saw millions of tiny entities forming into sound. Then I stopped. I felt you deep inside me. I knew at that time that we were one, together, and the same."

Shar Dea became silent as she looked gently at Michael's face. With tenderness in her voice and love emanating from her heart, she softly said, "Michael, you have a tear in your eye."

Michael had gone through some form of transformation, or

at least, was definitely in that process. He was a new person: sincere, honest with his feelings, and in love with a stranger who touched upon antiquity. "Shar Dea," he said, "I feel so complete with you. I trust every word and host every thought that you have to offer. As you were describing your journey, my love was joyously with you. Though now, I have discovered a secret question in life that I'd like to share with you." He paused momentarily, "While we were immersed, my soul was enjoying your presence and guidance. You, on the other hand, were far away from me. If we were one, together and the same, then is it true that our souls are in love at a higher plane?"

Shar Dea was deeply moved by his openness and quest for divine knowledge. "Yes! Three events were taking place at the same time. Your sexual ecstasy, my journey with light, and our souls joyous union to the wonderland somewhere in the Spirit of Ara E Hum. And all this was done simultaneously."

Michael's thirst for knowledge was clearly stated by his supportive expressions. "Go on," he nudged.

"Michael, I have to find out exactly what my mission entails and how you are involved. Tonight, we must journey into the Akashic Record and read the past. In the same fashion, we must also comprehend what the future holds for mankind. This time we must be serious in our pursuits for I feel the presence of Ara E Hum within my heart and about me. So, Michael, you are part of me, and together we must accept our mission with trust and love, regardless of the outcome. Peace must be attained or else the planet Earth will once again cleanse herself of all living souls indiscriminately."

Michael offered his unanimous commitment to follow her wishes. He held her hands with his, and said, "Let's go for it all. I'm with you all the way, Shar Dea."

Shar Dea was pleased. "Great, I feel your sincerity well within my heart too." She embraced him tightly as their auras exchanged the essence of love and truths.

"Michael, when we are in the Akashic Record we will be in an etheric mode. This means that we will function in a similar fashion as our real earthly bodies. OK."

"Do you mean that there are different levels of the Akashic Record?"

"Oh yes!" she said, "There are 49 levels, . . . well, as far as I know about it anyway." Shar Dea took a deep breath, and expressed the joy of knowing her own limitations: "There is just so much knowledge out there. It's always something new, time after time, place after place."

Michael was interested. "Well, tell me what you know about the Great Planetary Aura."

"Right! There are seven major levels and each of these have

seven sub or inner levels."

"Seven times seven equals forty-nine. Na! There's got to be more than that?" he said humorously.

"Michael, as you become more advanced, assimilation of knowledge becomes instantaneous. But for our first journey, it is most important to find out a few basics," coached Shar Dea.

\* \* \*

The night was exceptionally clear, cool, and silent. Shar Dea and Michael prepared for their journey. They needed to keep their bodies warm and well-protected, while they traveled in their astral dreams. They got a couple of blankets and pads and laid them on the beach deck.

Out on the deck they lay. Shar Dea lead Michael into a meditation. Then she recited this prayer, asking Michael to silently repeat each word with his deepest feelings:

"Ara E Hum, Lord of Lords
In Spirit dwells ALL THAT EXISTS
I give my love eternally to You
Your will is my destiny

You are The One Mind, and I am Your Power
You are The Divine Light, and I am the Fire
You are The Source, and I the Seed

Embrace me with Your Grace
The Truth is in Your Face
Together in Spiritual Peace
Eternally in Peace
Peace, My lord

PEACE"

Gently, Shar Dea and Michael ascended above their physical bodies. Their earthly faces were peaceful and virgin still. A faint pale blue haze encapsulated their bodies to protect them from any harm. A silver-blue cord, only visible through the astral eye, connected their bodies' sleeping consciousness with their astral minds.

Michael was confident and ready to travel. In their astral dreams, they were telepathic. Both prepared to accept the knowledge that awaited them. Shar Dea began to communicate with Michael, "We are ready to move into the Great Aura. Are you comfortable?"

Michael's mental mind clearly affirmed "Yes!"

Shar Dea spoke to him. "See yourself moving through space, faster and faster as you move through time. Seek a bright distant star that you want to see. We shall soon touch its shores, freely, with our thoughts and etheric bodies."

Not a word spoken, yet total communication and awareness towards each other was realized. Their etheric astral bodies moved outward into the vast voids of space. Higher and higher they soared. The reality of the absence of space-time continuum impressed Michael tremendously. Well within a moment's time, as if the 'will of mind' was the creator, the envisioned distant star was at their presence. It was very still, much smaller than the size of the Earth's moon. Michael's mind was in awe, for the little star was a perfectly smoothed round diamond, holding no trace of celestial collisions nor bombardment. He was captured in the brilliance of its luster and tranquility.

Shar Dea's voice echoed through his astral dream. "Michael," she said, "I'm with you totally, and this is what you wished to see. Wasn't it?"

"How did you know that?"

"Remember, Michael. Your will is the author of your reality in the astral dream. That's if you permit it to happen. So please be careful of your inner most subconscious thoughts, for they will be created."

As they hovered nearby Michael's newly created diamond star, they took a moment to talk. "My dear Shar Dea. I want to let you know that you are a wonderful teacher."

"Why, thank you Michael. It's my pleasure."

Shar Dea's astral dream caught on to something quite marvelous for her friend to experience. "Listen Michael," she said, "listen very quietly. You can hear the sun."

Shar Dea felt Michael soaring with ecstasy as he heard the pulsating chants of the sun emanate throughout the vast voids of space. The brilliant diamond star was gone. He then realized that so much can change.

Michael picked up a vision which was being generated in Shar Dea's mind. As he concentrated, he realized that her mind's creative powers were superb and potent. And within a few nano seconds of time, he became a vital part of her vision. The universe around them rapidly began to manifest itself into a space-time continuum unknown to Michael. First he saw a vast global horizon form around him. An ocean surrounded by high rugged cliffs became more evident. Soon his etheric body found itself in the midst of a most magnificent garden, in which there were hundreds of ancient looking trees and plants. He saw many birds flying nearby, most of which were captivated by his unique arrival. There was life all around. All was real, alive, and functioning without any discontinuity because of their presence.

56

Michael was enthralled by the transformation that had just occurred. In his astral dream state, he mentally began to communicate the message "Where are we?" to Shar Dea, who was beside him throughout the entire episode. However, her response shook Michael off his feet.

"We are in Atlantis, Michael."

After a few gulps of air, as Michael perceived it to be, he uttered, "I can't believe this!"

Shar Dea never did explain to Michael that in an astral dream, you can partake in any lifelike activity. This is done only with the understanding that you cannot take any physical property back with you, except the knowledge of it.

"Michael, we are in the gardens of Atlentium Dea. This is where I grew up and spent many days with my family."

Michael's eyes were still oscillating from the shock of the space-time transformation. His real physical body was about 12,000 years back into the future, lying quietly on his beach deck. Regardless of the awe of it all, Michael was experiencing simultaneous visions of his life. Shar Dea sensed his confusion and immediately said, "Michael, concentrate on the here-and-now. You're beginning to fade out. Concentrate on being here with me. Don't think of yourself back in the future until you have established yourself properly here. OK!"

By the time she was finished reaffirming his presence, Michael regained his composure. "Shar Dea," he said, "thanks for your guidance."

They easily floated around the garden then stopped. An old man was approaching them. They waited for him to acknowledge their presence.

"Shar Dea, can he see us?" inquired Michael.

"Maybe. If he is a wise man, he would see us. If not, he'll probably think he saw or felt some odd phenomenon taking place, but would easily dismiss it."

The old man walked right up to them, and then stood still. He stared right at them as if he was trying to focus on some object. He was dressed in a white robe, had a silver-gray beard, and was frail in posture.

"My name is Oughten. I'm beginning to see your astrals better now. From whence do you come and why?"

Both Michael and Shar Dea felt honored to be seen by the little wise old man. Shar Dea spoke to him first. "We are from the future, and I once played in these gardens as a child."

Oughten showed instant delight. "You are Shar Dea, the daughter of Atlentium Dea."

"Yes!" replied Shar Dea. "Are you not the high priest who was my brother's inspirator and guardian?"

"I am he."

"Please tell us of Dah Etro Dea," petitioned Shar Dea.

Oughten spoke, "Dah Etro Dea took on the White Robe of Peace and saved thousands of people from the evil ways of the Emperor Lur Atol."

The old man was very glad to see Shar Dea, but the frown and wrinkles on his forehead showed some apprehension. He then turned suddenly towards Michael and said, "I know those eyes." He then asked Shar Dea if she knew of her brother's fate.

"Wise old man, I know not of his fate, though I will soon journey to his side."

Oughten then said, "My dear Empress, you are at his side."

Oughten's statement didn't penetrate Shar Dea's thinking at that moment. Instead, she assumed that it was time and proper to introduce Michael. Proudly Shar Dea said, "This is Michael. He is from the land called America."

Oughten gently bowed to Michael. Michael in turn reciprocated.

"Shar Dea," said Oughten, "where is this land called America?"

She replied, "This land is of the future. It lies in the sunsets across the ocean, and against the Great Currents."

The old man's body took on a sudden wobble of instability. He didn't appear to be nervous, rather he expressed excitement. "How far into the future is America?" asked Oughten.

Michael offered the facts. "About 12,000 years or so."

The old man was taken aback by the tremendous span of years. He pointed westward to the ocean, and said, "Michael, say the name of your land slowly and softly to me."

Michael respected his wish and slowly said, "A-M-ER-IC-A."

Oughten was fascinated. Something was said that sparked life in him. His face aired with glee and enlightenment. He moved a step closer to Shar Dea and inquired, "Shar Dea, did your good father ever speak to you of the mysterious blue-eyed black man the walked our lands?"

Shar Dea said, "Yes."

Oughten continued, "And then after two years to the exact day, he left the lands and sailed westward on the ocean into the western sunset."

Shar Dea simply said "Yes he did, Oughten."

Oughten mumbled "Amerii Kai." Then he tilted his head upward, looked directly into Shar Dea's face, and said, "It's true."

Michael's mind was beginning to drift away from the place where they were standing. Shar Dea picked up on his fading concentration, and said, "We must be going."

With a desperate appeal written on the face of the old man,

these words followed, "What will happen to our Atlantis? Your brother has gone and the evil emperor has become ever more powerful."

Shar Dea offered Oughten one final promising thought, "Seek Peace in your heart, Ara E Hum is Eternal, my dear old man."

Then, as witnessed by the little wise man, his two visiting strangers transcended back into their future.

They were both in their etheric bodies, lingering somewhere in their astral dreams within the confines of the spiritual universe. Michael had performed well and was evolving into a proven traveler. In his mind, the same curiousity that intrigued the old man flourished in his own thoughts. If Atlantis was destroyed by a cataclysmic episode that cannot even be proven, then what in God's name can happen to America? His mind continued to ponder and fluster. Here I am talking to a wise old man living in Atlantis 12,000 years ago. I want to know about . . ."

Shar Dea caught his thoughts. "Michael, I can read your mind. You are seeking to experience the future. Remember, should your emotions get out of hand, and you become excited or fearful, then you will jeopardize your life. This may possibly cause you not to return to the earth, or worse yet, die on earth this very moment. I don't recommend that you demand to see your future in this mood."

She succeeded to calm him down. Within a few moments Michael spoke to Shar Dea, "But we need to know what The Great Aura foretells about our destinies."

Under control and challenged by Michael's sincere concerns, Shar Dea willed them into the future. Instantaneously they were about 100 miles above the cloudless skies over the North American Continent. Looking down, Michael felt at odds with what he saw. Shar Dea sensed his feelings, but was not familiar with the geographical interpretation of the sea and land masses. Michael's intuitive mind suggested to Shar Dea that there was once a lot more land between central United States and the West Coast, which was now gone. He also noticed that the Floridian Peninsula was only an island. Then he saw that the United States was divided by a large body of water which ran north and south where the Mississippi River once flowed.

They decided to go down to land and investigate the environment.

The contours of their etheric bodies began to appear along a mountainside dirt road. Nearby there was a small village. It looked somewhat modern and yet offered a primitive character to its varying architectural structures. In a few minutes, their etheric bodies were quite formed.

Michael heard a cranking sound approaching. It didn't sound harmful, but definitely suspicious. Around the curve in the roadway appeared a young boy peddling his bicycle. Soon, the stout little boy caught sight of the two aliens. He cautiously approached them with a courageous hold of fascination. He stopped his bike within three feet of Michael and Shar Dea and began to look curiously at them.

Neither Michael nor Shar Dea moved.

"Hey! Are you guys for real?" shouted the boy.

Shar Dea looked at Michael, and Michael looked at Shar Dea. All hands were now extended out with gestures of doubt.

"Yes, I guess so!" said Shar Dea.

The little freckled red hair boy's face puffed up with excitement as he sputtered, "Wow! Space travelers!"

Michael felt entertained by the boy's enthusiasm. "What's your name?"

"Marrody," the boy responded with delight.

"Marrody, huh!" mumbled Michael.

Shar Dea had an affinity with children and she was equally entertained by Marrody's eagerness. "Marrody, why do you call us space travelers?"

"Because your bodies are see throughs," he exclaimed.

Michael got Shar Dea's attention. "I think Marrody means that we are transparent."

"Oh yes! That's it."

"Marrody, can you tell me today's date?" asked Shar Dea.

"It's 2025, May, Spring, the 140th day of the cycle," rapidly replied Marrody.

"What planet do you aliens come from?" asked the boy with his nose up in the air, as if the answer would reveal a cosmic surprise.

"Earth," replied Michael with a sense of pride.

"No ya don't. Earth people have real bodies. Just like me."

Marrody tried again, hoping to find the real answer. "Where do ya really come from?"

"Earth, but in the year 1988," uttered Shar Dea. "You see Marrody, we are investigators of our future which is your past. We are doing this so that we can tell the people who live in the year 1988 what the year 2025 will look like."

"No. You guys are from another planet," retorted the boy. Then a jubilant thought passed through his mind, and he said, "Hey! Can I bring you two guys to school as an exhibit?"

"Maybe, Marrody. Maybe," speculated Michael.

Shar Dea was trying to find out a little more information about this space-time continuum. She addressed Marrody with an academic approach. "Marrody," she said, "are you a good history student?"

"Sort of. There's not too much good in history stuff, except Laurel and Hardy adventures."

"Marrody, what did they teach you about history?" prompted Shar Dea.

"Two things. First, that you must learn from it or else you must experience it all over. And the other is that most of the old history stuff emphasized war instead of humanity and peace. Brooks, our teacher, tells us that 'not so long ago, war was always threatening people'. Brooks says that 'now people are peaceful, and most of the work they do makes them even more peaceful'."

Michael enjoyed Marrody's academic defense. Mistakenly, he then asked Marrody a superfluous question which intimidated the youth: "Did you know that you use the word 'peace' an *awful* lot for a little boy?"

Marrody tensed up and puckered his lips. "Whoever you guys are, you shouldn't use the words 'peaceful' and 'awful' together. Brooks tells us that words of peace and people of peace are what saved the world from war. Don't you understand?"

The boy took Shar Dea and Michael by surprise, despite the fact that they were in full agreement with Marrody's defensiveness.

"Who are you guys, anyway?" demanded Marrody.

Shar Dea maintained her probing questions. "Marrody, how old are you?"

"I'm not old!" he retorted with a crude voice.

"I mean, what's your age?" insisted Shar Dea.

"Four!"

"What?" said Shar Dea in disbelief.

"Four!" Marrody impatiently responded.

"You're only four years old?" attested Michael.

"No!"

"Well then, how old are you?" forcefully stated Shar Dea.

"I'm not old. And you are starting to bother me. Bye!"

Marrody, looked confused and seemed quite perturbed as he turned away. With his back facing Michael and Shar Dea, he peddled his bicycle down the dirt road which was tunneled by enormous weeping willow trees.

Michael was dismayed. His face drooped with stupidity and frustration. He looked at Shar Dea and in remorse said, "Shar Dea, we goofed. That kid was a delicate little creature and we peaceful adult jerks scared him off. How could we do such a callous thing like that?"

"I guess we were too much into ourselves and not in his frame of mind. We also underestimated his educational process. He must have thought that we were some really dumb aliens," commented Shar Dea.

61

"You're right! Did you hear him defend the concepts of peace?" said Michael.

"I sure did!"

"Michael, there was one very good thing he did say."

"Yeah! That there was no major war after the Middle East Crisis period," claimed Michael.

"True, but why has the North American Continent changed so much?"

Shar Dea sighed as she said, "Michael, I think Mother Earth rebelled."

Michael hesitated for a moment, then said, "Why so, Shar Dea?"

"Apparently, the collective social consciousness of most global civilizations must have been quite negative and full of fear. Something was potent enough to instigate a rebellious and cataclysmic reaction from within the planet. It definitely must have been a major event." She paused for a moment, then said, "Michael. Let's go home. I need to think a few things out."

"Fine!"

# CHAPTER 14

# THE MISSION

*"God has no eyes. He sees the world*
*through our eyes and by the feelings*
*emanating from within our hearts . . ."*
*—Shar Dea*

The cool night warranted the warmth and coziness of the fireplace. Michael gathered up some wood and Shar Dea prepared a little something to eat. In order to comfort the ear, Michael turned on his stereo system. The melodies of the instrumentals spirited the soul and echoed throughout the beach house. To Shar Dea, these musical sounds were appreciated as gifts from the heavens above.

"Michael, I can't stop bouncing all over the room. Your music is great!"

While they were eating, Michael switched tapes. About five minutes later, Shar Dea tilted her head slightly upward and to the side, as if her ears were honing in on something. "Who's that playing?"

"That's Kitaro, a crusader from Japan, and is fantastic on the synthesizer," informed Michael.

"It's very interesting to feel and see such sounds. These were so similar to the sounds I heard when I was astral dreaming in the Akashic Record," commented Shar Dea.

Michael loved music so much that he viewed it in the same delight a child would a gigantic ice cream cone. Michael looked sharply at Shar Dea, and with his cheek to cheek smile, he simply replied, "Yea, it's great!"

Exercising more sophistication, Shar Dea said, "Music is the language of the universe, and the musicians of today capture it so properly."

"I'm glad you appreciate it."

After dinner they sat together in front of the fireplace and became more acquainted. They talked about Michael's former girlfriends and his preferences for women. Michael got the urge to make use of the bathroom and while getting up said, "Yow! I almost forgot. I need to go to the office tomorrow. Do you mind being alone for a while?"

"No, not at all."

"Michael, speaking of which, I need to ask you something too."

"Yea, what's up?"

"It's about being alone. Tomorrow, I must travel alone and get a precise definition of my destiny."

"And?" he said.

"I want to know if you will be my protector?" she humbly asked.

"What for?" he said with puzzlement.

"'Cause I could encounter some problems."

"Shar Dea, what are you talking about 'Encountering some problems?'"

"When I astral dream!" she divulged.

"Oh!"

"Michael, my father told me that 'to understand your past completely is to know your destiny'."

Michael took on a challenging viewpoint. "Do you remember every little single incident in your life?" he questioned.

"It's not necessarily the question of remembering, rather learning," rebutted Shar Dea. "Did you learn from every incident? That's knowing your past."

"That's a hard one."

"If in my astral dreams, I don't return, it means that I have discovered a moment of self hate in my past—that which I choose to cling on to. It must be removed before I can journey further or I will automatically die, and probably be reborn somewhere in your past. Or, I may return in a different mental frame of reference which was not indicative of the way I am with you tonight."

Michael looked perplexed and almost slaphappy. He sarcastically said to her, "You manage so well to lose me in all your 'heavy stuff' that your father told you. Why?"

She kept her composure, and said to him, "Each of us journeys continuously in LIFE. My journey is quite mature and seeks a new beginning. Like a child, yours is but a wonderland of trials and errors. Its destiny is in the exploration of LIFE, and mine is the final acceptance by Ara E Hum, and entrance into the next universe."

"Regardless of all that! What about your safety?" he insisted.

"Michael, if something should happen, then only your total dedication of love and peace for me could save me. Otherwise, I am a trapped person inside a body that isn't really mine, like those poor souls who are hospitalized in the mental institutions."

Michael was still defensive and stressed. "Shar Dea," he said, "how did you know about the people in our mental hospitals?"

"Michael, every minute that I sleep or travel in space, my brain works diligently fast to absorb all the knowledge which surrounds me. In about two more days, I will know almost everything that you know. Remember little Marrody? His aura was mostly white when we first met him. My etheric mind was so preoccupied with absorbing his knowledge that I had trouble communicating back to him. His aura started to turn to light yellow, but it was too late for me to pursuade him to open up and trust us."

"Yellow?"

"Light yellow! Michael, it meant that he was getting a bit nervous and emotionally scared."

Michael rolled his eyes once more, mumbling "Yellow, light yellow, white, pink, striped red and black."

Shar Dea moved extremely close to Michael, and said, "I hope this doesn't become a Pavlovian mistake, but the only way to shut you up is . . . ." She proceeded to tantalize Michael, then she embraced him and presented him with a very potent kiss.

A little later on, all was neutralized and calm. Shar Dea was rapidly learning about the beauties and weaknesses of masculinity. Most of all, she had a good hold on Michael.

"Sweetheart," she said romantically, "I must make my voyage soon. I feel a slight amount of anxiety chilling my bones."

"Where are you going?"

"Atlentium Dea told me that the Earth's greatest energy forces are at the opposite sides of the Equator, which divides the electro-magnetic force fields. This balances out the electrical current surrounding the planet and separates the positive fields from the negative fields."

"Forget this stuff, Shar Dea, it's over my head."

"Fine! But I must tell you that I will spend ten minutes of earth time each night for seven nights traveling in the Akashic Record. On the first night I will migrate to the outer shell of the Earth's Aura, which your scientists call the Van Allen Belts. I will be high above the North Pole Region. The second night I be at the outer limits again, but at the South Pole Region. I will alternate this pattern five more times. When it's all over, we will need to go to some mountain area for twenty four hours."

"Then what?"

"I will begin my mission."

"And what about me?" he asked with an expression of hopelessness.

"You must protect me with your masculinity, not your power," she said commandingly.

"Oh, Shar Dea, I'm lost. What's a man without power?"

"An angel of peace. Like he was before he dominated the women of this planet."

"Remember the stories my father told me about Amerii

Kai?"

"Yeah."

"This most beautiful planet was totally in peace. Recall, it was once named Heart. What you call the Milky Way, your Solar System, is just one aspect of Ara E Hum. Every star, planet, and conscious soul within this known body is part of ALL THAT EXISTS. The Heart of the solar system, IS, if you will, the Heart of Ara E Hum.

Peace must come from within the HEART. For the solar system to survive, peace needs to be restored. Do you understand?"

"Not quite! But, I will," he retorted with enthusiasm.

Shar Dea prepared to expressed the seriousness of her beliefs. "If the planet Earth underwent a nuclear war, it could very well blow up or possibly disintegrate. If that didn't happen, then it could become cold, barren, lifeless and die. Should any of this happen, then the entire solar system would also undergo death, for all depends on the continued life of the planet Earth.

"Michael, if your heart stopped pumping blood to the brain because it suffered a heart attack, could you still function normally? Or, would you drop dead, or at best, be a vegetable?"

"I'd croak!"

"So would the solar system. Get it?"

"A little."

Shar Dea attempted another view point. "Think of it this way. If the planet Earth and all its civilizations died, then it would have a profound affect on our solar system. The solar system has a life too. It breathes, gives birth, and has it's place among other solar systems within the universe.

"There is no other way to EXIST. Do you understand?"

Shar Dea sensed that Michael understood the importance of her statements when he expressed, "I can feel it in my heart."

"Good!" she said.

For the next couple of moments, they did not speak. Then Shar Dea said, "Obviously, my destiny could not be fulfilled on Atlantis. Michael, I know that I am the last Empress of Peace. And . . . ," she momentarily contemplated, ". . . and, somehow I found myself in America. It is not all clear to me now, but when I return from my journeys, I will definitely know."

# CHAPTER 15

# IN SPIRIT, I WILL KNOW

*"The harvest of righteousness is sown in
peace by those who make peace."*
—James 3:18

Michael woke up around 7:00 A.M. that Monday morning.
Shar Dea lay fast asleep. He leaned over to cover her and keep
her warm. His penetrating eyes noticed her face becoming tense.
Michael sat up on the bed beside her and closed his eyes. In the
still of his thoughts, he telepathically began to pick up on her
dreams. She was locked up in some kind of cage, screaming for
help. Michael concentrated on the horrid scenario. He noticed
that it wasn't Shar Dea who was screaming, rather it was Sherrie
Dailey, the heroin addict, whose body Shar Dea revitalized in
spirit.

Then the picture began to crystallize. It was not a cage; it
was a jail. A policeman came over to ask Sherrie where her
parents lived. "Please let me go," she cried. "My parents were
murdered in their garden two years ago by the will of a corrupt
politician." Sherrie started to scream louder. The nurse helped
restrain her. "I hate the system; it's brutal and unfair," she cried.

The officer asked her if she had any brothers or sisters.

"Yes, one younger brother," she said sobbingly.

"Where is he?" asked the officer.

She wept further, and with tears wetting her face, and said,
"He went after the evil sons' of bitches, and now he's gone, too!"

The police officer got down on his knees and held her hands
saying, "My name Marrody, Sergeant Marrody, that is. And if I
can help you in any way, please consider it in friendship, OK!"

Sherrie shook her head up and down rapidly in full
agreement.

"In the meantime," Marrody said, "I'm going to take you to
a rehab house where I do some volunteer work. My good friend
Martin Foster will help get you back on your feet. OK?"

Sherrie looked into Sgt. Marrody's eyes and said, "Thanks a
million, Marrody, some day we will meet again. But right now, I
just want to die and get out of this body. It's been bad luck for
me since I was born."

Within a moment's silence, Michael felt Shar Dea's hands on
his face. He opened his eyes, and saw Shar Dea looking sincerely
into his eyes, saying, "So that's the connection. Do you

understand?"

Michael gently shook his head expressing doubt. "Not quite, please tell me how you and Sherrie look so much alike. And, unless I am mistaken, didn't the policeman and the little boy we met in the future have something in common?"

"Yes," replied Shar Dea. "It's starting to materialize somewhat for me. But Michael, please let me hold off on some of these explanations for now. What I must do is focus on these personalities, including the wise old man from Atlantis, and try to link them together. It's a great start for me."

Shar Dea's eyes grew passionate and loving. "Michael, come closer to me," she said softly. "You have become the greatest loving adventure I've ever known. I'm beginning to marvel at you. I guess that's the first time you ever performed a telepathic read?"

"Yes, and it was truly accidental."

"I know," revealed Shar Dea. "Didn't you come to comfort me and desire to relieve me from my bad dream?"

"I did. But when I saw you in a dream of agony and turmoil, my love prompted me to change the pain into peace. Somehow and for some reason, I read your mind."

Shar Dea reaffirmed for him his masculine traits of protectionism. "No, you did exactly what you should have done. You didn't let emotions get in your way. Instead you got the facts and saw the truth of what was happening to me. In the ways of a wise spiritual person, you learned from my sorrow. That's the way to become a leader for Peace."

Monday morning's awakening adventure set the pace for a week of hard work and little play. A rough schedule and trying times were in store for Shar Dea and Michael, who played a secondary role to her efforts and studies. Not much was to happen for Michael, except a lot of research.

As they were getting dressed, Shar Dea asserted, "Michael, let me tell you of our plan. And please do be patient with me, for this week will initiate potential global changes for humanity."

Michael put on a bold and stern face. "Shar Dea, so far you've taken me on a journey from a beach bum looking for some quick action all the way to an Assistant Savior. I'm one hundred percent behind you. Please let me in on your secret mission, if you can?"

"All right, my man. As far as I can comprehend, my job is to first find out about my past. Second, to find out about the history of the world from the day I mysteriously left Atlantis to this very day. And third, I must touch upon the Spirit of Ara E Hum and accept my destiny."

"Which is?" interrogated Michael.

"Michael, I think I'm supposed to deliver a message to the

world."

"What kind of message?" he insisted.

"A message about survival and world peace."

"Oh! Good luck! See you in Sing Sing!" he said sarcastically.

"Michael, I'm very serious!"

"I'm sorry. There's just been too much of that stuff floating around. It doesn't help nor does it get people to think a bit harder."

"True so far. But I'll tell you that this time it's for real. I'll prove it to you. Ready?"

"Yep!"

"You're going to sneeze in a moment. And in about three minutes, your mother will call you. She's going to hit you with the question that makes you shiver."

Michael didn't budge one iota until Shar Dea said, "She's mad at you for neglecting to call her since you last did. Do you remember the last time you spoke to her?"

"No! So big . . ." Michael's body went into sudden convulsions as he prepared to violently explode with the inevitable sneeze. "A . . . ah . . . chew!"

"See!"

Michael's eyes were red with embarrassment. In a few seconds he got his breath back and sternly said, "Shar Dea! What is going on here?"

Shar Dea immediately took on an innocent look. She shrugged her shoulders as if to indicate neutrality.

"How did you know about my last phone call to my mother? . . ."

R-I-N-G! R-I-N-G!

Michael's entire body went into its second convulsion. His chin dropped, his mouth opened, and a swift rise of redness blanketed his face.

R-I-N-G! R-I-N-G!

"Shit! I don't believe this." He went over to the phone and picked it up. "Hi, Mom! Not now please! Listen, I've got to call you back. Give me ten minutes. OK! Thanks!" He hung up immediately, expressing his anger by banging the receiver down on the phone. "Shar Dea, are you fooling around with my head?"

"No! No! No! I mean what I say about survival and world peace. I am their last hope. Do you understand that?

"OK. You win. You've got my respect, and my love." He walked around the sofa, and came right back to Shar Dea and said, "Hey, you're also going to get a lot of my masculinity, too."

"Fine."

"Let me call back my mom before she croaks. Then we will do some serious planning. Ok!"

Michael had a lot of explaining to do. After an hour or so, he said goodbye to his mother. He was exhausted and needed desperately to relax his mind. He turned on the stereo and started a cozy fire.

"Who's on, Michael?"

"The Alan Parson Project."

"What's that? The name of a scientific project," responded Shar Dea.

Michael threw in a curve. "Yea, the Secret Service."

She came back with a more eloquent reply. "They wish! If they could produce such fine tunes like that, the government would be in good shape."

"Yea, really!" supported Michael.

Shar Dea motioned to Michael to come to her. "Michael, let's get on with the plans for this week."

As he approached her, his palate prompted him to suggest some wine. "Want some Cabernet Sauvignon?"

"That sounds good."

The wine was poured and they positioned themselves for a lengthly conversation. Shar Dea initiated the plans. "I need for you to work very astutely for me this week. Your task will consist of preparing leading information for me to focus on. What I need is for you to gather as many names as possible of individuals involved in global decision making. We'll need names of famous and important people. These people are the leaders and activists, such as the Pope, Heads of State, radicals, poets and writers, and most importantly musicians. By doing this, I can easily target my mind absorbing skills onto any particular person I choose, enter his aura, and read his entire life history. Once I complete that process I would know every single belief, behavior, and thought of that person."

Michael lifted up his eye brows and said, "Now that sounds a little far fetched."

"Remember that little boy on the beach with the burn injury? Didn't I know about him and his mother?"

"Hum . . . your right, Shar Dea."

"Most importantly, Michael, I could tell whether or not the person was speaking the truth from his or her heart. Do you understand the importance there?"

"Very much so." He paused for a moment, then said, "Okay, you want me to read newspapers, magazines, watch the news, investigate movements, good or bad, and become Mr. Cronkite."

Shar Dea's face showed approval, until she flinched at the word 'Cronkite'.

To express his enthusiasm, Michael took the long stemmed wine glass and converted it into a microphone, and humorously recited, "Good evening, this is Michael Walter Cronkite, of the

Shar Dea News Media Service, reporting world and local news to you, on this day, December 8, 19 . . ."

"Cut the bull!" ordered Shar Dea without any soreness.

"I got carried away."

"You're not a ham, Michael, but funny."

She gave him a big smile. "Anyway, you got the picture. I'll need at least fifty names or events happening around the world each morning. We'll discuss the specifics of each right after breakfast. During the day, you go your way and gather the information. I'll do my thing."

"And what's that?" asked Michael.

"I'll be meeting all the people on your list. If it's an event, like a terrorist bombing or the signing of a document or pack, I can focus on the real purpose, intent, and truth of the event. This way we can find out if it's for good or the usual bullshit!"

"Shar Dea! Your mouth is rattling off some pretty awful wordage. Do you realize what . . ."

"Say no more, you're right. I'm amazed how easily a person can acquire lower thinking habits. Just imagine how adults can pollute the innocent minds of our children with substandard wordage."

"Let's get back to our plan," prompted Michael. "How exactly are you going to find out about an event that has already happened?"

"Easily. But first of all, there must not be any interruptions whatsoever. I'll be on the back deck most of the day investigating and recording information."

Michael coached her on. "Tell me a little more, my imagination is limited."

"Michael, you never fail to poke a little finger at me when I say something that's not simple. I take it for granted that your thinking is as acute as mine."

"I'm teasing," he said cautiously.

"Each day I'll be diligently astral dreaming, but this time with great amounts of concentration. When I do this, I consume tremendous amounts of energy and usually get exhausted. That's why I need all your support and love."

"More, please!" Michael edged on.

"While in these forced dream states, I am able to read auras, thoughts, see and listen, and even learn the environment. In a matter of a few moments, I'm able to scan a person's lifelong activities. As I incorporate all the information that I want, it will become permanently part of my aura and memory."

"That's unbelievable!" commented Michael.

"There's a couple of things I just can't do," she claimed.

"What's that?"

"Remember, I can't touch or do anything physically.

Michael played upon Shar Dea's seriousness and blurted a kind of ridiculous comment. "So if you do this to all the people in the world that I chart for you, Shar Dea, just how big would you be?"

Her rebuttal came swiftly. "About the size of your big fat head, Michael. Can't you get serious?"

"Sometimes not! It just sounds too kooky to me. How can you visit fifty people and places in a day, all over the world, and record it all? It just sounds impossible to me. And I am very serious about what I mean!"

Shar Dea respected his plea. "Let me put it to you this way. What's a God?"

Michael said, "A Supreme Being."

"Why do civilizations pray to them and make sacrifices for them?"

"Ah . . . because they fear God," replied Michael.

"It's because the gods know everything about everything! And, there's a mighty power behind all that which makes mankind shiver at the magnitude of the mind of God."

Shar Dea paused for a moment, then said, "But, it's all written. It's just a matter of learning how to read the unseen, whether telepathically, astrally, or while in the Akashic Record. Christ did it! The Bible speaks about it! But, why on earth do so few believe in it?"

"True, but you're not a God!" retorted Michael.

"Look, I know it sounds a bit over your head, but by next Sunday, I will have more information in my head than the the Central Intelligence Agency's computer will have in all it's databases combined! And that's a fact!"

"Well, I'll give it a try. I'm behind you regardless. You mean well, and that's the important thing."

With Michael's vote of confidence supporting her good intentions, Shar Dea summarized her plans. "Michael, during the day I'll be travelling in the astral world. You will need to make sure that my physical body is safe and comfortable. We will have breakfast and supper together. At night, between 1:00 A.M. and 3:00 A.M., I'll be in the Akashic Record learning about myself, and my destiny. I can't tell you any more, but please have faith in me."

# CHAPTER 16
# THE THREE DESTINIES

(Civilization's . . . Earth's . . . Shar Dea's)

". . . The time has come when we may
choose to die for Mother Earth, but it's
unlikely we'll remain in the Piscean Age
justifying war as good . . . it takes 5 billion
conscientious objectors to invalidate the
thought of war. ". . . Mother Earth has
received some injuries, but we care, and we
now see how we can change patriotism into
enthusiasm for healing the Planet."
—Andrea Kay Smith

For seven days and seven nights, Shar Dea performed a
strenuous campaign to catch up on the history of the world. In so
doing, she realized her place and purpose. She also saw into the
future and it was glorious. However, she did see some major
changes.

Other than normal hellos and good-byes, Michael and Shar
Dea spent little time, if any, together. They had minor
interaction during the seven day campaign; both were busy doing
their thing and compiling the data.

It was around 4:00 A.M. Monday morning when Shar Dea
returned from her final journey. She opened her eyes and stared
across the length of the bed for about three minutes looking
mysteriously into the void of the room. Slowly she put her feet
on the floor, got up and walked to the bedroom balcony, which
overlooked the ocean.

The three-quarter moon was crystal clear and pulling away,
rising higher and higher, southwestwardly. Her concentration on
the moon was mystifying. While grabbing the wooden railing, she
tilted her body slightly backwards, and said, "Moon, what a
beautiful child you are, hovering around your mother for
comfort, and receiving light and guidance from your distant
father, the sun. You're no different than human beings, the
process is only a billion times slower. Can you hear me, distant
child? How painful it must be to see all the misery and wars
which take place on your mother's land?"

"Shar Dea, are you up?" said Michael in a half dazed mind.

He got up and on the way to his mystic traveler, he grabbed

her white-laced nightgown. Ever so gently, he draped the nightgown over her shoulders and caressed her in admiration.

"I'm glad you're back, my Empress," he said.

She touched his hands in a comforting maternal manner and said, "So am I."

With a pose of diligence, Michael asked, "What's the word?"

Her reply was simple. "The WORD is good."

Michael said, "Even though I understand what you mean by 'good', I doubt if the WORD will be appreciated or even perceived as good by the rest of the civilized community. Tell me more."

"My journeys revealed to me some kind of migration of souls, that is, from one civilization to another.

"Souls undergo lifetimes of development and take on physical human shells which must be respected as the soul's Tabernacle in Peace. Should the soul subject its Tabernacle to pain and disrespect, then only through learning how to overcome pain and disrespect can the soul survive. This means that there are no guarantees on the eternal life of the soul. It must be prepared to survive and learn to love unconditionally if it seeks eternal Peace."

Michael was listening with great intensity. "Go on," he said.

"Michael, my travels traced the history of my soul; the beginning of which was a bit beyond my comprehension. I felt the colorful vibrations of Peace and Love, as I know of them today. But I could not grasp them. My father, always spoke of Ara E Hum as an energy life force. I remember him saying, "Shar Dea, LIFE is constantly moving in the highest unseen forms; you can not grab them or stop them, for then, they wouldn't be LIFE."

Shar Dea began to tell Michael some of the scenes which she had encountered. "Before Atlantis was Lemuria, a large Pacific island which flourished under the primal pink sky. The Lemurians were mostly new souls experiencing the planet of Love and Emotions. They knew little about physical matter, and ignorantly became subjected to it, only to find themselves separated from Ara E Hum, and eventually, fearful of the unseen. Their beliefs deteriorated and so did their civilization, except for a few developed souls who migrated elsewhere."

Figuratively speaking, Michael said, "I wonder how many civilizations in recorded history lost their beliefs in the spirit, and consequently vanished?"

Shar Dea's eyes moved upwards as she realized another important aspect of developing the soul.

Still somewhat dazed until Michael moved his head between her eyes and the ceiling, and spouted out, "Ancient Empress, who and what were you on Lemuria? Please, it's exciting to hear

74

one's history."

Slightly stunned, with her eyes still enlarged and rigid, she regained her awareness, and told Michael to rest his bottom brain on the chair. He did, of course, without a return compliment.

"Listen, Michael, there is so much to say. So I'll be brief, and tomorrow, I'll fill you in on all the rest. But I am extremely tired now and need some sleep soon."

"Okay Empress, how about a class of Beaujolais to smooth your voice and serve as a nightcap?"

"That would be fine, Michael."

Michael went over to the bedroom selection of his choice wines and poured two glasses of his favorite beaujolais.

While sipping on the delicious red wine, Shar Dea began to talk about her travels. "In Lemuria I was the only son of the Empress, Eram, and the brother of twelve younger sisters. My name was Haram Dat, and I was called the 'Speaker'. This was my first physical life form on this planet. My mission, as ordained by the Empress, was to speak of the physical universe and its relation to the planet Heart. Most of the inhabitants of planet Heart were females. There was only one male per twenty females.

"I lived for over five hundred years, and left the peaceful land in a ceremonial transcendence. My next three lives were not on this planet. During that time, I was well aware of the beginning trend of metaphysical and spiritual deteriorization of the people on Lemuria."

"Shar Dea," asked Michael, "How did you know that was beginning to happen?"

She replied, "I saw myself looking on Lemuria from a place high above in a different solar system. I was learning how to use my Inner Eye, which you see me use quite often in your presence.

"Michael, this is very important. While in another universe, I learned something very secret and sacred. Now it is for us to share this to all."

Shar Dea stood up in front of Michael, paused, and took a sip of wine. Then she rested the glass on the table and calmly shared her knowledge with Michael. The planet, Earth is alive and has its own consciousness, and she is a proud female. Originally, males were not of this planet. Females were the principle dwellers of the planet. Men would migrate here from several sources in spirit, and take on human physical form."

"Shar Dea, do you actually mean that females had their own civilization on this planet before men came around?"

"Not exactly like that, Michael."

"Try this, Ara E Hum created all life and in so doing this, the laws of perfection and balance were also created."

"So far, so good."

"Assume for a moment that this planet is truly proven to be of female origin. Its function, behavior, and physical expressions should therefore reflect femininity. Now, would a man start that kind of operation?"

Spontaneously Michael replied, "Don't ask me!"

Shar Dea's lips puckered up. "Michael," she said, "Without man, what's the purpose of a woman?"

Michael's face lit up like a red balloon. "Right!"

"So, what's the purpose of a man, without a woman?"

With a little white returning to his face, Michael simply replied, "Frustrating, Shar Dea! Frustrating!" His comment followed a little nod from Shar Dea, who was well aware of Michael's low thresholds of sexual frustrations.

Then in a loud tone of exasperation, Shar Dea spoke out, "Of course the planet was created for both male and female, but the whole point of it is that this planet belongs to females, not males. And as your own eyes can see today, it's the selfish, powerful and ignorant male who is screwing up the whole planet!"

"Wow! Calm down, Shar Dea!" demanded Michael, as he got up to caress her and ease her emotional outbreak. She started to cry. Michael was taken back for a second. He grabbed a couple of tissues to wipe her tears from her cheeks. Michael absorbed her pain.

A few minutes later and in a more relaxed mood, Shar Dea looked straight into Michael's eyes, and said, "Who's going to believe me?"

She sipped some more wine. Then with a quick turn, moved her hands in front of Michael, as if to stop him from moving, and said, "Let me continue, . . . while in Atlantis, I was being educated by my father and mother to learn the ways of the Supreme Ara E Hum. My parent's mission was never explained to me, but they knew quite well that I would, someday, be required to become the 'Speaker' of the people of the promised land. I loved and obeyed my parents, and I cannot recall one bad mental utterance or thought towards them. I felt feelings of frustration many times, because as I grew wiser and more loving, I saw my people lose faith in Love and Peace. What I really saw was the realities of Lemuria being repeated in Atlantis.

"I sought to 'Speak' to the ailing society, but my parents told me to wait, for it was not my time. I must have to admit, I was getting a little punchy about that restraint.

"What actually happened in my ancient land of Atlantis was that eventually most of the civilization chose the same paths as did the Lemurians—fear and war against each other. The planet Heart had no choice other than to protect herself. She chose the only method of cleansing her ailment, and that was a natural act on her part. She destroyed the entire continent and all its people, except for a few developed souls. It all happened in one day and in one night. As horrifying as it might have been for those poor souls, it was truly an awesome sight to behold. This all happened five hundred years after my mysterious disappearance from the beach—the night of the electrical storm.

"America, the land of new hope, may very well be the child of the civilization of Atlantis. It carried with her many of the same beliefs and principles which Atlantis was founded upon.

"Amerii Kai arranged for his people to settle there in order to protect and continue the spiritual heritage of the ancient Atlanteans and Lemurians. But, today, this child civilization, America, is repeating the same deterioration as her mother civilizations."

Shar Dea took a deep breath, then continued. "Michael, it's my inherent right and honor, to fulfill my destiny."

Michael paused for a couple of moments and asked Shar Dea, "So my lovely Empress, what is your destiny?"

Her reply was swift and concise: "To become the 'Speaker of Peace'!"

# CHAPTER 17

# UNITED FOREVER

*"And when is man called "one"? When he
is male with female and is sanctified with a
high holiness and is bent upon sanctification;
then alone is he called one without blemish.
Therefore a man should rejoice with wife at
that hour to bind her in affection to him, and
they should both have the same intent. When
they are thus united, they form one soul and
one body."*
     —*The Holy Kabbalah*
    *Zohar Part III, fow. 8ia; V,224*

It was after 2:00 P.M. in the afternoon on Tuesday before
sunlight entered their eyes.

"Oh boy, it's late," mumbled Michael, as he stretched his
arms outward while sitting up in bed. The contour of his dear
friend could be easily observed with the naked eye. Her hip was
the target of a wake-up love tap. Down went his beastly hand.
Whack!

"Michael!" shouted Shar Dea. Patter followed, "I'm getting
up, really, I am."

Not a budge. Whack!—number two. "OK! OK! I'm up
now," was her next best defense.

"It's past 2:00," said Michael.

"Food, Michael! Food! Please! . . . Please! . . . Please!" sang
from beneath Shar Dea's sheets.

Michael said, "Sure, anything for you, my Empress." And he
said it with all the sincerity in his heart.

Eggs benedict was his delight and his specialty. Michael's
subconscious mind shouted out: Heck, why not give it another
try?

Just has he finished pouring the hollandaise sauce over the
eggs, Shar Dea walked into the kitchen area. She trapped her
arms around him and said in a haphazardly serious tone, "We've
got a lot of hard work ahead of us today, my man."

He turned immediately at her and saw sparse pickings for
clothing. In his little childlike mind, the sense of play was
awakened. With an attempt to defend his well prepared
breakfast he said, "Breakfast is ready." That was an unsuccessful
statement.

Her response was convincing, "So am I."

The beauty of love was bestowed upon them. In their hearts a new awakening transpired. Gently and ever so gracefully they ascended into the spiritual realities ever so sought by mankind. Few achieve this splendor; it was theirs to enjoy.

Slowly, sounds and colors of ecstasy appeared before their eyes; spectacular visions of a world visited by few. For Shar Dea and Michael, the beginning of a new life was in the making. Each move, each touch, each heartbeat brought them closer and closer to an inevitable destiny of oneness. Slowly, the music of life filled the room, all temptation and lust gone, only innocence and tranquility of the minds prevailed.

Then, from the distant universe, a small bright light began to approach them. Their souls focused on their unification, and in a most passionate rhythm of LOVE, they became mystified by the brilliance of the light. Hand on hand and soul on soul they readied themselves. The light echoed with magnificent sounds of the heavens and captured them in awe. Soon it was upon them and engulfed them. In its midst, the power of Ara E Hum electrified their souls and made them one. Its deliverance was monumental and full of splendor. All was united into one. The sounds of multicolored crystals displayed full spectrums of gold and silver-blue light rays: each traveling through their transparent souls and far beyond their sight. Deeper and deeper they traveled with the light until they saw all of the worlds of LOVE and PASSION before them. Moment by moment they knew the secrets of LOVE and its beauty unfolding. It was there that they consciously experienced infinite pleasures of sharing unconditional Love and Acceptance.

Slowly, in the total ecstasy of stillness, silence begot their hearts. Their eyes now at rest, and in the depths of serenity and tranquility, they became surrounded by the protection of PEACE. It was then that Shar Dea and Michael experienced the feelings of eternity.

Out of this eternal sense of PEACE came a cool and moist breeze accompanied with faint sounds of crystals echoing in the distance. Shar Dea opened her eyes only to capture the love in Michael's eyes, as he saw the love in her eyes. Each face was pictured with tears upon its cheeks. Nothing need be said.

Shar Dea walked over to the shower room and Michael soon followed. Afterwards, they hurried downstairs and uttered their first words.

"I'm starved, Michael."

"So am I."

Shar Dea went over to the table and once again rested her eyes upon poor Mr. Eggs Benedict. With an apologetic smile on her face, she said, "We're sorry, but you always manage to encourage something special for us. Thank you kindly."

Michael was in the kitchen working by the counter area fixing up a couple of mushroom and cheese pocket bread sandwiches. Shar Dea came up from behind him, rested her chin on his shoulders and said, "Michael, I love you."

"My Empress, I love every bit of you too."

"Michael, I feel most ready and exhilarated to share my life with you. I want your hand."

"My dear Shar Dea, my love for you has grown beyond my imagination. I am in awe with you presence. Ever since I first met you on the beach, I heard a compeling force say to me that you're a part of me. Now I know you are. You are me, and I you. There's no doubt. I love you Shar Dea. My life is yours."

"Let's go into Charleston and get married," said Shar Dea.

"Fine!" he replied in delight.

* * *

On the drive back to the beach house, Shar Dea and Michael were unusually quiet.

"My Empress, how come so quiet?"

"Oh just thinking."

"How about sharing some of it?" Michael said with encouragement.

"Sure, I never had a relationship with a male before, spiritually or otherwise."

"And?"

"Well, what about you?" inquired Shar Dea.

Michael was a little confused on her questioning and said, "What are you trying to get me to say? I really don't catch on to this?"

"Michael, it has often been said that lightning strikes the earth somewhere every second. Then is it possible that people engage in sex, but not necessarily out of love, about every second?"

"Oh! I see what you are asking me," said Michael. "There is no denying that I've had other women before, and thoroughly enjoyed them, as well."

"Well did you love them?" she asked with a bit of remorse.

Michael's reply was sincere, "Shar Dea, you showed me what true love is. I never experienced such love from anyone in my life," he paused, "nor could I have given someone such love, until I met you."

"Those are kind words, Michael."

"So is your soul, Shar Dea."

# CHAPTER 18

# THE NEW TRIAD

*I am my beloved's,*
*And his desire is toward me.*

*—The Holy Scriptures, The Song of Songs, 7:11*

"Michael, let's go out for dinner tonight. It's a treat to our oneness," suggested Shar Dea.

Michael joyfully responded, "I agree! I could really get my palate into some lobster, a delicate salad, fresh baked bread, and some Mouton-Cadet."

"Sounds romantic."

"I'll take you to the Sounds of the Sea restaurant. It's on the intercoastal waterway on the northern part of town. Maybe about a forty minute drive from here."

"That's fine with me," Shar Dea blurted out with glee.

They arrived at the beautifully decorated restaurant about 7:00 P.M. that Tuesday evening. They both looked spiffy. Michael was dressed in an outlandishly casual outfit; any passer-by would subconsciously term him 'a man of leisure'. Michael's mate wore a tempting low cut satin dress, which she bought that afternoon for her wedding. She pursuaded Michael to believe that she wore it as a token of women's identity and independence. Actually, Shar Dea was pushing her gifted body a bit much. As it was, neighboring, jealous eyes were about. Several men were committing minor accidents: they were not concentrating on what they were doing.

The setting was definitely romantic and the dinner delicately prepared. It was a treat for them and quite an experience for Shar Dea.

With the candlelight in their eyes, love was pulsating throughout their bodies. A final toast was made. The wine glasses clung together and brought a farewell to the superb and exquisite dinner.

The drive home was along the winding two lane beach road. The waves of the Atlantic were peaceful and a white satin glow appeared on the ocean's horizon, in advent of the rising full moon.

The ride was truly enjoyable. Both of the newly weds were quite relaxed and and quite happy. Shar Dea felt content about her accomplishments: a feeling of self-satisfaction. She looked at

Michael's profile as he was driving, and said, "Michael, do you realize how much I learned about myself, you, and the history of the planet in such a short time?"

"Na! It never impressed me one bit," he hinted.

Shar Dea began to snuggle up to his cheek. "For that, you deserve a big kiss."

Without hesitation, Michael pulled over to the side of the road and parked his red convertible. The only thought on his mind was to take full advantage of his new bride's kiss. It was a romantic scene as the satin and yellowish moon broke the horizon and began its slow and glorious ascent into the sky.

Back in the beach house, Michael started a fire in the brick fireplace. He got some more Mouton-Cadet from his bedroom collection. Shar Dea was sitting on the oriental rug, with her back leaning on the sofa. The fire began to crackle and distribute pulsating colors around the room.

She held up her glass so that Michael could pour the wine into it. While pouring, Shar Dea saw the image of the fire concavely being reflected on the back side of her glass. Instantly, her body shrilled. The visions she saw alluded her thoughts to forthcoming traumatic cataclysmic events that she'd gained knowledge of in the Akashic Record.

She became tense and emotional. "Michael, hold me, please quickly," she begged.

"What's wrong, my Empress?"

She explained to him what happened in her mind. However, what was more devastating to Michael was her knowledge of future.

"Michael," she said, "we need to become more involved with the everyday flow of life, people, and governments. This must be done quickly, for our time is short."

Michael took his hands and placed them on each side of Shar Dea's face. He offered these words of oneness to her, "My Empress of Peace, though you are officially my wife, I yield to your beliefs and ways that you profess. I love you dearly, and I am truly your servant."

"Michael," she replied, "you should have been with me during the days of Atlantis."

"I probably was, from all that you said."

"Shar Dea, how do you propose to begin your mission as 'Speaker of Peace'?"

"Maybe you can tell me. Your background and work is in journalism, right? Well then," articulated the Empress, "how would you rattle the attention of the masses?"

Michael sarcastically giggled, then he cracked a deceiving smile, and said, "In the usual way, my dear, just make the headlines! Arouse the public! Call a spade a spade! You must assuredly, point the finger at the world's political and religious leaders. These are supposedly the delegated speakers of the people. Unfortunately, they got lost in the process and became self-centered and untruthful to the cause of PEACE."

"Very well," shouted Shar Dea. "I'll need you to offer me some more good suggestions real soon."

"Hey, lady," retorted Michael, "I was serious when I said those words about pointing the finger. However, you'll need to be very careful to whom you point at and what you target for the challenge. 'Cause some of those folks could very easily put a stop to you and your mission! Do you understand?"

Shar Dea quickly responded, "But that's my mission. I can't stop because of a challenge. It probably is the essence and source of major problems and deterrents of peace."

"Shar Dea, I think we might need a little help from the outside. Do you agree with that?"

"Sure do. I'd like to see every human being stand up and fight for peace and harmony throughout the world. Wouldn't you?"

"Be serious, Shar Dea!" exclaimed Michael with a chant of pessimism.

"Michael, you're great. I used to tell you to be serious, now . . ."

Michael interjected. "Donna. Donna Champlynn. She's my senior editor! That's who can help us. She knows a lot of important people nationally and abroad. I'll give her a call right now."

Michael was excited by his suggestion. Shar Dea, on the other hand, tried to share his joy by putting on a smile, but was actually somewhat taken by Michael's aggressiveness. As he skimmed through his personal phone book for Donna's secret home listing, Shar Dea interrupted him, and said, "Let's talk this over for a minute, okay?"

Michael, paused; turned around to Shar Dea, and said, "I'm part of you and am here to serve you. Trust me on these matters, OK . . . Please."

"I'm sorry, Michael. I guess I'm caught up in the awe of the whole mission. Your aggressiveness frightens me. It reminds me of how the aggressive males in Lemuria acted out behaviors which the females were ignorant of and by which they were eventually overruled."

Michael's response to that was: "Oh! So that's man's hang-up."

"Not really, Michael. It's really fear on the part of women. They can't cope or compete with that aspect of male aggressiveness consistently. Therefore, they have learned to withdraw and obey."

"Ah, I see more of the male-female problems surfacing," expounded Michael.

"Your friend, Donna. Do call her," requested Shar Dea.

"Let's see. Ah! Here it is . . . 555-2247," mumbled Michael to himself, as he put the telephone receiver between his shoulders and left ear.

"Hi, Donna . . . It's Michael . . . Fine . . . Sorry about calling so late at night . . . Yes . . . Well I've been extremely busy working at my beach house . . . Everything is fine here . . . Listen, I'm kind of curious to know if you would like to meet my wife . . . Yes, I got married! . . . Aha! . . . She's beautiful . . . Shar Dea . . . Shar Dea! . . . It's an ancient name . . . I'll explain it to you sometime . . . You don't believe me? . . . You would . . . Fine."

Michael turned to Shar Dea, and said, "She doesn't believe me and wants to talk to you personally. Is that Okay with you?"

Shar Dea looked at Michael, shrugged her shoulders and said, "Fine."

"Hi, Donna . . . This is Shar Dea . . . Yes, we are really married and in more ways than you may presently realize . . . It's hard to believe it too. It's been a long time in the waiting . . . No, he wouldn't have mentioned it to you before . . . Why, because . . . Hey, would you like to get acquainted tonight, if possible? . . . Great, we'll drive over to your place. The moon is just too beautiful to let go by so silently into the heavens by itself . . . Great, I love herbal tea . . . Can't wait to meet you . . . Bye!"

"How did you do that?" questioned Michael while raising his hands above his head in wonderment.

"I don't know. She sounds wonderful, intelligent, exciting, and she's not a man," replied Shar Dea.

# CHAPTER 19

# THE BOOK—PART I: A Start

*"Whatever you can do or dream you can,
begin it; boldness has genius, power and
magic in it."*
—Goethe

The drive over to Donna's home was delightful. The moon proved its friendliness by providing some magnificent and serene scenes. Shar Dea was in a talkative mood and was curious to know more about Donna's way of life.

"Does Donna work with you Michael?"

"More than that," replied Michael, "she's my boss."

"Oh!" nodded Shar Dea. "Do you get along with her?"

Michael grinned, "Better than she does me."

Shar Dea's eyebrows instantly became uneven, "Why the difference in perspectives?"

Michael looked at Shar Dea, and said, "You should know. Remember how I used to behave? You know! Regarding my sexual desires and my boyish attitude about girls and things?"

"Ah yes! And, I'm glad you've outgrown that attitude," complimented Shar Dea.

"Well, Donna knows me as the other guy—the boy! She perceives me as a rich mamma's boy who's preoccupied with playing around and having fun. There's only one thing that saves me; that's her respect for my excellent and creative work."

"Michael, it seems to me that she does have some good feelings for you. After all, you are very handsome. More so, you have an attractive masculinity about you."

"Okay. Some of that may be true," offered Michael, "but all too often I found myself chasing after her, and without success!"

"Aha! She's curious to see how I fit in with you. Better yet, she's anxious to see her competition."

Michael got a little annoyed, and remarked, "What's this women stuff you're chattering out?"

"Michael, please don't mind me. I'm sorry. I guess I'm a bit nervous, too."

They parked their convertible in the underground parking lot, and walked over to the elevator. As soon as the elevator got underway, Shar Dea expressed her sensations, "Yow, this is new to me. It's feels like we're going to fly away."

Donna lived on the twenty-first floor of a luxury high rise

condominium. The building was located mid-way between the downtown area and the country side. It's architectural design blended well with the environment. Each of the apartment units accessed three balconies which welcomed nature in and out.

Michael's finger swiftly pressed the gold and black plated doorbell button. The doorbell rang and reminded Shar Dea of the heavenly crystal chimes she heard in her love travels with Michael. Shar Dea giggled, and said to Michael, "She's got a head start on her men." Michael looked at Shar Dea, and said, "What's come over you?"

The door opened. A bright, cheerful and loving face appeared. "Hi! . . . You must be Shar Dea?"

Shar Dea acknowledged with a smile and yielded a slight yes motion with her head.

Donna continued. "I'm Donna . . . Happy to meet you . . . Hi Mike!"

Michael was not going to let an opportunity like this pass him by without taking some good notes. He watched them interact with extreme sensitivity. His eyes were as sharp as an eagle's. The two ladies rapidly began exchanging their first words. Their mouths were rattling at full speed. However, Michael was in third place, and he realized it too. Then he astutely gestured a friendly courtesy, and said, "Hi, my name is Michael, I'll see you both in a couple of minutes. I'm getting hungry." He disappeared out of sight, heading straight to the refrigerator.

The exchange between Shar Dea and Donna was efficient and thorough. They had no obvious incongruencies. Friendship was imminent.

It was the first time since Michael had met Shar Dea that he found himself shared. Actually, he enjoyed every minute of it. His chest inflated with a sense of pride, for captive in one room were his two favorite ladies.

They sat around Donna's fireplace and engaged in exploratory conversation. It took a little convincing to prove to Donna that Michael and Shar Dea really did get married. But soon Donna accepted their marriage as a fact.

An hour had passed since the newlyweds arrived, and Shar Dea began to shine with an aura of gentleness. In a very tender fashion, she asked Michael if he would excuse Donna and herself. She was suggesting to him that they needed to speak woman to woman.

Michael headed for the records, while the two ladies walked out to the balcony. Outside, the breeze was cool and offered a slight chill. The moonlight put the finishing touches to a night that Donna would never forget.

"Donna," candidly asked Shar Dea, "what do you think of

me?"

Donna was taken by surprise. She showed a little hesitation, in order to maintain neutrality, she replied, "I think you're a lovely person."

"Donna. Really! Tell me how you feel about me."

Donna said, "I don't know. But you are strange." Donna contemplated for a moment and reconciled her statement. "I'm sorry," she apologized. "I mean you certainly act different."

"How so?"

"You seem to know me too well. However, I don't feel uncomfortable or intimidated about it," remarked Donna. She then paused for a second or two, then said, "Shar Dea. Why did you marry Michael?"

"Because he and I experienced oneness while in love, and I was taught to recognize the miracle in Life by my spiritual fathers."

Donna stood back and looked concerned. Then in a rather harsh tone said, "You've only known this man for a few days, and made love to him a couple of times, and then married him!"

Shar Dea held her comments and remained silent for a couple of breaths. Then she said, "Yes. But it's not exactly that simple, Donna."

Donna puffed-up while maintaining the same expression of concern, and blurted, "Sweetheart. Only four weeks ago, he tried to get into my pants. He's a nice guy, but aren't you moving a little too fast?"

"No!"

Donna prompted Shar Dea again. "Please don't be offended, but you asked me to say what I feel. Michael is a hunk, but I've always known him to be a rich wimp. I don't want to hurt your feelings, but you do come on strong about things yourself."

"Are you finished, Donna?" hinted Shar Dea.

Donna was stymied. "What are you asking me now, Shar Dea?"

"I want your help."

"Aha! I knew this would come, but not so soon," acknowledged Donna.

"I want you to write a book for me," petitioned Shar Dea.

"A what?" shouted Donna.

"A book!"

"You're kidding me. I don't even know you yet," stated Donna defensively.

"Then why such inconsistent, painful, and factitious statements about my ability to choose a man whom I've been waiting for thousands of years?"

Donna's mouth hung open and positioned itself in utter confusion. She walked into her living room and sat down on the sofa. Michael came into the room sensing that Shar Dea had altered Donna's stubborn thinking process and put her into a mesmerized trance.

Donna sat up, but looked very pretentious. She looked repeatedly at Michael and Shar Dea. Wondering what she was getting herself involved in, she exclaimed, "OK guys, what's going on here? I'll listen, but it better be good!"

Michael hinted with a touch of enthusiasm, "It's a very special event, and we welcome you to join us in a spiritual adventure in life and the pursuit of world peace."

Silence befell the triad. Michael and Shar Dea remained still and peaceful. Then Donna lamented sarcastically, "A book, uh?" She delicately nodded a very doubtful yes.

Michael shouted out, "Great!"

Immediately, relief fell upon them. They began to smile, relax and converse. The newly-formed triad knew that they were about to make something major happen.

# CHAPTER 20

# THE BOOK—PART II: The Theme

*"There is perhaps only one hope for the future. That is that the people will learn the facts in time, and that an aroused public opinion will force the politicians to gain control, to stop the nuclear arms race and to reduce armaments."*
—*Olaf Palme*

About 10:00 A.M. Wednesday morning Donna called and suggested that the triad meet around noon for lunch. The plan was to meet at the beach house and prepare an agenda for action.

Both Shar Dea and Michael were overdue for some rest and relaxation. They put on their bathing suits, grabbed a blanket, and walked to their backyard beach. There they rested, stretched out, and consumed the sun. Soon they heard Donna's Japanese sports car pull up in the driveway. As she got out of the car, her eye caught Michael and Shar Dea lying on the beach. Donna shouted out, "Hey! Why didn't you tell me to bring my bathing suit? Shar Dea, do you have a spare one?"

"Yes, in our bedroom, in the top right hand drawer of the large dresser. Take any one you want."

Shar Dea had her new reflector eye shades on and was lying perfectly still in order to absorb every possible ray of the sun. Then she heard a street corner version of a 'high-there-babes' whistle emanating from Michael. His target was Donna. She was wearing the largest bathing suit that Shar Dea owned. However, Donna was about four inches taller and had a lot more contents to pack. Shar Dea turned around, and said, "Donna, Michael doesn't need this! Remember what you said last night."

"Oops! I forgot," replied Donna.

"Hey! Do I hear the sounds of a conspiracy here?" clamored Michael.

Michael's eye beamed in on Donna's beautiful qualities and slipped out a dangerous anecdote. Shar Dea heard it and rebutted, "What do you mean? You forgot how great she looks in a bathing suit." Shar Dea took him quite seriously and offered him a frown, but it was more like a warning.

Michael could do nothing but retreat and try to regain some color on his boyish face.

Donna accepted it all too easily, and said, "Listen you two, how about a short swim out into the deep blue sea."

Michael jumped up, looked at Donna, and said, "Beat you in!"

They swam straight out about 500 yards then returned. In the shallow waters they began splashing and playing around—dunking one another and having fun. Soon they were lying on the beach blanket utterly exhausted.

After some general lazy conversation, Shar Dea suggested that they all go inside for a quick lunch. They did and afterwards, they went into Michael's main study, and sat around his newly inherited mahogany table, which his grandfather gave him.

Shar Dea lead the conversation. "Donna," she said, "We need you to write a book for me. It will be titled 'Earth vs. Heart: Are Males Earthbound?' The theme will focus on the historical and current inability of males to lead the planet Earth towards Peace. The plot is what we have to work on. As journalists, I'll need your working knowledge on how to get this book to the masses. We will need to know a strategy of how to get the leaders of this planet to unite in Peace. Are you with me?"

Michael retrieved his forty pounds of research and dropped it on the table. He looked at Donna, smiled, and said, "Here we go! There's enough research to start a world wide coup d'etat."

Donna looked up at Shar Dea and Michael with an expression of utter remorse. "Do we get killed in the process, guys?"

Shar Dea got up and walked over to Donna. While putting her hands on Donna's shoulders she softly stated, "I've only known you for a few short days, but seeking world peace is my destiny and possibly yours too."

Donna's eyes rolled upwards to meet with Shar Dea's line of vision. Then she said, "Now I know what you meant about searching for a man for thousands of years. You're dead serious, aren't you? Can you prove to me that your claim to be the Empress of Peace is true?"

Shar Dea paused for a moment, and then pointed to Michael. She asked Donna to comment about the changes in Michael's personality. Donna replied "Yea! Now he would be of interest to me. Yes, he has changed, and I could easily see him as my masculine partner."

"Donna, what do you mean by a masculine partner?" asked Shar Dea with a curious overtone.

Donna responded while holding onto a doubtful expression, "I don't know. I've never said anything like that before."

"Think hard for a minute, Donna," prompted Shar Dea.

"Well, maybe deep down in my heart, I really yearn for a

masculine complement to my own existence."

"Good thinking!" complimented Shar Dea.

Donna looked up at Shar Dea and slowly let out a smile of content. Then she said, "Keep on convincing me, Shar Dea. Keep on."

"OK. Are you satisfied with the way world leaders are managing our world affairs?" asked Shar Dea.

"Absolutely not!" shouted Donna. Then she got up and walked around the table, firmly rested her hands flat on it, and said, "Who are we kidding! Those fat bellies have done nothing but fought each others egos, manipulated laborers, stripped the lands of its life giving mysteries, raped the women, and started wars. They are even cunning enough to have other men die for them. Yes, I'm convinced; we need to do something that will knock the pants off these so-called leaders of people, businesses, governments . . ." Donna gasped for a breath of air, and continued. "Who in God's name is the governance of this planet anyway? . . . I'll bet . . ."

Michael never saw Donna lose her composure. He was taken a back and saw her rattling on and on. So he interjected, and loudly said, "Wow! She's D-Y-N-O-M-I-T-E!"

Donna immediately stopped. She turned towards Michael, and said, "Thanks! I don't know what got over me. I've had this blasted subject hidden and suppressed so long inside of me, that I just had to explode."

Reflecting Donna's anxiety, Shar Dea ran her fingers through her silky hair in frustration. She moved closer to Michael, and whispered for him to give her a big hug. It was his pleasure to do so. Tightly they embraced. Donna sought not to invade their privacy, and turned away, moving closer to the window. Michael's fraternal love for Donna made him aware of her loneliness. He caught the staring gaze in her eyes. She was lonely and without masculinity. Never did he imagine that she would permit herself to show that side of her personality. He felt a surge of love for her. Around the inner embrace of his arms was the woman of his dreams. Just a few steps away, the erotic lady of yesterday's love and lust yearned for his comfort.

He tapped Shar Dea softly on her buttocks, kissed her on the forehead, and gently eased away.

He slowly moved towards Donna and innocently passed in front of her. Michael abruptly stopped and consumed Donna's attention. "There's something that I wanted to do for a long time, but didn't have the privilege to do. Now, I am open, honest and loving." He moved slightly closer to Donna, took her by the hands, and said, "Hey lady! It's about time you and I let go, and exchange a couple of good loving hugs." The energies of love and friendship finally awakened between them. A true sense of honesty and respect was restored. The comforts of loyalty and admiration had begun. They held each other tightly and felt the spirit of life flow around and through them.

Shar Dea waited for a couple of minutes, then walked between Donna and Michael, and lovingly concluded, "I love you both, but enough's enough."

They meandered downstairs into the living room. For the most part, none of the three said much of anything important. Then Shar Dea made a statement, "Donna! Michael! Permit me to be candid. Upstairs was somewhat emotional for each of us in our own ways. The point was well made—that within each of us is a burning desire for change. However, it is our own human weakness which defaults our gut level feelings to find the answers for change. Instead we request proofs or avoid what we must be responsible for.

"The truth lies within our hearts, and we truly know that this planet is heading for potential natural disasters, unless something is done to stop it. Let's unite tonight in a ceremony that will bond us forever, and may Ara E Hum guide us towards WORLD PEACE."

# CHAPTER 21

# THE BOOK—PART III: The Plot

*"Mankind can find peace and harmony if
it is pursued without fear, rather with love."*
—Shar Dea

Shar Dea asked Michael and Donna to give her a moment of silence. Then she said, "OK. I've got it. Listen closely to this. The book must be written in simple and understandable language. All must be able to read it—from the intelligent to the ignorant, regardless of their natural colors.

There's still time to divert some of the forthcoming global disasters, which are being called to order by the planet. If man elects not to change his subconscious mind and pronounce a peace loving way, then the planet will abide by its own intuition. She will seek her own destiny, with or with out mankind."

Donna was scratching out some notes. She thumped her pencil a few times on the table and was thinking out loud to herself. Shar Dea was waiting patiently for Donna to say something. But Donna didn't. It was Michael who expressed his thoughts. "You know guys, it sounds as if Mother Planet Earth has taken over our minds and wants us to do her dirty work for her."

"Oh no she doesn't!" defended Shar Dea.

Donna interjected, "Listen you two, I'm already deeply involved in something equally as strange. Are we really the few chosen children of this planet, calling out to all our brothers and sisters for one final petition for help?"

"Yea, feels like if we fail, our Earth is determined to spank us all the way into hell—a day of infamy, so to speak," lamented Michael.

Shar Dea perked up. "Well let's get on with the book. It's already apparent that there's going to be an unrealistic amount of questioning going on between us."

In a very sarcastic overtone, Donna said, "Imagine what the publishers are going to say?"

"Screw them," Michael said pessimistically. "It's the bewildered reader who's got to act on this stuff."

Shar Dea angrily stated, "Let's quit now! Do you know how you both sound?"

"You're right, Shar Dea. This is not an easy assignment for us, for the publishers, or for the readers," said Donna confidently.

"Good! Now we are back on track," said Shar Dea with a new surge of vigor.

Michael left for a moment. He returned with some fresh squeezed orange juice. After one sip of the delicious natural treat, Shar Dea said, "Here's proof of what we are trying to save—our natural resources!"

Donna's face crunched up. "Natural resources? That's not a natural resource!"

Michael arrogantly interjected, "Oh yes it is! Soil! Soil and water are our most precious resources. They make food and support life. Think for a minute, without them, gold is worth shit!"

"Right on!" said Shar Dea.

Michael looked at Shar Dea and uttered, "Right . . . on?"

Donna look a little bewildered. "I think I understand, but tell me more," she pleaded.

Shar Dea clarified Michael's facts. "Donna, the leaders of the world must put their priorities in order. Industrial pollution, nuclear fallout and waste, deforestation, overpopulation, and worldwide poverty are but a few critically important issues which demand immediate attention. All these require accurate long range planning and resolutions. However, politics and military conflicts unfortunately interfere and receive the bulk of most governments' time and money.

"Based on the knowledge gained while in my astral dreams, I regret to say that if humanity is to survive, it must take an imperative and intense stand to overcome these issues. If not, then as I have seen, the integrity of the planet's own conscious mind will see to its own survival and force the issues on humanity."

Donna's response to Shar Dea's profound statements was captured in her expressions of absolute awe. With reverence and humbleness, Donna said, "'Force the issues on humanity'?"

Shar Dea shook her head up and down a couple of times, and said, "Yes! The truth of the matter is that there will be no time left for major wars. Mother Earth has already consumed enough sense of fear, agony, and pain from the people of the world. She has already formulated a cataclysmic change. Quite frankly, it's already in the making. Even if mankind does a fast turnaround, millions of lives will be lost. But this is good in the sense that their deaths come not from man's wickedness, rather, the due process of nature."

A new sense of urgency emanated from the triad. Their minds grew more serious. Shar Dea lead their thoughts when she voiced, "The plot must be directed so that the readers all over the world are encouraged to confront their leaders. We must motivate people who live in small primitive villages equally as those who live in big cities to confront their leaders. They must bring their leaders messages of the need for peace and respect for natural resources. It must be done at their level, in their environment, and for their own sake."

"There are thousands of different languages around the world," said Donna. "I guess I'll need to find some earthbound slob who loves humanity and the planet enough to translate this stuff."

"Well, there are plenty of 'earth bound slobs' out there who would enjoy the privilege," said Shar Dea.

Michael looked at Shar Dea, and said, "If we keep this book down to about fifty pages, the reading comprehension at a sixth grade level, and have a few good animations drawn, then we've got a chance."

Shar Dea agreed. "That sounds good to me."

Donna also agreed.

Shar Dea was smiling and becoming more excited. She sensed that Donna and Michael were starting to get more involved and accurate in their thoughts. She got up, and said, "Excuse me guys, I need to go to the rest station," and then quickly departed.

Donna leaned back on her chair and gave Michael a quick scan with her eyes. She felt completely involved and comfortable with Michael and Shar Dea. "Michael," she said, "you've changed so much since I last saw you at the office four weeks ago. Is it because of your relationship with Shar Dea?"

"Donna, with all due respect, I've been trying to date you for a long time. And as you well know, not with too much success. If you weren't my boss, I'd have tried some of my stupid macho tricks on you. But I didn't want to jeopardize my job. However, all my lust for women came to an abrupt end when I picked up Shar Dea at the beach. She was lost, and a stranger in a new land. Instantly my subconscious mind and mental faculties were sent into motion. I have been living in the state of awe because of her. After we started to know our histories and purposes, I've grown to love and admire her. Now she's my wife, but in reality, my Empress and Guardian. Need I say more?"

Donna kept her eyes affixed on Michael, not in disbelief, but in a sense of fascination. In a tenderly fashion, she softly uttered, "I feel her too. She's in my heart and my mind. I am open and trustworthy of her guidance. I will follow her to the end, wherever our destinies may be."

Michael looked into Donna's eyes and saw the voice of truth. A new person was in front of him. Gently, he moved closer to her and kissed Donna on her forehead.

Meanwhile, Shar Dea returned and saw them together. She walked up to them, and said, "Fine! I'm glad that you two great people are real true friends. Now you can see, as I do, that mankind can find peace and harmony if they pursue it, without fear, rather in love."

# CHAPTER 22

# THE BOOK—PART IV: The Outline

*"I know of no safe repository of the ultimate power of society but the people. And if we think them not enlightened enough, the remedy is not to take the power from them, but to inform them by education."*
*—Thomas Jefferson*

Shar Dea was pleased with Donna's and Michael's sense of growing loyalty to her cause. If anything was proven to her, she sensed accomplishment and fulfillment between her two friends. The task that she saw in front of her now was to convert four and half billion more folks. She was very cognizant that the success of the whole matter was contingent on the beliefs of the leaders of the world—getting the leaders to seek peace wholeheartedly.

Shar Dea turned to Donna, and asked, "What about an outline for the book? Any suggestions?"

"Yes, as a matter of fact, I have," aspired Donna.

Donna got up and began to walk slowly back and forth. She took ample time to think this one out. Her eyes opened wide, as if she got her thoughts lined up for a thought provoking statement, and uttered, "You see, the essence of it all is in the first few pages. Each word that appears on the first two pages must relate to inner peace. It must be captivating, definitely must not be threatening, political, religious, complex, boring, and . . . oh boy! I'm thoughtless." Donna lost her monumental suggestion. Redness creeped up her neck and around her face. She sat down quietly.

"Michael. It's your turn," edged on Shar Dea.

"Well, big letters are a must. Maybe a different title too. Like 'Man versus Peace', or 'Peace Now—Or Never', or 'I PEACE', or how about, 'I Am Peace'. Regardless, it's got to be simple!"

Shar Dea's posture stiffened. Her eyes locked into a trance. "Most of the world's population is existing below a decent standard of living."

Both Donna and Michael instantly agreed.

"Worse yet," retorted Shar Dea, "an extremely high percent are living outside the realm of a spiritual developmental process. Only a handful of well developed souls live a life in peacefulness. All but a few know in the end."

"Shar Dea, 'in the end' of what?" asked Michael.

Shar Dea instantly replied, "The end of their lives." She paused for another moment, and then said, there is no guarantee on life. In a given instant—say death—you must be in peace. I know that as truth. It is each soul's responsibility to learn and know the essence of life, as it pertains to its own development. This is expressed in the soul's ability to exist in peace with other souls. Soul development doesn't come to you, you have to go and get it."

Donna was still. She was analytically deciphering what Shar Dea had just said. Looking on as well was Michael, who also concurred.

"We shall write an outline which will kindle the Spirit of Peace within the soul of each individual reader," directed Shar Dea. She collected her thoughts, then offered, "Okay Michael, you asked for simplicity. How's this for an outline?:

Peace
Feel Peace
Seek Peace
Live for Peace
Dream Peace
I am Peace
Die in Peace
Enemies of Peace."

Michael was a little curious about the context of the final chapter. "Shar Dea, what do you intend to say in the 'Enemies of Peace' section?"

Donna gave Shar Dea all of her attention. Michael readied himself for her orientation. Firmly Shar Dea suggested, "This final section is by far the most critical, for it may generate stiff opposition. Donna, you will have to take my thoughts, and rewrite them in the most simplistic, comprehensible, succinct manner possible. There can be no mistakes or pretenses whatsoever. Any misinterpretation could prove deadly for the reader and movement. We must direct the sparks of 'life' right back onto the reader, where it truly belongs.

"In its simplest form—this is the 'How-to' chapter. There are three categories which must be addressed. For the first, we will need to identify the most salient realities that negatively inhibit the collective social subconscious minds of the masses, from those who live in the cities to those in the tribes. The second group of enemies are the local community and religious leaders. Here we must enhance the relationships among small groups, and aim to ensure proper representation of the masses. Finally, we need to target the big ones—the world rulers and political monsters."

Shar Dea's hands were rigidly extended in front of her. Her lips were slightly puckered, and she looked like she was in a cold sweat. Innocently she said, "I'm not trying to condemn anybody." She took a breath of air, and continued. "Just get them to realize . . . that if the conscious and subconscious pursuits for global peace are not immediately undertaken, then we will all be witnessing a major cataclysmic retaliation by nature. I am absolutely serious about what I saw in the Akashic Records."

"Do you think we can do it?" Donna lamently asked.

Michael responded with a more positive attitude. "Listen, Donna, it's not a question of how we think; rather, how we WILL it to be done."

"That's a solid statement of truth, Michael. I'm enlightened by your thoughts," encouraged Shar Dea.

# CHAPTER 23

# THE BOOK—PART V: It is Written

*The universal principles of education are consistently defining war as an obsolete answer to the quest for world peace. Power comes from those individuals who are connected to these universal principles . . . and it has become self-evident that this magnificent birthright is available to all. The power flows not from the top, but from the consent of the governed. The Great Seal of America says it clearly: "E Pluribus Unum—Out of Many, One."*

Donna did an excellent job of translating Shar Dea's potent and formal verbiage down to a simplified comprehensive level. Michael had a special flair for using a poetic style and eliminating any possibility of threat from the words offered by Shar Dea. Michael's ability to draw animations and scenarios were tactfully used. Each drawing emphasized some form of eye contact, which sparked the subconscious thought.

The front and back covers of the book were veneered with a silver foil substance. The title "World Peace" had its raised lettering in dark navy blue. The lettering was in large block form—bold and easy to read. The words were imprinted with a slight vertical slant towards the right. As agreed from the very beginning, the book consisted of exactly fifty pages of written content including all the drawings.

Trying to get a publisher was, in fact, harder to do than writing the book. Some editors felt that Shar Dea couldn't give the book away; others felt politically jeopardized by affixing their names to the book. Fortunately, a small publishing house in San Francisco finally agreed to give it a try. The publisher, Aubree Press, specialized in publishing small books on religion and spiritual stories for children. The Editorial Director, Tony Yera, was a good friend of Donna, and was an ex-priest who relocated from Naples, Italy. He insisted that a copyright statement should be omitted, and that was easily agreed upon.

On August 1st, 5,000 copies were printed and released throughout the San Francisco, San Diego, and Los Angeles areas in California. In order to offset the cost of the book, Michael and Donna subsidized the publishing costs with their private funds. The established price of the book was a mere one dollar.

# CHAPTER 24

# A PERIOD OF SILENCE AND CONTEMPLATION

*"The unleashed power of the atom has changed everything save our modes of thinking and we thus drift toward unparalleled catastrophe."*

—Albert Einstein

Twelve days after the first release of "World Peace," all was quiet. Not a single call or inquiry from any one—not from the publisher, the readers, or the press was heard. This was a time to regroup, to collect their thoughts and to prepare for the future. In a sense, it was the calm before the storm. As far as Shar Dea, Michael, and Donna were concerned, they needed a break anyway. They were exhausted from the eight weeks of hard mental labor preparing the book.

The phone rang. Michael went over to pick it up. "Hi there Donna! . . . What's happening with you tonight? . . . I'm game. Let me ask Shar Dea . . . Hold on a minute." Michael asked Shar Dea if she would like to meet with Donna at the Fortune Dragon Restaurant for some Chinese food. Shar Dea enthusiastically agreed with the invitation: "Sure, I would love that!"

Michael jubilantly relayed the message: "Donna, we're on for 7:30 tonight. Better yet, we'll pick you up a 7:15, Okay?" The plans were set for that Saturday night.

In the restaurant, the triad was in a lazy-drawn-out, but humorous and sarcastic conversational mode of play. They each raised their hot saki, and drank a toast to "World Peace." They ordered some delicious food. Michael got his favorite, chicken in black bean sauce. Shar Dea did her usual risk-taking and ordered the specialty of the house, Lo Mein with lobster. Donna got her favorite, Moo-Goo-Gai-Pan.

Within two hours the sins of thoughtlessness and gluttony were upon them. Not only were they stuffed, but quite tipsy. Their favorite waiter, George Wong, came over with the 'exit' menu and four fortune cookies. George said, "One of those is for 'World Peace'." They each randomly selected one and broke open their cookie. The usual philosophical and intellectual statements of wisdom were jokingly read aloud. Then Michael nudged Shar Dea, and said, "Here! Open this one for the book."

Shar Dea began tapping her hands on the table to simulate a drum roll. Then she broke open the fortune cookie. The message read: "You will travel worldwide as the Peacemaker." Her chin dropped about two feet and Michael and Donna stared in amazement. Shar Dea saw George approaching a nearby table and signaled for his attention. He caught it and advanced to their table. "Want more saki?" he jovially suggested.

"George," said Shar Dea, "may I ask where did you get these cookies?"

He replied, "Lady Shar Dea, I got three off the top of the big fortune cookie bag." He used his hands to dramatize how large the bag was. Then he continued, "I thought of all your hard work writing that book, so I put my arm deep into the bag and pulled out a fourth cookie especially for you. Okay!"

Shar Dea thanked him for his sincere best wishes, and above all, his thoughtfulness. Soon afterwards, they left the restaurant.

Donna invited Michael and Shar Dea up for a nightcap. This was never a problem for Michael, and the invite was welcomed. They all arrived at Donna's condominium apartment and made themselves comfortable. Shar Dea decided to sit outside on the balcony. Donna and Michael soon joined her. It was a beautiful night with the breeze feeling a tad cooler by the minute.

"Crisp, fresh air is what the soul needs more often," said Donna.

"Yea, your right about that," seconded Michael.

Shar Dea turned to Donna, and said, "What we need . . ."

At that moment, the phone began ringing. Donna immediately interrupted Shar Dea, excused her self, and left to answer the phone. In the background, her surprised voice was heard all the way out from the balcony. Then she came running through the living room and onto the balcony. Her body was twisting and wiggling, and she shouted out, "What we need . . . is . . . what we got." Donna was out of breath and tried to get her wind back. She beat her chest a couple of times to order her lungs to properly perform, and said, "That was Tony Yera. He just got a call from New York for an order of 10,000 copies. He wanted us to know ASAP! Wow!"

The triad felt rewarded and relieved. Up to this time, they were left kind of high and dry. But now felt assured that the the book would really start to catch on.

For the next couple of weeks, things returned to a steady calmness. Donna returned back to her office in order to catch up with her other work. Michael decided to stay at the beach house with his wife and enjoy her company. In spite of Michael's assumption that he had newlywed privileges, Shar Dea did not stop her endeavors to understand the ways of the world, except to be with Michael. She began to probe through all of Michael's research papers a second time. Each day she had a new book in her hand. She was captured by Carl Jung's works on precognition, imagery, and especially, his viewpoints on universal collective consciousness.

She spent many hours experimenting with the ancient Chinese masterpiece, "Book of Changes, I Ching." At one point, Michael had to hook up a special 5x5 foot poster board so that she could chart the key to the hexagrams and write in comments which pertained to the upper and lower trigrams. She was fascinated with the ways in which she could get a more intuitive understanding of the future, though to her, it was another perspective.

Each night, Shar Dea would sit in the stillness and meditate. Many times Michael would join her. Afterwards, they would engage in extensive conversations until three or four in the morning.

All was well for them and that was good. For, soon they were all to be challenged, especially Shar Dea.

# CHAPTER 25

# HER COMPANION

*"One of the greatest gifts given to mankind is the ability to demand honesty and truth from a fellow person."*
*—Shar Dea*

As each new day arrived, Shar Dea awakened to new mysteries and thoughts. Most of these moments brought her closer to why she was alive and to the clarity of her destiny as well. In the true sense of it all, she felt oneness in the relationship among three entities—the world above, the world below, and the world within.

Shar Dea drove over to Donna's condo early on Sunday. It was a clear and most pleasant morning, just a perfect day for a good lesson in tennis. Donna introduced the game to Shar Dea about a month ago. Since that time, Shar Dea was proving herself to be a competitive and challenging partner, which was probably due to her incredible learning abilities.

The door was open, and Shar Dea walked in. She yelled out to Donna, "Hi! I'm here, Donna."

Donna returned a yell from her bathroom, "I'll be out in about five minutes. Please make yourself comfortable."

Shar Dea felt an urge to go out onto the balcony and grasp the morning wind. Autumn's tribute to mankind was magnificently being displayed. It was peaceful for her to see the colors scattered about the countryside, forming majestic patterns of beauty.

Turning her head downward towards the neighboring city, she saw a sleeping population begin to wake up. Gradually, the coastal city was changing from a tranquil night to a hustling place under the sun. "Imagine what it's like in a big city?" she thought. She wondered how many of those busy city inhabitants down below showed interest in their surroundings, to say the least, even cared about their neighbors. How dreadful a realization this was for Shar Dea.

She left the balcony, feeling melancholy, and slowly walked into the living room. She glanced at the Sunday morning newspapers which were lying on the ottoman. She skimmed the headlines, and uttered to herself, "Here we go again in the land of dying beauty and frustrated leaders."

The headlines spoke about the recent renewed upswing of

civil war activities in the Middle East. Shar Dea's thoughts began to run beyond herself. Rived with anger, she mumbled, "It was once a land where the Sacred Golden Stairway stood. It was beautiful. There was always a rainbow there. It stretched from the sea across the lands and into the mountains. It was where the peaceful people spiritually climbed to meet the Great Father. Now under millions of dead bodies, fallen temples, ancient ruins, and burnt earth do the great nations of Isreal, Lebanon, Syria, Iran and Iraq decay. And painfully I witness their Moslems, Jews, Christians: holy and non-holy, and paid heros and non-paid heros, frolic against peace. It is only because they all have fear in their hearts, and fear perpetuates death, destroys Golden Stairways, falls temples and rots the good earth."

Shar Dea broke her spell momentarily. She surfaced for more air, as if drowning, but was pulled back into the article once again, feeling her thoughts swirling deeper into agony as she saw the world in turmoil. Shar Dea was mesmerized as she stared directly into the papers. Her mind began to talk through her envisions:

I see a dirty child staring into oblivion.
What does the child see? Has his love for life
been spewed with the blood of his neighbors
along the sides of the streets?

Here is a land where mothers are scared of
what the future brings—the absence of their
childrens' dreams. A land which is numbered in
days. Where man fears to extend his hand and
bring peace to the land.

Saddened and troubled religious souls
viciously seek a home in the land of hopeless
thoughts. Above them all, sits an omniscient and
loving God, who wishes not to be fattened by so
many sacrificial lambs. How can these ignorant
and poor souls work towards peace?

They have become devoid of the ability to see
themselves as individuals. They have permitted
themselves to lose the meaning of civilization.
They talk defensively about their gods who love
them all. Can their religious and spiritual
pursuits ever come to an agreement on peaceful
coexistence—at least within their own hearts.

Leaders seek survival of their tarnished

dreams, yet forget that their children die
because of these dreams. The fear is so great,
it masks itself under self-pride and
desperation. There has been just too many smiles
of innocent women and children senselessly and
savagely ripped from their faces. They are not
animals for slaughter—they are the offspring
of beauty and life.

The subconscious minds of leaders know that
they would rather die before they will give the
enemy a moment of love. Here is a land with
artificial kings and temporal majesties. Below
them, a despot of bewildered and mislead souls.
Above them, a frustrated God.

Then Donna came triumphantly marching out into the living
room, saying, "Good morning!" A sonic boom echoed through
Shar Dea's brain. Her body was shrilled by the shock wave, her
heart pulsated vigorously, and a cold sweat immediately fell from
her forehead. Shar Dea then snapped out of her trance. She was
still aloof and looked incoherent. In a low key tone, she said,
"Oh. Hi there Donna. What time is it?"
    "Shar Dea! Are you all right?"
    "Yes! I need to sit down."
    "What's the matter? Are you sure you're OK?" repeated
Donna. "Are you up to tennis? Maybe some breakfast first?"
    "Donna! Please give me a minute!" begged Shar Dea.
    "OK! OK! Shar Dea," apologized Donna.
    Shar Dea sat quietly for a few minutes as Donna stood there
helplessly.
    "Listen Donna," stated Shar Dea, "Did you read the papers
this morning?"
    Donna drew her face inwardly, pressing her chin down
towards her chest, and retorted, "Damn! No way in hell would I
read the rag sheet this early on a Sunday morning! On my day
off! Do you think I want to ruin my day?"
    Shar Dea, now partially revived from her trance, commented,
"That's the point, Donna. You don't give a damn!"
    "Wait just a minute, sweetheart! You came over here so we
could play some tennis, not to put me on trial because I don't
give a damn about reading the Sunday papers!"
    Shar Dea's face turned expressionless. "I'm sorry, Donna. I
got a little upset about the Middle East crisis."
    Donna lifted her head up in disgust, and uttered, "Oh, that
shit again!"
    "Donna! Please be patient with me!"

"OK."

While sitting, Shar Dea put her hands to her face and began massaging her cheeks to relieve some of the mounting pressure. "I'm upset over what's happening over there. If this crisis is permitted to proliferate, your ass, my ass, and every other ass in this beautiful, but chaotic world, will be fried! And, I am scared stiff knowing that this is a truth."

"What's a truth?"

"The war."

"What war?"

"The war that's going to take place in the Middle East," replied Shar Dea.

"How do you know that there is going to be a war in the Middle East?"

"Because I can see it happening in my heart right now, and I am hurt by what I see," claimed Shar Dea.

"Shar Dea, you said to Michael and me that there would not be another world war."

"Right, there won't be a major nuclear war. But we all shall see tremendous build ups of little wars and skirmishes all over the world—every day of the year. Collective mental agonies are like bombs, waiting to explode. As each soul deteriorates into hate, animosity, and anger, it sends out horrifying survival signals to other souls in the area.

The more powerful the person, such as a leader or general, the greater the signal. The momentum geometrically grows out of proportion, it blows-up like a bomb. Love and Peace have no belonging in this state until death eliminates the fear."

"Woo!" lamented Donna.

"Worse yet," implied Shar Dea, "is that whatever I am feeling this very moment is the same exact feelings of the planet's consciousness too! Just like nature instinctively gives its creatures warning signals for survival, so it does the same to herself as well. These are the killing feelings that help cause natural disasters."

Donna and Shar Dea stood idle looking at each other for a moment or two. Then Donna's face tensed with frustration. "Shar Dea! You have said many things that provoke deep thoughts, but this is just a little too far fetched for me."

"Donna, please help me for a moment?"

"Sure Shar Dea. Go ahead. I'm with you."

"I've never really told you about my visions, have I?" uttered Shar Dea.

"No, not really."

Well, it's a long story, but in brief . . . I have special powers and know about many things that occurred in the past," explained Shar Dea.

"Like what, for instance?"

"You!" blurted out Shar Dea.

"What?"

"You and I have been acquainted with each other for over several thousands of years. Do you remember Sherrie Dailey?" asked Shar Dea.

"Yea! That's the girl who's body you entered," replied Donna.

Shar Dea probed Donna more. "What were your feeling for this Sherrie girl?"

Donna's face expressed curiosity and intimidation.

"Huh!"

"Go on. Say what you feel," pursuaded Shar Dea.

Surprised by her own feelings, Donna said, "I feel tremendous pain and love for that person. For some reason, she affects me and I'm grieved."

Immediately Shar Dea blurted out, "You were Sherrie's guardian and overseer in three of her past lives."

"Yow there! Miss Shar Dea. Come again on that!" demanded Donna.

"During the Roman Empire, just before the days of Christ, your role was that of her mother. In 1675, your name was Timothy, her older brother. You were very dominant over your little brother, Jon. Sherrie was Jon. Today, you're my dearest friend. And, as in your usual fashion, my guardian and protector, and Michael is too, as a matter of fact!"

"Stop! I don't have to buy this, you know," defensively uttered Donna.

"But you will. I know," offered Shar Dea in a consoling way.

The rest of the morning went on with conversation about each others roles, purpose and destiny. Shar Dea explained to Donna about how souls dwell with the same souls through many different lifetimes, explaining the phenomena of 'soul families' and 'soul migrations'. Each time in the process, souls are exchanging other aspects of themselves. Either they are serving as a teacher or participating as a student, that is, always learning and developing their souls' wisdom.

As the day went on, it became apparent that tennis took second place to their intriguing conversations. Donna and Shar Dea grew extremely close. They were becoming more inseparable and telepathic.

# CHAPTER 26
# THE POPE

*"Fear is the dogma of religion, and of
war and rumors of war, and of endings. And
the dastardly entities that profoundly make it
their knowingness are exacting Gods. The
other pole shall be in joy, of life, of loving
the moment, of being, of the ongoingness of
ISNESS. What is the tomorrow unless it is now
seen?"*
—Ramtha

The autumn coastal breeze blew crisp that Sunday night. Shar
Dea found herself mentally preoccupied about the newspaper
headlines she had read earlier that day. She was restless,
confused, and needed comfort. She sought Michael's masculinity
and strength.

While having dinner with Michael, Shar Dea talked about her
day. She explained the anxiety experienced because of the
headlines and her heightened closeness with Donna. Michael's
conversation with Shar Dea was comforting. His love for her
relieved her anxieties. He was elated about the news that Donna
and Shar Dea's friendship grew firmer, sensing that his own
relationship with Donna was probably doing the same.

It was close to 8:30 P.M. that evening when the doorbell
rang. Michael got up to see who was there. It was a courier,
dressed in a commanding white and red uniform.

"Special telegram for Shar Dea! Please sign here sir!" insisted
the courier.

"Just one minute, young lady. I'll get Shar Dea," replied
Michael.

Michael walked back into the dining room. While waving his
hand in a motion to come, he said, "They've got some pretty
looking couriers these days. It's for you, my dear."

When the courier saw that Shar Dea was an extremely
attractive female, her eyes popped out with surprise. "So you're
Shar Dea!"

"Yes I am."

With the element of surprise and glee, the courier
commented, "My manager, Mr. Jim Reed, read your little book.
And he said in a dramatic tone: "The guy who wrote this book
knows what the hell he's talking about." Then the young lady

impetuously said, "I can't believe he's a she!"

Shar Dea was spirited by the courier, and said, "Would you like a personalized copy?"

"Me?"

Shar Dea instructed, "Wait just a minute, I'll get . . ."

Just then, Michael had already figured out the conversation at the front door, and brought Shar Dea a copy. The courier was very appreciative of her encounter with Shar Dea, and left with a sense of accomplishment.

"Well, what does it say?"

"Let's see who's it from," mumbled Shar Dea. "Here we go, Michael. It's from (pause) . . . the Vatican! It reads:

Dear Mr. Shar Dea:

The Vatican wishes to advise you of the
displeasure expressed by the Pope because
of the ambiguous statements made regarding
the Catholic Church.

The Pope also wishes to congratulate you on
your bold petition for world peace.
It is not the intent of this letter to
present arguments relating to any specifics
discussed in the book. However, The Vatican
Council will be in touch with you in the
immediate future concerning many of the
statements written therein.

Respectfully,


Archbishop Emilio Giovanni Ormati
Chancellor of the Vatican Council
Office of Public Relations and Press

"Shar Dea, do you sense good or bad?"

"All good! If the Pope read it, we're in. That's the greatest news yet!" shouted Shar Dea with glee. "Let's see if we can find out what the Pope got hot on."

Michael got his work copy of World Peace. He flipped to the controversial chapter, obviously, 'Enemies of Peace'. With his finger zig-zagging across several pages, he came upon the part which spoke about the Catholic Church.

Shar Dea grabbed the book from Michael, focused her eyes over the words, and exclaimed, "Oh! This part is a bit sarcastic! It reads:

'. . . There are over 600,000,000 Catholic
people throughout the world. The Pope,
their leader, lives in a city called the
Vatican. It is located in Rome, Italy.
The Pope is a very good man, but he
doesn't devote enough time leading his
people toward peace. The Catholic Church
says that it offers a way to heaven. Should
that not be the way of peace, then the path
to God does not exist. We must ask the
Church: "What is the way to Peace?—Show
Us!"

The Pope must show to all nations that
all Catholic people, world wide, seek and
live for peace—in honor of God. That is
the Pope's true and only mission—world
peace . . .'

"Do you think that's what the letter is referring to,
Michael?"

Michael's response to her question was inconsistent with her
trend of thought. "He needs to humble down to the most
simplistic levels of thought. Furthermore, he needs to realize the
great powers which are rendered him, and practice them in
accordance with his teacher and predecessor—The Christ."

"I didn't ask you that."

Michael puckered his lips and wobbled his head in vain.
"Well then," he explained, "the Vatican's letter was vague. I've
got a feeling that they like some parts, but definitely don't like
to be told what they must do."

Shar Dea perked up. "Yea, that's it! It's a matter of politics!"
She strolled towards the balcony door and squashed her nose
against the glass as children do. She became mesmerized by the
site of the ocean's magnificent horizon. Shar Dea stared out the
window of time, and into deep thought:

. . . across the sea is the great little
man of heaven. He perceives himself as an
advocate of universal brotherhood and
peace. As he moves from one place to
another, the multitudes find themselves
temporarily elated in the ecstasy of
heavenly rapture. But as time moves on, and
reality returns, the people beyond his
blessing hands find themselves even more

111

confused and depressed.

Did this great man bring love, or did he
bring the promise of love. He does not come
as did his first Father and Wayfarer of
Peace, who in His time understood the
planet and her need for Peace. This was so
beautifully told by the day of the Cross—
Christ's resurrection, and the moment of
Thunder and Lightning—the cry and the
pain of the Earth's soul. I feel the pain;
I understand the sorrow.

Every possible thought that emanated in
Christ's mind was reality. Every single
word spoken was exactly the same as his
thoughts, and was demonstrated by his
deeds.

If love and peace were to be within our
thoughts, then hope for mankind would then
be realized.

Oh! . . . Mr. Pope. The times haven't
changed, only diplomacy and the sense of
personal security and safety. Christ, not
you, chanced life at every moment. I beg of
you to take the Divine Powers of your
Christ and march vigorously forward into
the diplomatic jungles of politics, greed,
and power.

Oh Mr. Pope, take off your rings of the
past. Wash your hands and feet, and march
into the sight of tomorrow. Falter not
under the threats of the blue suited
leaders who sit under the protection of
guns and might. Knock on their doors and
represent the people and their birthright
to life.

Hold the Cross tightly to your bosom,
but not to theirs. For the Cross served to
wake your soul, and not to host a
government. Speak to them of the laws of
the planet.

I see tears on the face of your soul. I
see the singing bee hovering over the rose.
I see the innocent smiles of children
playing in the fields. I see Peace.

Michael came up to and behind Shar Dea. In a soft spoken
voice, asked, "Shar Dea, what are you envisioning?"

"Imagine, Michael," she said, "if all the people in the world
focused their thoughts for world peace, then over a short period
of time they would obtain it."

"That sounds idealistic to me, Shar Dea." Michael's voice
suddenly changed into sarcastic overtones. "Most of the people
are starving and think about one good meal and a roof over their
heads. Others think of political and racial freedom. And in the
free countries, most people think about making more money.
How do you propose to persuade them otherwise?"

"I hope the book will be the catalyst—the spark that starts it
all," she humbly replied. "It must provoke the key leaders of the
world, if it is to succeed."

Shar Dea turned around to Michael and enthusiastically
professed, "The Pope is truly our best hope. He could
demonstrate the best example of a leader who would react in
defense of our book."

Michael responded quickly. "First he must step off his
throne and humble down, get back to basics. If the world gets
any more chaotic, who needs a big expensive religion anyway?"

"Be more specific, Michael," insisted Shar Dea.

"Look, the man is so preoccupied as the leader of the
ecumenical council and ecclesiastical matters. What's the sense?
It's become a full scale bureaucratic government constantly
bickering between lard headed conservatives and risk taking
social minded liberals. It's a big mess of intellectual and ongoing
theological crap that doesn't help anyone on the planet. Isn't it
true that the Catholic Church seeks to enforce discipline and
theological orthodoxy?"

"You're right, he must become more cognizant of the actual
needs of the people, and get down to earth."

"Thanks," replied Michael. "And, the Vatican has become a
religious bureaucratic center. About the only thing the people do
there is drown in inspirational first class tourism crap! The next
thing you'd probably see is a priest selling Vatican pizza!"

"Michael, show some respect! You are getting emotionally
pumped up. Don't forget, we seek peace, not revolution!"

Michael paused for a moment, and said, "I'm sorry, Shar
Dea. You've done something to me that excites my intellectual
aggressiveness. And I . . ."

Suddenly, Shar Dea interjected, and said, "Hold it right

there, my man. That male aggressiveness you speak of is 'public enemy number one'. I would prefer that you do not show or behave that way. It is without question a very touchy topic in my heart—males and their damn aggressiveness!"

Michael closed his lips real tight. His eyes and chin dropped, and he humbly said, "I'm sorry, your Empress. Please forgive me."

She walked over to him and kissed his forehead. "Let's take a break from all this stuff. Then we can come back and really hash it out with some good facts. I think it would be wise to prepare ourselves for the press anyway."

"Good idea. I'll put on some music. Why don't you cut up some jarlsberg cheese, slice some apples, and grab some crackers."

"Fine."

They were munching away and sipping some beaujolais when the door bell rang. It was Donna. It didn't take too long before she was sipping wine, munching out, and engaged in conversation. Donna was brought up-to-date on the dialogue about the Pope and the flaccid role enacted by the Church.

Donna got hyped-up real fast about the Church's role in Third World countries. "If birth control is evil and immoral, so is starving and watching your children die, Mr. Pope!"

Michael looked at Shar Dea who was just about to reprimand Donna.

"Donna, we can't afford to be rebellious in our statements, feelings and emotions. We know the world is sick out there. What we need is to prepare ourselves for making statements which offer logical solutions to these matters. OK!"

Then Shar Dea got on a roll and began to express her viewpoints. "Listen guys! The Pope is a chosen leader. He is a good man, and very spiritual, too! His mind is devoted to managing the Church and the Vatican bureaucratic clergy. Here lies the problem; he's dedicated to the survival of the Church, not World Peace. On one side, he has the conservative forces which advocate perpetual ecclesiastical stability. On the other side, he's got the liberal clergy who's efforts are for ecclesiastical innovation, economical and social morality."

Donna interrupted, and added, "And they all seem to have left the responsibility for spiritual development up to the five and ten cents brochures!"

Michael chuckled at that one. "Yea! You get two for a quarter. Light a candle for some poor soul, while you're at it."

Shar Dea got infuriated and threw up her arms. "Fellahs! Didn't we agree not to talk like that just a few minutes ago? If you think I'm exaggerating now, wait until the press gets a hold on you. You'll fall apart, lose credibility, and hinder the quest for world peace." Then she quickly walked out of the room.

"Well Michael," said Donna. "I think we've really blown it this time. Why is it, that you and I always seem to have an arrogant and nasty attitude about religion?"

Michael justified her comment. "It looks like we're both sarcastic, pessimistic, and experienced journalists. We see and write about a lot of negative shit everyday. I guess we are non-believers."

"That's right! You don't sell good news too often. Do you?" responded Donna. "Now we must get our Empress back on our side, otherwise we'll get fired!"

"How do suppose we do it?" petitioned Michael.

"We simply need to get serious about the whole thing. May I suggest," offered Donna, "that you and I get our heads together and lay a few good comments on Shar Dea. Then she might ease up on our child like rambunctious behaviors."

"That sounds good to me."

Shar Dea returned into the living room to see if her two associates had cleaned up and matured from their childish mannerisms. She said, "OK! Are we ready to continue with our conversation about the Pope, or should I get you both cookies and milk?"

Michael's response prompted Shar Dea to throw a sofa pillow at him. Then they all seemed to burst out in laughter, released a bit of anxiety, and began to feel relaxed.

Shar Dea got the conversation off to a fast start when she said, "If the Pope could only walk the streets and lead by example, as Christ did, he'd be fantastic."

"Shar Dea," said Michael, "what he needs to do is switch his focus from a religious campaign to an overt physical demonstration for peace."

Donna interjected with a positive overtone, "He needs to personify peace on his face, show energy with his hands, and speak to all with conviction, advocating the will of God."

Shar Dea offered more to Donna's statement. "He must confront each and every world leader, one-to-one, face-to-face and not by a silly letter of recommendation, as he usually does. He must do so with the same vigor and conviction as did his Lord, Christ—even if he has to die because of it."

Donna picked up a pencil and started to thump the eraser on the coffee table. Both Michael and Shar Dea reacted in silence to the thumping. Then simultaneously they spoke out the same words, "And what's on your mind?"

Donna looked up, and remarked, "There's no excuse for for the Vatican's bureaucracy. It has taken the form of a spiritual bureaucracy. It has evolved into a superficial and pompous milieu."

"Yes! You're right, Donna," claimed Michael, as he massaged his face. Michael paused momentarily before he continued, "What really is the mission of the Pope and the Catholic Church anyway?"

Shar Dea responded, "I know what it should be!" She further added, "If the Pope is truly serious about the need for world peace, he must be bold, inspired, and determined to represent the will of God continuously."

"Putting it bluntly," said Donna, "thirteen percent of the worlds population is Catholic. A good number of them are politicians, especially in America. The Pope needs to put some heavy pressure on these folks, and get them to start advocating a change. It's his responsibility and birthright."

"It's his destiny, too!" said Shar Dea. "When you come to the bottom line of it all—the challenge is in the vision. The key to his success is to share the vision with other leaders. And in the process, demand the respect for TRUTH—unequivocally."

Suddenly, Donna jumped up and began narrating:

"Think of it. The Pope announces to all
Catholic clergy worldwide: 'I request
that each one of you diligently and
openly advocate peace as your number
one priority.'

'Demonstrate peace in your hearts and
daily works. Begin inwardly with yourself,
in your church, and throughout your
community. And continue this until world
peace is at hand'."

Donna looked enthusiastically at her friend, and exclaimed, "Wow, wouldn't that be great!"

Then Michael got his two cents worth. "Hell, the Catholic Church has enough money to educate people from all corners of the earth on the need for peace. Instead of building more symbolic religious artifacts, the Church can support national educational centers for peace throughout Catholic communities world wide."

"That's not a bad idea," uttered Donna with reinforcement.

"True, this all seems pretty good to you two guys, but the real question is that the Pope has to believe in it first. Educating people is a very slow process. It doesn't necessarily maintain the best track record either," refuted Shar Dea. "What the people need is a new philosophy which can be accepted as a belief. Now you're talking big time."

"So what you're saying Shar Dea is that if the Pope stands

116

firmly behind a new and stronger philosophy for world wide peace, we have a good chance," remarked Donna.

Michael quickly added, "Then educating people would have a better success record, because the people would realize a better understanding of who they are and their place in the world."

"Precisely," said Shar Dea. "The people of this planet need to understand the fact that the universe is expressing its own self-consciousness through humans. Then maybe they will also realize the importance of their destiny '*IS*' the same destiny of the universes; we are only but an expression of it."

Michael looked apologetically at Shar Dea. Lamently, he inquired, "Shar Dea! Why are you so critical of the Pope?"

Her answer was sharply stated, "Because the Pope represents a universal code for hope."

"Go on Shar Dea. I need a little more than that."

"OK!" She said. "It's a fact that the Pope is a harmless critter. In the eyes of most leaders, it's a good political gesture to show respect for the Pope. Right?"

"Yes! I guess so," mumbled Michael.

"Why then is it so?"

"Don't ask me. You're the one with all the answers," rebutted Michael.

"All right then," blurted Shar Dea. "First of all, the word 'pope' tells you what?"

Michael's response didn't enthuse Shar Dea one iota. He said, "It rhymes with 'hope'."

"More so," replied Shar Dea. "The 'O' stands for maternal care, global, and for wholeness. The 'P' stands for power, people, or potential. And the 'E' reflects ascending thought and deity. Altogether, 'pope' means 'inspirational power of the people'."

Donna critiqued these words with a fleeting compliment, "It sounds somewhat convincing to me."

Shar Dea went on, and said, "Put it this way. The essence of 'hope' is peaceful survival—a good life. So whenever the Pope speaks or travels, he subconsciously represents hope for the world. Simply, there is a subconscious reaction process being exchanged. The Pope is the key to world unity, inspiration, and peace. His life and mission is not to be the leader of a bureaucratic Church. The Pope represents the Christ, not the mayor of the Vatican!"

Michael commented, "It would start a chain-reaction amongst world religious leaders; the quest for peace will serve as the common bond for mankind."

# CHAPTER 27

# THE PLAN

*"We are all one. It's only fear and the lack of peace that separates us."*
—Shar Dea

Sunday night's conversations went into the early morning hours. The triad was exhausted and one by one found themselves falling asleep. Michael was lying flat on the floor with his nose buried in the thick oriental carpet. Shar Dea was cuddled up in her plush velour chair, and Donna was half exposed as she lay awkwardly asleep on the sofa.

The morning light broke and in the background, chattering could be heard from the neighborhood creatures, but it did not seem to wake them up. It was about 10:15 A.M. when the phone rang. Shar Dea's inner sensitivity to mechanical contraptions reacted sharply, as she proceeded to limit the number of echoing and irritating rings. Halfway into the third ring was quite an accomplishment for a Monday morning dash.

"Good morning! This is Shar Dea."

It was Tony Yera, calling from San Francisco. He apparently was excited about something very important. "Shar Dea, it's me, Tony. It's a little past seven out here, but I had to let you in on this."

"Well how are you, Tony?"

"Never mind me," he said. "I just got a call from New York. They want to market 100,000 copies internationally over the next six months. Isn't that great!"

"Blessed be; it's happening."

"Listen Shar Dea, you and I need to talk about strategy and get some business details out of the way. When do you think you can come to see me?"

"How about Thursday?"

"That's fine with me," said Tony. "Give me a call so I can arrange to pick you up at the airport. I'll get things in order for you. See you then. Bye!"

Shar Dea leaned against the refrigerator and let go a big sigh of relief. She was excited to know that things were ready to break loose. Her mind was relieved from the many mounting doubts and tensions about the acceptance of the book. Her body felt recharged with new energies and strengths.

She walked passed the foyer and caught a glimpse of her

image in the mirror. She stopped, and took a step backwards. Facing the mirror, she saw herself in a different mood, not quite like her usual self. Her eyes were slightly red and her face was drawn with an expression of numbness. Shar Dea kept staring at her eyes in the mirror, and began to contemplate. Then a potent thought struck her—it was an affirmation that her destiny was within reach and that her time was dimensioned.

She felt lonely and pondered about the house for a few minutes while Michael and Donna dreamed on. As she passed the living room, Shar Dea saw her husband innocently aloft in his dreams. She felt like a mother who adores her children just before they awake.

This little boy was her handsome husband. His face showed courage and strength, though soft skinned, it accented conviction and protection. His lips offered gentleness and gratification. Michael's unusually long eyelashes hosted a delicate character who sought to conceal his romantic visions of passion. The urge for intimacy trickled throughout her body. She wanted to be next to Michael and feel his warmth. Her legs began to weaken as her knees quivered from the passion of her impulses.

Michael's body began to rise comfortably off the floor. It offered no resistance whatsoever, as if it knew its fate. Shar Dea's quest for masculinity brought her ancient powers to call. Her desire to make love brought his muscular body easily upstairs to the side of her bed. There, her aroused and impetuous body removed each of his garments slowly and silently.

As Michael awoke, he felt a tremendous surge penetrate throughout his body. Shar Dea released her passionate energies, and Michael was enveloped by her love. Without resistence or restraint, he withdrew from his conscious mind, and permitted Shar Dea to escape into a reality of total sexual immersion. He was captive by her erotic love, and felt paralyzed by her joy.

The smell of bacon and hot coffee worked its way upstairs and through the house. Michael's appetite was easily activated. He turned to his side and saw Shar Dea's contented face peacefully resting on her pillow.

He kissed her cheek and whispered in her ear "Sweetheart, time to wake up. Donna has got something special cooking for us."

Shar Dea stretched her arms out and around Michael. "You hunk of a man," she said.

"Who me?"

"I just feel so complete with you in me. It makes me realize the importance of love, passion, and the power of creation." She then sat up, kissed him on his neck, and in an enticing tone said, "Imagine what it's going to feel like when we are free of these bodies?"

"Like screwing in thin air!"

Shar Dea jumped out of bed and started to scream. She began to beat Michael over the head with the pillows, while shouting: "You idiot. That's the last time you'll ever get it from me. Can't you let your imagination relax into ecstasy just once? Sex-brain!"

He grabbed her and caressed her so firmly that she began to sink once again into deep passionate love.

Meanwhile, Donna had the privilege of eating brunch by herself. She did have the courtesy to keep the food in the warmer for the newlyweds. Soon afterwards, Michael and Shar Dea came down the stairs, grinning like two disobedient children.

"Thanks for keeping lunch warm, Donna," said Michael.

"I really wanted to share it with you guys, but unfortunately, you had embellished yourselves in lust!" commented Donna. "I'll need to head off to the office after I shower. There's a three o'clock appointment. Some dude from Dallas. He probably wants some free publicity or something. So, what're your plans for the day?"

Shar Dea turned quickly to Donna, and said, "That's a good point! We need to make some detailed plans for the next couple of weeks. I've got a feeling that things are going to get really busy around here."

"Donna, can you make it back over here tonight?" asked Michael.

"Sure can."

Michael happily grinned. "Good! Can you bring a map of the world with you?"

"Sure can."

And with a big grin, Michael chanted, "Good! Can you bring dinner?"

"Sure, Michael. What would you like—fried grasshoppers, with or without rice?"

"Well, I tried," Michael humorously gestured. "OK! You win. I'll get the Chinese take out."

After dinner that evening, the three peace pioneers got down to business. Michael stretched out the world map across the den wall. All his research and reference notes were organized on the back table for quick referencing. It looked like a civil defense emergency room. The group was ready and anxious.

"Okay," said Shar Dea, "our plan is to put the initial burden of responsibility on America—which needs to be the center of our campaign for world peace."

Donna immediately asked, "Why America?"

"Because of the freedom of the press and media. It will give us the exposure we need," replied Michael.

"Not so fast," said Shar Dea. "America at one time was the land of new hope. It has defaulted on its promise."

Donna quickly interjected, "What do you mean 'defaulted'?"

Shar Dea had trouble giving Donna an answer. She looked as if she was grasping for knowledge hidden in her memory.

"Well, let's skip it for now," suggested Michael.

"No, No! It will come," replied Shar Dea. "Something is there; I know it!"

"We'll wait," teased Michael.

"Wasn't America once considered to be the land of new hope?" questioned Shar Dea.

"Yea! I remember reading about that in our American history class," said Michael.

"Well, can you still say that it is the land of new hope?"

"No, not really," said Donna.

"Can you sense that it has defaulted?" asked Shar Dea.

"Sort of . . ." replied Donna.

Shar Dea contemplated for a couple of moments, then began to reminisce. I remember a story someone told me a long time ago about the people of Luroppus. Shar Dea became stiff and silent. Suddenly she exclaimed, "Damn it!" and bounced to her feet. Hitting her head with her hands, as a gesture of knocking sense into the cranium, she said, "Bene Dea, of course. That's what she was preparing me for. Now I've got the picture."

"Please clue us in, Shar Dea," petitioned Donna.

Shar Dea offered Donna and Michael an explanation. "My mother, during the time of Atlantis, must have known about my destiny in America. She had these special clairvoyant powers, you know. She told me a story, when I was about five years old. It was about the new land of hope, called Amergin."

"Was that a true story?" asked Donna.

Shar Dea shrugged her shoulders. "Whether or not there's truth in that story isn't the question. It's the crucial point made by my mother which concerns me."

"What may that be?" probed Donna.

Shar Dea's response was curt. "Amergin disappeared under the sea and earth, as if the planet was ordered to rid herself of a dreadful sickness."

Michael interrupted, "Yea! The same damn thing happened to Atlantis."

"That's speculation," said Donna.

"No! He is right, Donna," retorted Shar Dea.

"So what's the point, Shar Dea?" challenged Donna.

Shar Dea looked deeply into Donna's eyes, and said, "Isn't it true that the early settlers of the United States were Europeans?"

"Yes!"

"Didn't they come to the promised land to find freedom,

opportunity, and hope for a new life?"

"Are you trying to say that Luroppus is analogous to Europe, and Amergin to America," commented Michael.

"Precisely!"

Donna took a big breath, and said, "What you really mean, Shar Dea, is that America is destined for cataclysmic destruction."

"Not quite, Donna. It's my destiny to help prevent that from happening or at least reduce its impact," Shar Dea firmly implied.

"Well, I guess we ought to get down to some serious business on how to avoid this potential catastrophe," astutely petitioned Michael, while Donna seconded the motion.

Shar Dea asked for a moment of thought. Then she softly spoke to her two friends, saying, "I've always been cognizant of my role in life, even from my first physical human life form on Lemuria. Many times, such as in this life with you, I find myself challenging and denying my subconscious knowledge of my role. All through my journeys of soul development, I knew that some day, somewhere, and for some reason, my purpose would be to return to Ara E Hum a special deed. Now I know my fate, for I am, was, and always will be privileged."

Michael's face showed hesitation and apprehension. He wanted to make a motion to cross examine Shar Dea's statement. However, Shar Dea immediately picked up on his thoughts, and said, "Be calm, my dear husband. I sense your opposition to my statement."

Michael withheld his rebuttal.

Shar Dea continued, "I am a human, just like you. A most critical fact is that I am well aware of my past lives and purposes. Remember, the more you know of your past, the more you can reason to know your destiny.

"Human and soul development are both alike and subjected to CHOICE. I could have chosen to use my knowledge to gain untold amounts of wealth and fame. Instead, I have chosen to have faith in Ara E Hum. Realize now that I know from whence I came, where I am, and where I am going. Do you know your trinity of life?"

"What you are saying is quite impressive and honored, Shar Dea. But do you know exactly what's going to happen tomorrow?" questioned Michael.

"It will be good, at least for me, for I have faith," replied Shar Dea.

Donna was carefully watching and listening to Shar Dea and Michael's interchange of comments, as if it were a ping pong match. She moved forward in her chair, and said, "I love both of you guys, and would like to add a statement in here, if I could."

Then she said, "It is without question that we have a person in this room who has kept her divinity and spirituality elusive. I feel awed by your presence, Shar Dea. Are you the GAIA—Goddess of the Planet?"

Shar Dea's face went through a few rapid changes as she tried to regain composure after hearing Donna's comment. She stepped back a couple of feet and in a humbling gesture said, "I'm just me. I know who I am, and where I am going. I know that Ara E Hum exists and I know my purpose. Does that mean I am a Goddess?"

Michael was getting a little upset with the conversation. He showed signs of being edgy. He got up and began to move around. Then he turned to Shar Dea and said, "Shar Dea, I love you. I love all the good you're trying to do. I even call you Empress." He paused for a moment, then petitioned, "Are you really a Goddess?"

Tears trickled down Shar Dea's cheeks. She was hurt by the challenge emanated by her two closest friends. Both Michael and Donna were perplexed and lost for words or consoling gestures.

There was a brief confrontation of the eyes. Shar Dea made an appeal. "I am of peace; please believe me. If you fear the presence of a Goddess, then you most go, not I. I am that I am. I can't change that because of your inabilities to be at my side, and share my life's dreams and destinies. Go if you want. But if you choose to stay, please consider me your equal, as I do my parents, Ara E Hum, and All That Exist. We are all one. It's only fear and the lack of peace that separates us."

Donna and Michael were taken by Shar Dea's words of wisdom, and quickly went over to hug her and offer their compassion.

Soon the triad of peace began to map out a strategy. They were on the same wave length, feeling better about each other, and ready to work cooperatively together. Shar Dea lead off the opening statement: "It's initially important for us to make sure that we agree on the role of this nation. The American people and its government must understand that the quest for seeking peace, world wide, is and will always be the true destiny of their collective consciousness: not wealth, good will, or passivity."

Michael interrupted, and said, "Does this mean that every effort must be made to keep America at the center of the campaign?"

"Quite frankly Michael, that's a yes!" said Shar Dea. "Keeping America responsible is most important. As the collective consciousness of the American spirit changes towards harmony and peace, the greater the chance that the planet's consciousness will absorb these feelings. Once that process is consistent, then she will begin to abort the negative and paranoid feelings of doom she's been feeling for the last three decades.

"Are you saying that the Earth is in fact considering the destruction of mankind already?" asked Donna.

Shar Dea looked at Donna with reinforced confidence, and said, "Very much so! Haven't you noticed all the major natural disasters, wars, and human turmoil that have been taking place around the world? They are not just coincidences, Donna; they're deliberate!"

Donna prepared to voice a rebuttal, but Shar Dea knew her thoughts and continued. "Don't bother defending the thoughts claiming 'premeditated murder'. It's a pure case of survival. If you knew that someone was going to kill you, would not you protect yourself as best as possible? Despite moralities, it's already happening and needs immediate attention."

"We need to continue with the plan," clamored Michael forcibly.

"Right!" responded Donna. "A crucial element is that the Pope will publicly rebut or defend the issues stated in the book. Either way, it will get the American media and press hyped-up with a good second page story—that's publicity!"

"Then what?" asked Shar Dea.

"Our next step is to get the President of the United States involved. Once he agrees, we've got to get him and the Pope to join together towards one common goal for peace," explained Donna.

"Oh boy!" sarcastically exclaimed Michael, "I can see the Southern Baptists now."

"Hold on! Michael. We're only trying to see the basics of the plan, not each detailed step and obstacle along the way!" criticized Shar Dea.

"Excuse me! But I couldn't let that one get by without a touch of reality."

"All right! But let's try to link together some creative strategies behind this complicated scheme. OK!" suggested Donna.

Shar Dea clapped her hands together and vigorously stated, "Within the next several years, people need to change the way they think and behave about world peace. I dread the consequences otherwise."

"That's not much time, is it?" replied Donna.

"Despite the urgency and the stakes involved, America as a nation, will resist the most," stated Shar Dea.

"Why?" asked Donna.

Pessimistically, Shar Dea said, "There are just too many opposing cultures, an abundance of security minded and outright selfish people. The President's position would get substantial opposition—that means lots of procrastination. America is not a homogeneous nation—not yet anyway."

Michael raised his brows and commented, "the United States is becoming more of a melting pot these days. Each subculture has it's own origins, concerns, and goals. Except for prosperity and pleasure, their goals are not necessarily shared nationwide with other subcultures. The Blacks are reinforcing issues of equality and fair representation. The American Indians are concerned with survival of their culture and retribution for their lands; the Asians seek education and a chance for non-exploitation. It goes on and on, each seeking a piece of the American Dream. World peace, though a good concept, is not a primal concern for most Americans; it is taken for granted."

Shar Dea agreed. She further added, "Nations which are solid in culture, like Japan, Finland, Canada, and Mexico, will have greater acceptance of world peace once their governments become actively involved. More surprising, nations such as Russia and China, though each with many subcultures, are more prone to respond to their government's dictates. Therefore, the quest for world unity could be better realized in these countries verses the United States. There's just less opposition and potentially a greater quest for the people to vision and support."

"Many smaller countries, especially African and South American nations will move inwardly to each other. This will form a solidarity, never experienced on those continents. India will play a very critical turning point . . . "

"Why?" asked Donna curiously.

"Because the roots of 700 million Indians are Islamic, Hinduism and Buddhism. Indians and other Asians make up over half of the world's population. They are the silent majority of collective social consciousness. At this time, the planet Earth will truly know for sure that her existence is less threatened.

Politically speaking, Russia, would have resisted as long a possible. Not because they don't seek peace, quite the contrary, but their lack of trust of the West dictated so. When they join, we will see another major shift in world affairs. The focus of attention would now move towards the Middle East where the great religious confrontations prevail."

"So it really is religion that keeps the world in disharmony. Isn't it Shar Dea?" articulated Donna.

Michael jumped up from his chair, and said, "That's it! Isn't it?"

Donna looked completely lost and felt as if she was far behind Michael's thoughts. "Well, clue me in on your findings, Michael."

"The problems that face the world are not necessarily the political, economic, or military threats: Russian and American bombs. It all boils down to one thing: it's the Battle of the

Gods—a damn mythical war between the gods."

"Hold your tongue, Michael," said Shar Dea. "Those two Gods that you speak of are man made versions of a supreme entity. Buddha, Sri Krsna, Christ, Mohammed, Ghandi, and King were among the many great Speakers who were sent to this planet and spoke of peace, brotherhood, and the mysteries of the planet. Regardless of what revelations were brought forward to humanity by these Divine Souls, much has gone to naught. Over time, their followers took it upon themselves to dictate religious righteousness. Religious supremacy cannot exist on this planet, except that of knowing the planet's own consciousness—a belief in all natural laws seen and unseen.

"The sin of life is our conscious ability to ignore knowledge of our past lessons. More precisely, we fail to apply what we have learned in life's travels, and attempt to lie about the future of our reality—twisting the truth to accommodate our preconceived fate."

Michael broke out of his mesmerized stance, and commented, "So you mean, religious killing is justifiable—ignorantly speaking?"

Shar Dea offered clarification. "As they perceive truth, yes, it's justifiable. However, there is no greater disservice to one's self and the whole of humanity as to commit a lie. The greatest power given to mankind is the right of THOUGHT and CHOICE. To misuse either is direct confrontation with Ara E Hum and nature. Literally, there is no escape.

"The real measure of peace will come when an Arab can welcome a Jew into his home and toast to peace, and the colors of all people can form a rainbow of brotherhood."

"Hey! There are other problems in the world besides those relating to Arabs and Jews," fostered Donna. "They're in Africa, Pakistan, Cambodia, Nicaragua, and all over the world, too!"

"True," said Shar Dea. "The efforts of peace will eventually focus soley in the Middle East, because the religions of those lands are so diametrically opposed."

"In fact," said Michael. "In recent years, both Chinese and Russian governments have been painstakenly focused on making their nation reactive, single minded in purpose and culture. Socialization and the common good of the State are all important and enforced. But, you rarely hear of the individual's dream or spirit from these countries."

Donna looked quite captive by what she was hearing, and said, "Now I see what you're getting at. It's less difficult to change the masses which are homogenous and single minded, then a radical, divided, or rebellious nation."

"Right!" said Shar Dea. "When the time comes for a major change, that is, for peace, nations such as Japan, China, and

Russia will be less cumbersome, than say, Lebanon, or the American Bible belt."

Michael needed a break. He got up and went to look out the window. "Look guys! The ocean has gotten quite rough; it's exiting. Take a peek." Soon the two ladies joined him and together they embraced each other's shoulders as their minds escaped into the beauty and roar of the night's ocean.

# CHAPTER 28

## San Francisco

*" . . . To forgive is truly a vision of
intense and consistent betterment of humans to
serve a Godly purpose. It is a more
sophisticated and profound action than to
simply excuse somebody's error of the past.
Rather, it is a sense of hope for a peaceful
future."*

*—Shar Dea*

First their lips touched, then they embraced tightly.
Departing was not Michael's favorite activity. He had some good
old down to earth coping problems and was wetting his cheeks
with child like tears.

"You should be happy, my man," said Shar Dea. I'll be back
in a couple of days, and then we can spend a day or so making
love and being together. How's that for a return gift?"

Michael's mind caught on to the images easily painted by his
bride, and with a boyish expression of hope, said, "Yea! That
will be fine."

There was not a minute to spare. The newlyweds scurried
passed the reservation desks, sped through the electronic booby
traps, and came to a streaking halt by ticket Gate # 22. The
ticket lobby was empty. She had to leave immediately.

This time their kisses were exact replicas of the latest
romance scenes coming out of Hollywood. Michael's growing
deficiency of possession had just arrived, and would be settling
in for a few lonesome days of pain. Shar Dea made the final
break from her husband. She showed a very satisfying smile, and
encouraged Michael humorously when she said, "Good-bye, my
man. You really need this break from me. I'll bet you'll even
grow from it."

"Bull!"

"No No!" she warned, while pointing the finger at him with
a loving smile.

The plane would soon be traveling with the morning sun,
working its way along the pre-dawn horizon towards San
Francisco. It was the first plane ride for Shar Dea, though not
necessarily an enjoyable ride for her to experience. She grew
steadily impatient and felt restricted.

She brought the Christian Science Monitor, her favorite paper, in order to catch up on the world issues. Michael gave her his favorite book "The Prophet" by Kahlil Gibran. He knew that she would enjoy this masterpiece. About an hour and a half into the flight she opened the book. After reading the first chapter "The Coming of the Ship" she closed the book, and meditated for a few minutes.

When she returned, she reached into her attache case and got a pad and pen. She wanted to write a little thank you note to Michael. It read:

> My Dear Love,
> For each day that passes
> You become dearer to me.
> I thank you for your precious
> book, the one that speaks of the
> spirit of life, moves you through
> the tenderness of love, and
> defines peace within the soul.
>
> I love you for your understanding
> of me, my quest, and my destiny.
> For you are 'Almitr' and I
> 'Almustafa'. How thoughtful of
> you.
>
> Eternal Love in Spirit,
> Shar Dea

She sealed it in an envelope and drew a little heart with two smiling faces on each side it. Her love message would be mailed special delivery at the airport. She then sat back, and drifted into a light sleep.

In her sleep, she saw herself as the ancient empress, standing bright and majestic, fully garbed in a white satin and chiffon robe drapped with pearls and rubies. The wind was blowing across her face and the eminence of spiritual royalty was surrounding her, as she addressed the crowds. Her words were virgin and pure, as if she was still a child, but her words were also of awe, for she spoke in absolute truths.

She heard her own words echo back from the crowds, and this enthused her more. With her hands raised to the heavens, she said, "I come to free you from despair and offer you the hope of peace. Raise your hearts and minds from out of the ground. For the earth is for your feet and nourishment, but the heavens are for your mind and your eternal soul. Seek fear my friends and the earth will tremble beneath you, and consume you as dying fruit. Seek peace and see your children ascend into the brightness and joys of the heavens above. For each soul brings to the universe a star, and each star a soul unto Ara E Hum."

The plane bumped and shook a bit because of the turbulent weather. This prompted Shar Dea to awaken from her inner visions of her childhood. As she stretched her arms and legs she felt, once again, restricted and frustrated. Thinking to herself, she realized the message in her astral dream—her knowledge of the higher natural laws and powers. Then something came to her mind that excited her and sparked a sense of fascination and mischievousness. She sat as erect a possible, closed her eyes, and took off astrally. She willed herself at the airport in San Francisco. Presto! There she was astrally: no luggage, no attache case, and totally invisible.

"Now what?" she said to herself. Tony is not here yet, and even if he was he couldn't see me. Feathers! Back to the tin can. She thought of her place in the airplane seat, and soon she was there, without any disruption to anyone. It was 9:00 A.M. and destination was anticipated at 11:00 A.M., P.S.T.

"I know what I can do," she said to herself. "I'll get Tony to leave earlier and get the plane to arrive earlier, too!" She grew excited and telepathically got Tony to do just that. As far as the plane was concerned, she altered the weather and head wind conditions to favor the flight plans. And with a bit of magic, reduced the pull of gravity on the plane. Consequently, the plane was traveling much faster.

All of a sudden the stewardesses began to scurry around collecting things and acting strangely expeditious. At 10:00 the cabin bell sounded. Immediately, the 'fasten your seat belt' sign was activated. Within a moment or two, whispers and a few coughs were generated throughout the cabin by the passengers. Then it happened. The moment of truth. The captain was on the air "Ladies and gentlemen, I am happy to inform you that due to excellent weather conditions and minimal air traffic, Flight # 107 to San Francisco will arrive approximately one hour earlier than originally scheduled. We will do everything possible to accommodate you and your awaiting guests. Thank you and have a pleasant flight."

"Darn good, Shar Dea!" she silently whispered to herself.

Tony Yera was a distinguished looking Italian man. He had plenty of wavy black hair, big brown eyes, a robust and cheerful face which carried a sincere and warm smile. He was dressed comfortably for his first encounter with his client. As Shar Dea walked through the arrival gate, she saw that Tony had already spotted her and they exchanged their first visible hello's.

He approached her with a gesture of caution, just in case he might have mistaken someone else for Shar Dea, and said, "Hi,

I'm Tony Yera, . . . Shar Dea?"

"Yes!" she said. "We finally meet."

They began to walk through the corridors and to the baggage claim area. Some small talk was in order as they exchanged welcoming invitations, simple one-to-one comments, and the sort.

In the car, Tony began filling in Shar Dea with the business world and other peripheral matters. Then they came to a red traffic light and stopped. Tony pointed to the light, and said, "You know, Shar Dea? It generally takes me around forty-five minutes to get to the airport. That includes at least ten red traffic lights on the way. But not this time! Not one red light and less than twenty minutes—that's a miracle!"

Shar Dea looked at Tony, offered a very pleasing smile, and said, "To you my publisher friend, this may be true, but not to me."

"Come again, young lady?"

"I was bored on that tin can of a flying machine, so I played around with a little magic."

"I don't understand."

"Well, I'll explain a lot of this to you when we get to your place."

Soon they arrived at his home, which was remotely located on twenty acres of dense forest. His four level house was actually built on the eastern slope of a mountain. Its unique architecture caressed the grounds from the front view; the back view gave it the multi-level look. Each level had a sky view, and on the eastern side, glass walls were used to let the forest become part of each room's decor. Shar Dea was impressed. "Who built this beautiful home?" she inquired.

"It was a kit!" replied Tony. "You know, a mail order. They sent me the plans and supplies and we put it together."

"Who's we?"

"All the folks who work for me at the Aubree Publishing Company. They're great people. You will have a chance to meet them soon," he proudly acclaimed.

The day went fast, business was well presented and organized. Tony impressed Shar Dea by his precise manner of operations which delivered a feeling of confidence and trust to Shar Dea.

"Tony, how do you do it all so well?"

"Oh!" justified Tony. "It's the discipline that I picked up from the priesthood, at the monastery in Italy. You know, over there, not only do you work with the Almighty Father in heaven, but you must also work for the almighty clergy down here. It's two different worlds and shouldn't be."

"Am I to understand that you didn't enjoy working for the

Church?"

"No, no! The Church is fine. It's the clergy who run it like a bureaucracy that finally got to me. If you were not in an authoritative position, or some established intellectual, then you were treated like some kind of mindless and powerless zombie," Tony repulsed.

Tony asked Shar Dea to sit down, and he began to share his feelings. "You see, the mission of Christ was about two critical issues: the forgiveness of sins and the advocation of peace on Earth. Since Christ ascended into the cosmos, all the worker bees began buzzing around to build a hive. Do you follow what I am saying, Shar Dea?"

She positively nudged her head.

Tony continued, "But who was to be the Queen Bee? Ha! Since they couldn't find a Queen Bee, they settled for an intelligent and peace loving warrior. Soon he became Master Bee of the hive, but I do not know how a Master Bee can mother a hive. You see, Sister Shar Dea, The Church, as I believe it to exist, is the Silver Chalice of the Spirit, here on Earth. Its function is to give birth to the new word of enlightenment. The Church is truly maternal, yet a male sits at its throne. It is not the way of the sword to conquer lost souls; it's maternal loving care.

"Muhammed's mission was to fill the Silver Chalice—the final prophet to carry the divine message to the planet. Unfortunately, the Master Bee did not understand him. Instead, he became aggressive in the usual male fashion. As a last resort, the Master Bee sent out the Crusaders to stop the spread of Islam, because it was threatening the situation of Christians living in the Holy Lands."

"Tony, let me interrupt you for a moment, if you will," petitioned Shar Dea. "Religions seek perfection within themselves. Suppose one of the many hundreds of religions succeeded in its pursuit. If that happened, would it be just to say that all other religious pursuits were fruitless?"

"Seems so."

"True religion is one that honestly seeks the meaning of truth. On the contrary, what religions proliferate is the truth in their beliefs, not necessarily what is truth! This ambitious drive is the foundation of difference between religions. Consequently, religions spread their word by the sword, choose not to forgive, and cultivate deep rooted hate. Instead of peacefully spreading the words *godliness and peace*, they forced it upon others by the sword and through colonizations.

"As long as hate remains in the minds of the religiously chosen, peace of mind cannot exist—there's no place for it to dwell in the consciousness.

132

The ancient word of 'forgive' has a profound and indepth meaning. The 'F' means the province of the human; the 'O' means warmth; the 'R' means recurring; the 'G' means orderly growth; the 'I' means to add to one's higher self; the 'V' means cosmic content; and the 'E' means towards God. Altogether, the word 'forgive' is truly a vision of intense and consistent betterment of humans to serve a Godly purpose. It's a more sophisticated and profound action than to simply excuse somebody's error of the past. Rather, it is a sense of hope for a peaceful future."

Tony mumbled, "How succinct."

"Peace can only come to this planet," explained Shar Dea, "if and only if the Jews, Christians, Islams, Hindus, and all the other religions begin to unite. If they can't, then the collective consciousness of all religions will begin to deteriorate. You can witness this happening today, by observing the youths' and young adults' gradual breaking away from religion, as in the case in the Middle East. You know what the New Testament says, Tony: 'They that take the sword shall perish by the sword.'"

"I'm beginning to see your point."

"Think for a moment," she said. "Do you know how much oil and gas has been removed from beneath those lands? What would happen if the planet Earth decided to light a fire underground in that region?"

Tony lamently uttered, "Armageddon?"

Tony was taken. He couldn't agree or disagree. He just sat back and looked at Shar Dea, and said nothing. Shar Dea stood up and walked over to the window. "Tony," she said, "I can tell that you are lost for words. Please bear in mind that very few minds on this planet know of the tragedies that await the masses."

Tony put up his hand to Shar Dea and said, "Wait a minute. How do you know all this?"

"During the time of my childhood in the ancient lands, Atlantis, my mother, Bene Dea, clairvoyantly saw the world of the future."

"A few months ago, I taught Michael how to dream astrally and voyage into the future like my mother did."

Tony was taken aback. "Atlantis, uh?"

"Yes, Tony. Atlantis."

Tony looked uncertain about her use of the term "astral dream," and began to hesitate.

Before he could respond, Shar Dea continued. "Both my mother and I have read the same events." Then she added, "What is written within the conscious mind of the planet is 'that mankind will inevitably destroy himself and the planet'. And to the Planet Earth, that's the same thing as a 'death wish!'"

Tony stood up and started to scratch his head. He turned to Shar Dea, and said, "So what's the use. If that cannot be altered, then we are all doomed!"

She immediately replied, "LIFE IS CHANGE, Tony! We do have the gift of CHOICE. Don't we?"

"Yes, we do," he weakly commented.

Shar Dea got excited. "Well then, what's written in the Akashic record needs to be changed. The only way for that to change is for the collective consciousness of mankind to change it. Change for peace, that is!"

"And if not," replied Tony.

"Then the Mother Planet Earth will change it for mankind—her way and real soon!"

"How can it do that, Shar Dea?"

"She'll light the fires!"

# CHAPTER 29

# A TEAR OF HOPE

*"Truth is living, it is not static, and the mind that would discover truth must also be living, not burdened with knowledge or experience. Then only is there that state in which truth can come into being."*
—*J. Krishnamurti*

Christmas was just seven days away and Shar Dea was full of the holiday spirits. The experience of Christmas was all new to her. The folklore, fairy tales, Santa Claus and the celebration of the birth of Christ occupied her thoughts.

Aside from the festivities, the book "World Peace" had sold over 150,000 copies as of December 1st. It was in its second printing with an additional 25,000 copies scheduled for release. Above all, she was overwhelmed with joy, because of her invitation to appear on the Phil Donahue Morning Show on December 27th. This meant exposure for the book and a chance to advocate her cause.

Michael and Donna were not quite so lucky. They were busy prepping Shar Dea for the show. They even hired a public relations specialist to help train Shar Dea for such a challenging experience. John Rutherford, the PR man, was very emphatic and cautious on these subjects, especially when televised.

Donahue's Press Representative stated, ". . . that Mr. Donahue was interested in the intent of the book, but offered very little feedback on whether he supported or disagreed with its message . . ."

Shar Dea was advised not to permit herself to talk about esoterics. Shar Dea had some trouble with holding back the truths which she so dearly held to her heart.

"Be polite, and don't say anything beyond the simple," demanded John. "Or else, they'll bury you!"

"Well how about my visions? Michael even knows how to astral travel."

"No! Absolutely not! You're pushing your luck when admitting that you can remember your 'astral' dreams the way you do," pleaded John. Then he said, "Listen lady, I do not quite understand all that stuff you purport to know. I know the business of TV and how the audience thinks and responds. They want to hear what you have to say in the book. If it gets over their heads, which seems very likely, they will surmise you for a fake and wash you out. Remember, you're going to be on National TV, maybe five million people could be watching this show. It's the Christmas vacation period, and a lot of folks will be home," chanted out Rutherford.

Soon the day was upon them. In front of Shar Dea sat six television cameras, 250 people, and a bunch of microphones and booms. Her face was slightly colored, despite the efforts to fight off the make-up artists, who managed to get a little silicone powder on her face.

The initial welcome and applause was still ringing in her ears when Phil Donahue officially opened the conversation. He said to her, "Shar Dea, is 'Shar Dea' your pen name?"

Shar Dea was momentarily stunned, for she and her prep crew forgot to cover this question altogether, however, her response was swift. "It's my real name. My mother felt it appropriate to keep the family heritage alive from generation to generation."

Donahue knew she was discreetly avoiding something, but permitted the conversation to go on uninterrupted. He uttered back, "Oh! I see. It's not French then is it?"

Shar Dea mentally threw a "thank's" to him, and replied, "No! It's not French."

"I read your little book and can easily see why it's becoming a controversial hit," stated Donahue positively.

Shar Dea picked up on his cue, and immediately said, "Most intellectuals who respect mankind and the planet's request for peace will undoubtedly advocate reading 'World Peace'."

The question and answer conversations kept a steady pace. Shar Dea quickly caught on to the politics and mannerisms of the talk show.

Donahue's sharp sense of sustained dialogue caught on to Shar Dea's friskiness and agility for accurate interactions of thought. He then asked Shar Dea, "If the attainment of world peace was, 'in your opinion', a fantasized or probable reality?"

She looked at him directly, then turned to the audience, and said, "The choice is yours. It's how you perceive it to be. If the attainment of a loving society is important to you, then it's not a fantasy. Regardless, in the end, it's a matter of life or death."

This brought out an air of silence from everyone. Donahue broke the quietness by suggesting that the audience raise questions in response to the comment made by Shar Dea.

A very concerned woman raised her hand and was quickly called upon. Her opening question was, "I seek world peace, too; and I think most people do as well."

Donahue interjected, "Madam! What's your question?"

However, Shar Dea responded instead of the woman. "Phil! This is a good example of a situation. Please permit me to provide some feedback."

"Fine, if you insist," uttered Donahue.

Shar Dea offered some basic training to the audience. "First of all, I don't doubt that the woman wants peace. However, if we listened carefully to the woman in the audience, what we actually heard instead of asking me a question was a defensive statement. That kind of statement hinders our conveying the truth of the matter—most people do not actively seek world peace. Therefore, in order to pursue a loving humanity, we must be high-spirited, creative, and consistently diligent in the process.

"Now let's return to the lady in the audience. Madam, please give us an example of how you go about seeking peace?"

The woman hesitated and felt instantly apprehensive. Then she blurted out, "I like to help others."

Shar Dea knew that the poor woman got herself nervous and trapped, and offered the woman and audience a few kind words as to ease the conflict.

Then another woman asked Shar Dea to explain what she meant by, "The choice is yours."

Shar Dea's response went quickly. "If you fantasize on peace, you will see a world in chaos. Fantasizing is what governments do. However, if every day you diligently pursue peace, by thought provoking visualizations and imageries of peace, then there's a greater probability. The essence of visualization, imagery, and meditative prayer is 'action.' The essence of action is creating 'results.' Give your thoughts energy, and you will witness newness from within your heart.

Therefore, the choice is yours. Either passively gait around as a dotty fool fantasizing about peace, or think, speak, and perform some deed to advocate world harmony and love."

The questions went back and forth. Donahue interjected from time to time, but it was the audience who seemed to get themselves more involved with the intent of the book.

With under a minute left before the commercial, Donahue interjected to make a few closing comments. Looking directly into the T.V. camera, he said "We'd like to thank Shar Dea for joining us this morning. And most importantly for making us think more keenly of our roles and responsibilities for world peace. Finally, Shar Dea, we all hope that your little book will wake up a lot of you viewers, out there, wherever you may be."

* * *

As a result of this publicity, book sales soared and the demand for a fourth reprint was imminent. The show served her purpose and the movement toward peace really started to become prolific. Letters came pouring in. Volunteers to help out with the campaign prompted Donna to set up a second office for the movement next to her office. For the first time, a gentle and steadfast movement was being realized, and they were a part of it. In the minds of most readers a ray of hope transcended into their hearts.

Michael thoroughly understood the impact that would beget Shar Dea, and unselfishly committed himself to be her servant in disguise. He loved her and respected all that she stood for.

Tony Yera contracted to have the script translated into Japanese, Spanish, French, Italian and Chinese. By Easter Sunday, over three million copies were sold throughout the world. The Japanese were especially interested in the movement. As Shar Dea once pointed out, "Ever since Hiroshima and Nagasaki, the conscious minds of these people were to seek peace. Now, they appear to be absorbing the book and its nonviolent movement as a catalyst to their cause and moral obligation." The Italians demonstrated their own peculiarities as a nation. Shar Dea had predicted that the Italians would begin reuniting as a nation with a single cause. This was materializing, even though it was inconsistent with their past behavior; that is, despite the efforts of the governments and the Popes who had ruled over this divided land for centuries.

Slowly but surely, the Chinese opened up their hearts and were demonstrating an interest in the cause of Shar Dea's words and petitions.

It was not quite one year from the time Shar Dea appeared on the shores of South Carolina. During this period, many events took place, and the world was hearing a new voice.

\* \* \*

The Caribbean breeze carried itself up the Eastern coast of America. It was easily felt by Shar Dea as she lay outside the beach house. "Michael," she said, "Do you feel that breeze?"

"It feels good, sweetheart. Doesn't it?" he lazily replied.

"There is a certain ancient feeling that I get from the winds. It's like the winds I experienced when I was a child on Atlantis. I remember them well."

"They ought to be," said Michael, "those are the winds of the Gulf Stream—the eternal winds of the sea."

Shar Dea began to reminisce, "As a child, I would walk close to the edge of the high cliffs and let the breeze from the sea blow past my face. I would feel tugs from the Infinite, and hear the voice of Ara E Hum sing peacefully through my ears. When I closed my eyes I began to fly. Higher and higher I would go.

Into the astral dream and see only beauty. What a gift from Ara E Hum! I guess that children are still peaceful souls with bodies, 'cause all that I saw was in peace."

Then she turned towards Michael, and said tenderly to him, "Darling, you will soon see peace as I did when I was a child. For now you and I are one." Shar Dea contemplated momentarily, then continued. "I know that my destiny is fast approaching. I can see us in play and forever in peace."

Michael looked into her eyes and wanted to tell her something poetically beautiful, but instead he cried a tear from his heart.

# CHAPTER 30

# LAST CHANCE, AMERICA

*"The Age of Nations is past. The task
before us is now, if we would not perish, is to
shake off our ancient prejudices, and build the
earth."*
—Pierre Teilhard de Chardin

It was without question that the book World Peace was widely accepted throughout the world. However, it had a mixed impact on the American reader. On one hand, many of the readers were patriotic and enlightened to the realities it spoke of. The theme and driving force behind the little pocket book of peace renewed the founding spirits that once made America a great place to live, and an American, a great person to be.

On the other side, many of the readers felt that the book intimidated and tarnished the American way of life and its high standards of living. One of the main enemies, described in the book, was the American way of contemporary thought. It addressed this concept as passive and permissive. It looked at Americans as a nation which superficially or theorectically sought peace, and at best, claimed that the American viewpoint for peace could be attained by the efforts and tribulations of others. The dichotomy that it pointed out was given in the example animation drawn by Michael depicting the contented typical middle-class American saying: "Give me a house with a two-car garage, a couple of good remote control color TVs, a quiet back yard, and a fenced-in pool." Versus, the words of the world's majority population: "Please! Some food and shelter."

Except for the political incongruities of some countries, the affect of this little book created a spirited driving force which was contributing to the betterment of those respective nations. Things were materializing and starting to happen. People were reading the book as individuals, as groups, as communities, and as nations.

Unfortunately, in America, the book was on trial. It was a fifty-fifty deal. Pro-factions wanted more peace movement activities and government support. Anti-factions wanted the book censured and government support as well. It wasn't the "Right-To-Life" or "Prayer in the Public Schools" syndrome, anymore; rather, it was the "Are We a Peace Loving Nation or a Lazy

Affluent Nation?" syndrome. As usual, the legal ramifications took hold. Conservative-versus-Liberal, and Hawk-versus-Dove dichotomies began to get the full attention of the 'Proud to Be an American' and 'Not So Proud to Be an American' groups in rivalry. The American public was split, however, the major portion of the cross-cultural minority populations showed definite support for the movement.

For eight straight months book sales soared. One day late in August, a significant event occurred and the movement began to manifest its force. The doorbell rang and it was a Federal Express courier. Michael answered the door, and the young man asked for Shar Dea. Michael looked at the little guy, and said, "That's me, where do I sign?"

Afterwards, he tipped the courier and brought Shar Dea the sealed envelope. As she was opening it, she mumbled, "I wonder who's this from . . . aha! It's our friend Emilio, Archbishop Emilio Giovanni Ormati, the guy from the Vatican."

Michael was impatient. "Well! What does it say this time?"

Shar Dea read it aloud:

Dear Ms. Shar Dea:

Of first order, please accept our
apologies for identifying you as a
gentleman.

In light of your most courageous
attempt for world peace and universal
brotherhood, His Eminence, The Pope,
requests your presence to share in
dialogue with him.

His eminence feels quite positive that
you will attend. Therefore, he took the
liberty and asked me to arrange all
transportation and accommodations for
you and your husband, Michael.

The Pope will spend two days with you
in his private chambers at the Vatican.
He has designated the days of November
1st and 2nd for this occasion—All
Saints Day.

The Pope sees your work as a message to
the world and sincerely appreciates the
inspiration you have given him.

The Pope also wishes for me to convey
this anecdote to you: "Your
acknowledgment has already been
received."

Cordially,

Archbishop Emilio Giovanni Ormati
Chancellor of the Vatican Council
Office of Public Relations and Press

"Ara E Hum has responded," cried out Shar Dea. "I think
the movement is really going to happen."

Michael shouted a positive note. "And I think we've got ole'
Mother Earth's consciousness beginning to hear the cries of
mankinds thoughts, too!"

"Michael," said Shar Dea with an exasperated voice, "that's
two months away. Let's call Donna right now and celebrate." At
that very instant, the phone rang. Shar Dea ran over to answer it,
and said, "Hello!" Shar Dea's eyes rolled around as her face
glowed with joy and wonderment. "Donna!" she exclaimed.
"What? . . . Wow, this is fantastic!" Shar Dea turned to her
husband and clamored, "Michael! Michael! She actually picked
up on our thoughts telepathically." Shar Dea asked Donna to
come over to the beach house. "Great! We'll pour the wine for
you. See you in a few . . . Oh! Please do drive carefully! Love
Ya!"

Shar Dea ran over to Michael and hugged him. "Did you
hear that? She was with us all the time. I don't believe all this."
Shar Dea's body almost fainted from all the excitement. Michael
sensed her mood and held on to her tightly. As he did, Shar Dea
saw herself through his eyes and felt love in his heart. Her body
became limp. She softly uttered in his hear: "Please make love to
me." Enlightened by her love for him, he carried her upstairs
and rested her heart in his.

Donna did not bother to knock and easily worked her way
into the living room; shrewdly realizing that her friends were
upstairs celebrating their joy, she started a fire and put on a
little upbeat music. It was not long before they all joined in
order to review Emilio's letter. Afterwards they began to relax
and consumed a fair amount of wine. Donna got a little carried
away, drinking a bit more wine than she could handle. She
suggested that they all go skinny-dipping. Michael favored the
treat, but Shar Dea felt that it was out of place. With a little bit
of pride locked in her throat, Donna openly admitted that she
was a little lonely when being in the midst of Shar Dea and

Michael. This made Shar Dea's mind tremble. Michael sensed the seriousness of Shar Dea's concern for Donna. "What's up, Shar Dea?"

"Donna's drive for masculinity is extremely potent, yet she belittles men whenever she gets the opportunity," cautiously inferred Shar Dea.

Donna showed her defensiveness, and rebutted, "Show me a good vivacious, handsome and honest man, and I'll let you know how it feels."

Shar Dea pointed her right hand, palm facing up, towards her husband, and said, "Michael! You let him slip right through your fingers. He is one hunk of a guy. Sure! He was silly and immature when I first met him, but now he is part of me: in mind, body and spirit."

This caused Donna to ponder for a moment, while Michael listened with a sincere heart, hoping that Donna would understand the depth and of Shar Dea's intentions.

Then Donna said, "Are you saying that I don't give myself a chance with men?"

"Not quite that," responded Shar Dea. "A complete and fulfilled soul reflects all aspects of the universe—femininity and masculinity are perfectly balanced. You must find the masculinity of yourself to be complete. Somewhere out there is a missing male personality of Donna Champlynn embedded in a good man. The same situation exists for a man seeking his femininity."

"Yeah!" said Michael. "I never thought of it that way, darling. You bring out the woman in me, and I feel so complete with you."

Donna's eyes opened widely. "Are you trying to tell me that some part of me, little ole' me, is somewhere out there inside of some strange guy?"

"Getting close, Donna!" said Michael. "Here's another analogy for you to think about. Picture yourself as a person consisting of three parts. Put these three parts into the formula: $A + B + C$ = Your Entire Self, Okay! Part 'A' is your Soul and is worth 6 points, part 'B' is your Mind and is worth 2 points, and part 'C' is your Body and is worth 2 points. Assume mathematically that a well balanced 'Entire Self' is equal to 10 points. Note that the soul has a higher value placed on it, and that these numbers can vary. Let's say that God took one third of your soul, part 'A', and mysteriously placed it inside the soul of a male personality. Thus your equation would look like this . . ." Michael sketched out the equations on a tablet for Donna to see. ". . . $(2/3\ A\ \{Female\} + 1/3\ A\ \{Male\}) + B + C$ = E.S. In order to keep things in balance, God also did the same to the male, so we get this equation: $(2/3\ A\ \{Male\} + 1/3\ A\ \{Female\}) + B + C =$

E.S. Thus in your case, Donna, we would have this equation: (2/3 A {Donna's soul} + 1/3 A {some male's soul}) + B + C = the Entire Soul of Donna Champlynn.

"Now listen carefully, in your pursuit to find your total self, one of your jobs in the process of soul development is to find the missing one third of part 'A'. By setting up this spiritual responsibility, all personalities must seek the opposite sex in order to become complete. This magic sex formula guarantees balance, proliferation of life and race, social interaction, and cosmic play, just to name a few by-products of it all. Therefore, all men need women and all women need men. To consider yourself above this magic formula, you must be a highly developed soul, which in earthly terms, you would be called gods."

"Michael, that was beautiful!" complimented Shar Dea.

Donna was a bit surprised by the conviction of perceived truth behind Michael's narrative. She also took a good look at what Shar Dea had said, too. Donna sipped some wine and walked over to the window next to the fireplace, and humorously blurted out, "All I wanted to do was go skinny dipping. And you two cosmic whiz kids dump a bomb on my head that truly makes a lot of sense. So, what I really have to do is seek a man who holds the secrets to my all."

Both Shar Dea and Michael responded with, "A Ha!"

"My mission is to find my other third of my soul-self. What you are telling me is that in order to do that, I must forget my selfish needs, open up my heart so he can see what I am, and most importantly, listen to his heart."

"Right!" agreed Michael.

Shar Dea looked maternally at Donna, and with a sincere tone, said, "The reality of equality between the female and male remains law. The process of balance is up to the individual. How you do it and how long it takes to achieve it is all within the game of LIFE. The choice is yours."

* * *

Several hours later, the triad recovered from their philosophical stupor and decided to have a bite to eat. In the dining area, Michael spread out an array of delicious edibles and a kettle of hot water for the herbal tea.

As they were sitting around, Michael initiated a little humor to liven things up. He picked up the kettle carefully and lifted it over his head. Reading the little blue manufacturer's tag, he said, "Made in Japan." Then he moved to the tea bag holder. "Ah! This one is made in Thailand. Oops! This little wooden spoon comes from Tanzania."

Shar Dea frowned. "Where's Tanzania?"

"It's just below Kenya, in Africa."

Donna interjected, and said, "Poor Americans, they're not represented on the table. Unfortunately, they have really let things get out of hand. Now they're trying to tell everyone to buy American, and get back into good old patriotism."

"What they really need to do is get off their lethargic asses," vehemently claimed Shar Dea. "They need to speak for quality, and honestly stand behind their products and services. Most of the stupid advertisements that you see on television are just short of outright lies. The characters modeling and role-playing on those silly commercials misrepresent the truth. It's a grand scheme of undermining the public. It's expensive crap and a waste of money. Make a good product, and advertise how it benefits the consumer. Talk sense instead of playing on the ignorant consumer's emotions and dreams. The whole process deteriorates the essence and importance of the validity of a vision and the importance of a dream. The Americans are getting what they asked for—mediocrity and sloppiness."

"Yea! If they don't get their act together really soon, there won't be much patriotism left in America to live for. America needs to press for high moral standards and human rights, and it can't sell that through advertisements. It's their last chance," exclaimed Michael.

Donna spoke in a humble manner. "Michael, I keep on hearing you say last chance for the Americans. I have a good idea where you are coming from, but can't seem to put my finger on it exactly."

"Well, let me give you a better understanding of what is approaching," offered Shar Dea. "What Michael is implying is that the focal point of world peace is burdened on to the Americans. Neither India, Russia, France, nor Japan can sponsor the fulfillment of world wide peace. It is the ultimate responsibility of the souls who have migrated to the land of new hope over the past five hundred years. It's their destiny. It is true that peace can be obtained elsewhere on the globe, but the integrity and strength of a world wide peace movement must be generated from American soil. It's their Karma and it must be attained.

"Recall the greatest moment in American history, the moment when all the freedom fighters and heroics united and announced to the world American independence. This was only made possible by the spiritual enlightenment received from Ara E Hum as the land of new hope. In essence, the discovery of the North American continent—epitomized by the Declaration of Independence—was actually a miracle granted to the people of Europe and the rest of the suffering world.

"The young American government began a crusade of liberty and freedom. Its endeavors were courageous and admirable, despite the aching pains in its evolution. However, as this establishment began to feel the comforts of security and the clumsiness of bureaucracy, the essence of the political spirit began to deteriorate.

"Hypocritical to its cause, the American government rationalized and raised the sword against the Red Man and their tribes—a sin that has still not been be dealt with.

"Next came the industrial revolution, where the aggressive males had a chance to show their might and power of rule. Most of the Civil War was caused by the awesome evil of industrial survival. Unfortunately, the poor people of the lands had to pay for this political nonsense, which was beautifully guised under issues of morality and racial freedom. How anti-humanity American valves have turned in such a short time."

"What you are saying, Shar Dea, is understandable, but I don't see why America warrants being the focal point?" commented Donna.

"Make believe that a very large mosquito landed on your left forearm. Written on his wing were the words 'USS Malaria.'And just as he stuck his sharp needle into your skin, smash! You swatted him, crushing every molecule the guy ever had. Look at his death. It was good! As you perceived it to be justifiably so. You probably didn't even think twice about it either.

"Now, think of yourself as the Planet Earth. Alive and with all conscious faculties working to keep yourself well and surviving. On your skin, excuse me, on your land, millions of people were thinking poison and dreadful things about the world. Wouldn't you protect yourself, and kill the little bunch of villains? Whereby you, the Planet, perceiving it to be justifiably so.

"Think openmindedly about it for a minute. Look at what's happening between Iran and Iraq: millions are dying for what cause, worse yet, for what victory."

Donna did just that. A few moments later Donna said, "I get the gist of what you are saying, Shar Dea, but how do you convince over four billion folks out there that the planet is alive and has a consciousness?"

"Hum! You got me," Shar Dea said remorsefully.

Michael came to her defense, and said, "Just about every individual who has some level of spiritual development could testify to the fact that nature is alive!"

"But that's just it, Michael. We can't prove it to be a fact, not in this scientific Western society," rebutted Donna.

"It doesn't make a bit of difference, Donna," said Shar Dea. "The truth still remains as is. The planet Earth is a living organism. It thinks, breathes, feels, and loves through its nature. The powers of the Holy Spirit are channeled through nature.

"The only difference between Mother Planet Earth and humans is that she is a billion times slower and a billion times more powerful. So, when she wants an electrical storm to light up the sky, she does it. If she wants an earthquake to scratch her back, she does it. She is not a helpless heap of dirt floating around the universe and lighting up the solar system with the most beautiful blue and white colors for nothing."

"Nevertheless," said Michael, "what are we really trying to accomplish in America, Shar Dea?"

"Good, let's get down to business," Donna urged with reinforcement.

Shar Dea agreed wholeheartedly. "We need to have the American people stand up for their rights as a prosperous and peace loving nation. This includes direct action and behavior on the part of the U.S. government and all those pin-striped blue-gray suited business gurus. They must join in mind, body and spirit to lead the world in this direction. It is so important for Americans to take up this responsibility. If they fail in this venture, then they will inevitably suffer from their passiveness. Just like the Babylonians, the Greeks, and the Romans—when all gets too fat and easy, permissive and legal, and the pursuit for the survival of peace is replaced with entertainment—existence is diametrically opposed and shattered."

Donna focused sharply onto Shar Dea, and declared, "You said that there wouldn't be a major war. Right!"

"Correct, it will come as in the guise of natural and economical disasters. Do you know what would happen to the American Nation if something drastic occurred?" Donna looked quite perplexed, and simply and doubtfully shrugged her shoulders.

Shar Dea continued. "Think for a minute how messy it could all turn out. Rarely in this country has the American population or government had to confront a major disaster on a large scale level. It has even failed in trying to establish a major city evacuation plan, which would probably be more disastrous then the horrifying event that caused the evacuation.

"In most cases, Americans are usually the first to come to aid when other countries have natural crisis or some kind of political trouble. Unfortunately, most nations offer little to the Americans, as a whole. What do you think would happen if Los Angeles, San Francisco, New York City or Washington D.C. had suffered a major natural catastrophe?"

Donna lamently offered, "Nothing other that a couple of good tear-jerker letters from other concerned countries." Then Donna sarcastically added, "I can hear a lot of nations saying:

"Y'all got all the money, so now how does it feels when it strikes you, America?"

"Heavy words, Donna," commented Michael.

"I just don't think that the people in America realize how passive and permissive they have gotten. It's dangerous not to fight for your survival, or at least know what to do in case a major emergency occurs on a grand scale," remarked Donna.

"That's it, Donna!" said Michael. "Americans are like football coaches and military leaders. Their minds are set on power, strategy, and bigness. They've replaced survival instincts with military might and touch downs. They forget that what we are postulating is mind over matter—the quest for survival must be in the minds as thoughts of peace: not the tanks, planes and footballs."

Shar Dea emphatically pointed out: "Survival and the quest for existence are Rules number one and one—they are one and all the same."

"We need to get Americans to rise above their comforts and seek peace as forcibly as they seek profits and military might!" said Donna.

"Don't forget to tell them to rise above their friend, laziness, too!" commented Michael.

"It's kind of hard to believe that Americans could undergo such change and humiliation," said Donna.

Shar Dea stood up and covered her face with her hands, as if to wipe the pain of thought from her brow, and said, "History tells many stories. One story is told over and over: "Whenever a nation gets too comfortable, relaxed, and conceited, it falls." Let us focus our thoughts, for a moment, on the historic events that occurred in the profound city of Jerusalem. Ask ourselves: "How many times have the Jews been conquered? How many times have the Islams been conquered? How many times have the Christians been conquered? The Romans? The . . . ? Do we need to go on?

"Is it not true that whenever a nation becomes great, it eventually falls? And whenever a nation loses the vision for peace, it is overtaken, not by its foes, but by God?"

# CHAPTER 31
# THE BEGINNING

*"The great whore, as it were
—Fear—enslaves, encaptures and inhibits the
creative mind. It does not permit love to
bloom in its wondrous fields; it does not
permit life to be reveled upon; it stagnates
the emotions and kills hope. Fear is born
out of not-knowingness: whatever you are
in not-knowingness of you enslaved to, you
are in darkness about. This hour shall bring
not-knowingness forth in the clarity of our
wondrous light, to pursue it and find all the
answers that have kept us in the state of not-
knowingness. And then we are freed!"*
—Ramtha

The Pope was elegant in thought and spirit. Outwardly, he
seemed gentle, yet inwardly, he was annoyed by the bureaucracy
which surrounded him. He was a man who wore the white cloth
and saw peace on Earth as a mission. Together, the Pope and
Shar Dea sat in his private study room in the "Apostolic
Pontifical Palace" throughout most of the day. Food and
beverage were brought to them as to not distract their
concentration.

On the first night, Michael joined them for dinner and some
brief entertainment. But, soon afterwards, he left so that they
could continue talking into the night. And, that they did, non-
stop till 2:15 A.M.

The large mahogany door of their Vatican guest suite opened
quietly, as Michael heard Shar Dea tiptoe into the room. "God,
you must be tired," Michael said half asleep.

"No, just in ecstasy," Shar Dea said, as she took off her red
trimmed coat. "He is unbelievably a gentle little man."

"Are you up to telling me what you and the Pope
discussed?" asked Michael with a desperate sense of curiousity.

"Well, what we discussed is difficult to tell anyone. But, I'll
let you in on a few things as best as I can. Hopefully, you can
stay tuned in to me telepathically for the next few days."

"That's fine with me."

They sat around for a couple of minutes and Shar Dea
reviewed the essence of her conversation with the Pope. Michael

noticed that Shar Dea's eyes were beginning to roll more frequently into a closed position. "Let's get you into bed," he suggested.

With their heads safely tucked under the sheets, the last fleeting words were exchanged between them. Michael inquired about food. "What time are you going to meet with the Pope in the morning?"

"Oh, an escort will meet us at 7:00 A.M. . . . . We'll all have breakfast at 7:30 A.M. . . . . By the way, sweetheart, the Pope is quite impressed by the way you are handling your transitioning."

"What?"

"He's more spiritual then he shows himself to be. In our discussion he blatantly asked me if our souls were developing together during our previous life times. Then he came out with the statement that you're are my true masculine complement. I mean, Michael, the guy is really together on a lot of things for which his conservative clergy would impeach him."

"Is that why you cannot let things out between you and the Pope?"

"Emphatically yes."

"Well, keep your telepathic mind open tonight. I'll try to fill you in on the rest of what we said. But, right now, this girl has got to go to sleep!"

The lights went out. And the night's cool air filtered through the room. And without any superhuman feats, Shar Dea, in the midst of her astral dream, shared telepathically with Michael, her entire day's conversations with the Pope.

It seemed like only moments later, but a loud knocking sound was heard; it was the escort at the door. Michael and Shar Dea were ready and anxious to begin their new day. She was dressed in a light blue suit with a flared skirt, which was beyond the call of a liberal clergyman's domain. She knew it would get condescending remarks from the ultra-conservatives, but never imagined that the liberal would also find it offensive as well. It didn't matter which side of the fence they were on, for the Pope's opening statement was: "Bless the Lord, the color of the sky. You must feel special in that thing?" And, a thing it was. Michael held his giggles, though he almost admitted them when Archbishop Ormati's eyes popped out. After breakfast, Shar Dea and the Pope went off into his chambers. Father Berinelli, the Pope's personal secretary, followed them close by.

Michael headed for the museums and eventually the ancient ruins. In his mind he entertained the notion that in one of his past lives, he was a Roman Senator. Feeling quite attached to the historic events, his carefree attitude offered him companionship and made his time alone intriguing.

Around 3:00 P.M., Shar Dea and the Pope said their final

farewells. Michael met them at the front of his chambers, and presented the Pope a piece of petrified driftwood which he had received from his grandfather.

After a brief explanation of its heritage, he handed it to the Pope, and said, "Your Eminence, this could be an ancient token brought forward to consummate a new beginning for mankind. My heart tells me that it once was part of a tree on Atlantis, now it is but a reminder of a lost civilization. It has no value, except that which we put into it."

The Pope took it and studied its shape for a moment. Then he raised it slightly over and in front of his head, and prayed, "It is of the Earth, and tells us of a past life which has gone dry, and orchestrates naught. Let us pray to the Almighty Father that this ancient reminder will never drift again to the shores of the next civilization. We must have peace on Earth."

\* \* \*

The trans-Atlantic plane ride back to Atlanta permitted Shar Dea to explain some of the finer points exchanged between her and the Pope. A lot of note taking went on and plenty of planning as well.

Donna met them at the terminal, and then they hopped on a private charter Cessna for a short flight back to Charleston. While Shar Dea caught a short nap, Michael filled Donna in on most of the events and conversations which took place. Donna easily absorbed the details.

As the plane was descending on the approach pattern, Donna recommended that they go straight to the Fortune Dragon for some Chinese food. Her idea was readily accepted.

At the restaurant, the met their good friend, George Wong, and ordered their usual favorites. Donna was a little restless and appeared to be anxious to know what was forthcoming. "Well guys, what next?"

"We must wait for the Pope to call the next move," replied Michael. "The Pope said: '. . . that we must be patient for a few days, in order for him to prepare a workable strategy.'"

Donna inquired, "What do you think he will do?"

"We'll have to wait and see," replied Shar Dea.

The next day, Michael and Shar Dea sought to find seclusion for themselves at their beach house. Occasionally the phone would ring and a reporter would try to squeeze a little information from them. The national news networks were well informed of some upcoming papal event, and stayed close to Shar Dea and Michael. But despite all the activity around them, they did manage to relax and catch some mid-day rays from the sun.

Later that afternoon, Michael called Donna up, and asked

her if she would enjoy coming over to the beach house for a couple of days. She was delighted, and stated that she needed a break from the office madness and appreciated the invitation.

Donna arrived about 8:00 P.M. with three small traveling bags on her proper. "Here I am! Where's my room?" she said jokingly.

Michael gave her a hug and kiss, and said, "You're just in time to see something beautiful. Come here." They both went outside onto the back deck and looked southward. A thunder storm was moving up the coast and approaching the beach house. It was about ten miles away and they could see yellowish-white lightning currents erratically illuminating the skies. The height of the storm easily topped 40,000 feet. However, the awe of it all was that the storm was totally witnessed in silence.

After of few minutes of nature's gift of might and beauty, Donna proceeded to the guest room. As she passed the phone, it rang. She nonchalantly picked it up, and voiced a friendly "Hello." Then she yelled out, "Michael! It's the Vatican?"

Michael quickly ran to the phone and began to converse with the caller. "Yes . . . Aha! . . . We understand . . . It's going to be great! We will call you at 3:00 P.M. Saturday, our time. We'll touch base with you then . . . Superb! . . . Thank you Cardinal. Chao!"

While Michael was talking on the phone, Donna went upstairs to get Shar Dea. As Michael hung up the phone, Shar Dea was standing right beside him desperately awaiting the news. He grabbed her by the arms and gave her a big hug, squeezing her tightly. He spun her around a few times, and informed her and Donna of the good news. "Listen to this, you guys," he jabbered. "We're on! The Pope will address the public this Saturday afternoon. Cardinal Ormati said '. . . that the Pope will be making a statement about our talks and committing himself to the movement.' Ormati also stated that the Pope is going to officially challenge all the world leaders to fend for peace in their countries. The Pope told Ormati to tell you especially that he agrees with you on the issue of the American people's responsibility to lead the way for world peace. Being more specific, he's going to challenge the President, personally on the matter!"

Sunday morning's paper headline story read: "The Pope Seeks World Wide Peace: The President Is Challenged!" In addition to the cover page, two full pages and a dozen articles were written about the topic. It was so well performed that the Associated Press and most national and foreign news syndicates ran with the story, and in their usual fashion exaggerated it. Ideally, this was exactly what Shar Dea and the Pope had planned, anyway.

Tony Yera called about 9:00 A.M., and told Michael that an

hour after the Pope's speech, he had received three phone calls requesting copies of the book. One call came from New York, requesting an immediate 175,000 copies; another from Great Britain asking for 500,000 copies; and Japan sought an unprecedented 2.5 million.

The triad reviewed the newspapers completely and immersed themselves into conversation. They were picking out the details and trying to identify the level and potential strength of their supporters. Nation after nation, it all looked promising. Most importantly, most of the journalists and press syndicates vowed not to let this movement go by the wayside. Whatever was happening surely seemed to offer a sense of hope throughout the world.

It was close to noontime, and except for a couple of cups of coffee, the triad had nothing to eat. Donna decided that they should go out for brunch. "Hey, guys, how about a little nourishment?"

"That sounds fine with me," collaborated Michael.

"Really, what have we been doing that's so important to keep us away from FOOOOD!" Shar Dea resonated sarcastically.

They all made a quick dash to put on some warmer clothing. Within five minutes, they were in Michael's red convertible, and on their way.

While driving and engaged in cheerful conversation, they overheard part of a comment made by the radio DJ, who was saying: ". . . and the President was jokingly commenting about the Pope's speech." That was all they heard. Instantly, they all got upset and very quiet.

"What the hell was he saying?" angrily voiced Michael.

"It doesn't matter. Don't get foul mouthed, and look for the positive in what ever he said," demanded Shar Dea.

"Yea, Michael," interjected Donna, "maybe he was saying something very encouraging like: "If the Pope is going for it! Then so am I."

Michael painfully yielded. "Well, I guess you're probably right."

Shar Dea felt unaffected by the fuss that just transpired. She wanted to say something special, and the ride offered the best informal place for her to say what was dear to her heart. "There's something special I've been wanting to tell you two fine folks for a long time," she humbly mentioned.

"And?" said Donna.

"Do you realize how close you both have gotten to each other?"

"Hum!" murmured Michael and Donna simultaneously.

"See, right there! It's happening. It really is!" joyfully announced Shar Dea.

"What's happening?" petitioned Donna.

"There are some things I can't share with you in this life time, and that's one of them."

"Wait a minute, sweetheart. You and I are one. There's nothing between us that can't be shared."

"Michael, dear," retorted Shar Dea, "remember the time when I told you how secretive my mother, Bene Dea, was about my destiny?"

"Yes."

"Well, then I must be secretive about those things that I envision that relate to the destiny of others."

"Are we going to have another 'Catch 22' discussion which creates a high level of frustration?" commented Donna. "Shar Dea, if you know something good about us, then that's fine. We'll trust your visions and anticipate a day in the future when we can say: "I loved her for her well-kept secrets."

\* \* \*

Brunch was great, and the drive along the two-lane ocean highway back to the beach house was even greater. As they pulled up into the driveway, two dark gray sedans, of American make, were parked. Michael cautiously got out, assuming potential danger, and approached the cars. No one was in them. Shar Dea and Donna got out and walked behind Michael. Then, around the back, on the deck, three well suited men and two women gathered. They all seemed to be relaxed and presenting no threat.

"Hi there, can I help you folks?" greeted Michael.

"You sure can. We are Federal representatives from the White House," said the shortest man of the team. "My name is O'Hare, Agent Pat O'Hare. We come with good news."

"Sure, come inside," offered Michael. They all went inside and sat around in the living room. Donna started up some hot water for tea. An attractive young female agent, Kim Applefield, addressed the group, and said, "We come here to inform you that the President is one-hundred percent behind your movement. The Pope has already contacted the President personally. The President has vowed to go all the way with the movement."

"This sounds like there's going to be a lot of hard work ahead for the President," said Michael.

"Yes, your absolutely right," agreed agent O'Hare.

"What are the President's plans?" asked Shar Dea.

"So far, he hasn't said what is plans are to us. Our mission today, is to find out your plans and report them to the President," commented Applefield.

"Our plans?" said Michael disruptively. "We don't have

detailed plans of the sort to offer the President."

"You're kidding," clamored O'Hare with surprise.

"No, I'm not! Our primary goal was to approach world governments and religious leaders. We have not devised a formal plan for the people, other than to read the book," retorted Michael.

Then Shar Dea interjected, and said, "It was a critically important objective to get the Pope and the President to this point; so far, we're successful. Our next step is to make sure that the American people maintain pressure on their public officials. And, on the other hand, make sure that the President does not let this movement slip away into a bureaucratic hole and rot. Double pressure is the next important process."

"But you say you don't have any plans or strategy for this? asked O'Hare.

"Not at the moment," replied Donna.

Shar Dea responded with wholehearted honesty. "I'll assure you folks that the President will be informed of our intentions and suggestions for a strategy within a few days."

Then Agent Thomas Polanski asked Shar Dea a few questions which seemed contradictory to their previous words of welcome and good gesture. "Shar Dea," he said, "I was told by one of our agents that you graduated from U.C.L.A., and so did I. What years were you there?"

Shar Dea instantly knew of his intention behind the question, and wisely answered, "Your agent was wrong, Polanski!" Then she immediately directed her attention away from Polanski to see if it would arouse his temper. It did. And Shar Dea immediately became suspicious of their mission.

"Ms. Applefield," asked Shar Dea. "Did you think that the book was well written?"

"I suppose so."

Michael instantly responded, "Didn't you read the book?"

"Well, not completely."

Then the Senior Agent, Janet Cohen, interjected, hoping to break up the competitive verbal battle which was surfacing, and said, "Look, we are here to help you, not hurt you . . . ."

Shar Dea immediately interjected. "Listen, Ms. Cohen, and the rest of you; as I hear each of your words, I also hear your thoughts as well. Please do not try to deceive me any further. You came to tell us a few good words. But your real mission is to find out exactly who we are. Well be informed, and tell your Mr. President, that we are of peace. First and foremost, we seek peace in America—for America's sake. If your President hesitates for long, he will not have a nation behind him to govern. God will see to that! Our words, which the Pope has publicly stated, are not political but Divine. Now would you please go and encourage your President to listen to the Pope!"

# CHAPTER 32
## EYE-TO-EYE

*"The United States has chosen to play the
role of those who make peaceful revolution
impossible by refusing to give up the privileges
and the pleasures that come from the immense
profits of overseas investments . . . . A nation
that continues year after year to spend more
money on military defense than on programs
of social uplift is approaching spiritual
death."*
            —*Martin Luther King*


Tuesday morning brought in an unusual mood for the day's
beginning. The cool chill from the northern winds had finally
worked their way into the coastal areas of the deep south. The
flow of the Gulf Stream's currents began to face its northerly
opposition, and it couldn't warm the breeze as it was accustomed
to. The late morning sunrise warned to all that the days would be
growing shorter. Wildlife began migrating to warmer climates. It
was time to prepare for winter, and many hours of
contemplation.

Michael looked out beyond the deck and saw a wintery
frontal system nudge its way over the ocean. He was captured by
its graceful movements of the gray masses of clouds stretching
across the sea, slowly covering the blue sky and dimming the
brilliant yellows from the sun.

Donna was in the kitchen conjuring up some breakfast for
her friends, and keeping very quiet to herself. The smells of hash
brown potatoes, bacon and eggs meandered towards Michael until
his senses caught wind of his lust for food. As he began his
hurried walk to the kitchen he heard Shar Dea in the bedroom
yakking away to herself. He thought that was strange and
unusual for her to do. He kept on going and went into the
kitchen. "Good morning, Donna."

"Are you ready for some good hot food?" she offered.

"You bet!"

"I felt a little cold this morning, when I got up."

"Yea! Old man winter is moving in on us today. Better get
out your sweaters and gloves," hinted Michael.

Then Shar Dea burst through the kitchen doors while
rubbing her arms which were crossed, and said, "What's

happening to me? I'm chilled."

"Did you ever have a winter season in Atlantis?" said Michael inconspicuously.

"Oh! . . . Hush!"

"Yow!"

Shar Dea went over to Donna and gave her a big hug. "You doll, thank's for cooking breakfast." They sat down and began to enjoy the hearty breakfast. Their conversations were only a prologue warm up exercise of what was to come that day.

While Shar Dea was sipping coffee, Michael snapped his fingers, and said, "Hey sweetheart. While you were upstairs, what were you rattling your mouth about to yourself?"

"Oh, I was just acting out a little on my impatience towards the President. It's been three days since the Pope's speech and we haven't heard anything directly from the President, except for those goonies who made me mad."

Donna lowered her buttered toast, sat up erect, turned to Shar Dea, and in a challenging manner said, "Why don't you call him up?"

"Fat chance!" instantly and pessimistically commented Michael. "Do you know how hard it is to reach the President by phone?—all those . . . goonies." They all began to laugh.

After breakfast Shar Dea went into the living room to straighten out a few thoughts. Then she called Michael and Donna to join her. "Listen," she said, "I've got a little super stuff hidden in my sleeves that I have not shared with too many folks. I'll get right to the President. Watch!"

She dialed the White House number and waited a moment until some one answered. Then she firmly said, "Hi there! Please connect me to the President . . . immediately!" Her voice was about two octaves lower, more powerful, very commanding, and absolutely convincing. Above all, it was etched with a cosmic mystique, as if there was a subliminal dictate subconsciously attached. She began to speak: "Please hurry, it's urgent . . . No! . . . I need the President. Immediately! . . . I am Shar Dea, he knows me well." She looked up at Donna and Michael, and said, "It's working!" Then she returned to her serious side of business. "Hello, Mr. President!" she said. Michael and Donna went into shock. "Fine, thank you. I'll be specific: we need to talk—it's vitally important . . . That would be ideal . . . Thursday at 9:00 A.M. . . . Excellent! Have a good day, Mr. President."

After a few brief moments of recoupment from her accomplishment, Shar Dea could be seen returning to normal. "How in God's name did you do that?" asked Donna.

"Just that. In God's name!"

"You've really pulled one over all of us with that one, Shar

Dea," said Michael with a sense of knowing her secrets.

"Everything is natural, friend, even my mystical powers. I didn't tell the President what to say. By using a deep, low voice and subconsciously forcing the issues of truth, he understood my strength and conviction. We all have that ability."

Michael cringed. "I guess we really abuse meanings of truth in our conversations."

"Especially when we talk face-to-face," blurted out Donna.

"Michael, you were once a student of psychology. Right?" inquired Shar Dea.

"Yep."

"Do you remember the stuff you read about perception?"

"Ay?"

"How about you, Donna?" asked Shar Dea.

"Ay? Like Michael, I suppose."

Shar Dea smiled. "Do you remember about the secrets of 'eye-to-eye' knowledge?"

"Is that perception?" asked Donna.

Shar Dea offered an explanation. "A person's eyes and face, together as a working combination of physical matter, reveal to the keen observer, the inner secrets of a person. The face resonates whatever pressures, that is, stresses or elations, that the mind has just thought, just like a hi-fi speaker resonates sound.

"The eyes reveal sincerity, just like the lens of a precision camera, which can accurately focus on an image. So when a person is telling a lie, his face instantly resonates the negative psychic pressures, and the eyes forcibly glare from the spiritual strain.

"The observer who is properly trained on these detection techniques can easily determine where a person is coming from. This whole process also helps the observer to telepathically read the thoughts of others, too.

"One of the greatest gifts given to mankind is the ability to demand honesty and truth from a fellow person. To do this, you must devote absolute attention onto the other person's eyes and face. And as you speak the truth, you hear what the other person is hearing, see what the other person is seeing, and feel what the other person is feeling. There can be no divergent communication—in either direction."

Michael was beaming on Shar Dea. He leaned over and gave her a big kiss. Softly he said, "My Empress, you definitely had some good training in these areas. Did the Pope know how many beautiful colors your eyes are?"

"Very well indeed he did. As I said: He is a very special person."

"I'll agree to that," said Donna.

"Folks," Shar Dea said, "when you speak eye-to-eye, you

speak in the realm of truth. Only then do you know the liar, the fraudulent, and the evil."

* * *

In the White House stood more awareness to the past then some museums. It spoke not of the future, but of the accomplishments within history. Except for some tasteful poetics here and there, it was indicative of reaction and only a trinkling of hope for the future.

At precisely 9:00 A.M., the President entered the Blue Room for the interview. He was garbed in the usual dark suite and tie, polished and extremely diplomatic. He was on the defensive. "Good morning. You must be Shar Dea?"

"Yes, I am. Good morning to you, Mr. President."

They both sat down.

"Now what's all this I hear about the peace movement?" the President asked.

"I'm sorry you've said that, Mr. President."

This took him off guard and made him express an uncomfortable feeling. He repositioned himself in his chair, as to dislodge any nervous twinges.

Shar Dea came right back with: "Please be very openminded and hear me out, if you will, Mr. President."

"That's fine with me."

"I come raptured in peace. My sole purpose in this life is to speak of peace—nothing else. When my mission is over, I will be gone. My message to you and the Pope is that world peace can only be obtained providing that the collective consciousness of the American nation assumes the responsibility for peace."

"May I speak now?" asked the President kindly.

"Please do."

"First of all, who are you and where did you come from?"

"That's not important."

"Well it is to me!" he said. "What about my credibility and integrity with whom I am speaking?"

"As far as we are concerned, you are the credibility and integrity of this nation—not me. Whatever I say to you comes from three very sacred places: moral consciousness of the world's populations, the planet's own consciousness, and God. And if you want me to prove it, I can."

"Do!"

Shar Dea paused for a moment, then said, "Would you like for me to levitate the table up to the ceiling, or speak the truth?"

"No nonsense. Let's talk."

"Mr. President, look at me straight in the eyes—both of them: eye-to-eye." The President followed her instructions and

159

readily gave her his full attention. "Mr. President, do the people of the world want and hope for peace?"

He quickly responded, "Yes."

"Would you desire to see an end to natural disasters, world wide, as much as possible?"

"Yes."

"In your heart, do you believe that God desires world peace?"

"Yes."

"Then why do you doubt my sincerity?"

"I . . . don't really know what you're getting at?"

Shar Dea repositioned her energies. "Listen, did you not feel truth in your answers to me?"

"Yes, I did feel truth."

Shar Dea felt an inner surge of life pass through her, and she said, "It's not me sitting here—it's the people, it's the planet, and it's God! . . ."

The President was taken by her last statement. He pulled back and took a moment to think. His face became more relaxed and tender. He leaned forward, and said to Shar Dea, "We need to discuss what we have to do, and I still want to know who you really are."

At that moment she knew that he heard the Voice from the Rock, too. "Let me tell you Mr. President, that there are no solutions, just actions. There's only good ahead."

The President got up and walked around to the back of his chair. He stopped and rested his hands on the antique, then suggested that they go into the garden and enjoy the cool crisp day of Autumn. She cheerfully agreed, and together they left for the back lawn. On the way, one of the White House aids excused himself, and said, "Mr. President, the Secretary would like to meet you at noon for lunch and discuss . . ."

The President interjected, "Thomas, tell the Secretary that I have a special engagement. I will see him at 2:00 P.M."

"Yes sir."

Then they continued to walk, and he said to Shar Dea, "I feel we have something more important and more urgent to talk about. Don't you agree?"

The late morning air was invigorating, calm, and colored bright blue, clear enough to see the moon diligently watching its mother, the Earth, below.

"America defaulted on a miracle? Please explain," requested the President.

"Do you not agree that the signing of the Declaration of Independence was one of the greatest events of mankind, Mr. President?"

"It certainly was a landmark event, I'll admit that!"

"Could you fathom the notion that events like that are inspired by God?"

"Sure, that's a possibility."

"Then could you host the assumption that those courageous Americans were the recipients of a deed from the Almighty!" prompted Shar Dea.

"I guess so!"

"Then let's try something for a moment. Please concentrate with all your mental faculties on this next question, and rethink it through."

"Ok."

"See yourself signing the Declaration of Independence, actually writing out your name," guided Shar Dea. For about 15 seconds there was complete silence. Then she asked, "Who's name did you sign?"

The President stuttered, and leaned back, indicating some sensation of stress. Then he slowly looked up at Shar Dea, saying with a great deal of hesitation, "William Floyd." Pausing for a moment, he then commented, "Were you trying to trick me?"

Her reply was swift. "No sir! Just sharing."

"Well then, who was he?" demanded the President.

"William Floyd was a soldier from New York who happened to be one of the signers of the Declaration of Independence."

The President was dumbfounded. He said, "Is that true?"

"Yes! I wanted you to feel it through, and let the knowledge of the past teach you about the future."

Within a couple of moments, he realized that there was something much larger and more important to know about that great event. He saw Shar Dea in her true light. "My dear," he said, "it is beyond my imagination to comprehend the power of mankind's collective consciousness which drew all those courageous men to the pen—declaring a society's freedom, hope, and pursuit of peace." The President took a few steps towards a neighboring tree. Tilting his head slightly to the side, he reminisced. "Look even deeper. See how long and how much suffering and sorrow it took to arrive at that point. It took less than three hundred years from the time of Columbus for the declaration of freedom to culminate."

Shar Dea lamented. "That's all but forgotten now. America has become contented, permissive, lazy, and above all, forgetful of the source behind the miracle of collective consciousness."

"But look at the great progress this country has made."

"True, very true," she said, "but only in material things and good gestures. There's a lot more to survival than coping and helping. It takes a concentrated effort, a drive, good leadership, and most importantly, a vision.

"America had a Civil War, two World Wars, Korea, a

161

Vietnam, and scores of other death defying battles to warn us of the decadence that exists. The missing element is the collective consciousness of the American people for world wide peace. Within collective process is the necessary machinery to generate the vision we so desperately need."

"But that's not just for the Americans to hope for," he said.

"That's the issue," she said. "The last political and quite provocative movement for humanity and freedom took place in America, in 1776, against the most powerful nation at that time, Great Britain. It was a declaration of the will of mankind to be free and pursue happiness. It must be preserved!—that's the American Dream.

"Ever since the signing of the Declaration of Independence, people from all corners of the globe have traveled, and even died to get to America. All this collective mental well wishing helped make the United States what it is. Now many of these people are showing hate and animosity towards the United States and its people. The collective consciousness of the world is reversing. Worse yet, Americans are becoming frustrated about the chaotic world affairs and not even concentrating on protecting the American Dream. Rather, we are witnessing today, that Americans are reactively defending a dream that they don't quite feel anymore. Continued world peace comes from creating peace, not defending peace."

"That's because people from other countries are envious of our higher standards of living," he remarked.

"Not quite true, Mr. President," retorted Shar Dea. "That's because the Americans have created an image of wealth, and behaviorally take their freedom for granted. There are plenty of obnoxious and fat American tourists out there doing a great job of destroying our image."

"Well we in America have always helped the other countries, and will always continue to do so."

Then Shar Dea's face saddened with the pain of wisdom. The President sensed the agony withheld, and said, "What's wrong, Shar Dea?"

In return she said, "Let me paint a picture for you, Mr. President. The world knows that New York City, San Francisco and Los Angeles are the Nation's financial centers. They, in effect, are the hub of world trade and many financial matters. Should California suffer a cataclysmic catastrophe, and L.A. and San Francisco become devastated, will the United States be fortunate enough to receive aid and finances from other countries abroad?

"If not, how will America survive from the loss and abrupt destruction of its financial controls and trade. Will it be able to rush to the scene and salvage the remains of a fleeing and devastated population, to say the least? If you cannot accurately answer this, then we are all in trouble."

"If what you are asking me is if, in fact, I know how this can all be managed, then the answer is a flat—No!"

"I only used California as an example," said Shar Dea, "but other institutions have already well documented that a major quake is destined for that area. The point I am trying to make is this: the world's population could easily fall apart because of their dependency on us as a nation of stability! If America had to concentrate on its own survival, then the rest of the world could easily slip, especially those countries that are dependent on us for economic and political reasons. It would be an awful time for the planet."

"Yes, I agree, but who can stop natural disasters from happening? Certainly not me!"

"Wrong! What I know and believe from the wisdom that's been granted me throughout all my being is this: the collective consciousness of the masses is the consciousness of the planet. Therefore, whatever is willed through thought over time is manifested into an experience of planetary reality.

"Just as the people who have grown accustomed to expect an earthquake in California, prepare for the inevitable, so do those who live in poverty expect more poverty, and those who see war expect to die in war. Unless the minds of mankind are re-kindled with hope for prosperity and peace, they will receive that which is most on their minds."

"Mr. President," said Shar Dea, "in the little book 'World Peace', I mention many critical concerns which you and I need to discuss."

"Well, let's begin with some of them," he said.

Shar Dea began: "First, I would like to talk about the 'killers of hope'. Killers of hope are what deteriorates the spirit of life within our hearts. Soon, it suffocates the soul and life tends to cease.

"On top of the list is the absence of a vision. Martin Luther King had a vision for equality where white and black children could join hands in play. We need to think strongly about that role of America—a land which is providing the opportunity for the Black race to fulfill a vision. Mr. President, what other land has provided a sanction for that kind of miracle? We need to protect their movement, educate the ignorant, and eliminate the cancerous prejudices of our land.

"America needs to have within its eyes a vision of peace. This means she must dream and speak of peace, and not of fear, or war, or of death. You must rise and surge forward, spark the light and proclaim hope with all that you are. America needs your direction, not as a President, but as the Father of Visions."

163

The President expressed a sense of awkwardness. "You make me feel as if I were a prophet!"

"But indeed you are!" she proclaimed. "More people voted for you than they did Christ! At least half the world's population hears you. Imagine if they listened to you and were inspired by you. Don't you realize how important and powerful you are to the individual? Forget politics and government for a moment. You are the threshold to world peace. You are the Father of a Nation of Visions, Mr. President. You are a politician, and you are my friend," she exclaimed with the might and force of an Empress.

"You make sense. I can move the people. All I must do is believe in it myself?" he replied with a question of doubt.

"When I called you 'my friend', did that bother you?" asked Shar Dea.

"No, not at all. As a matter of fact, Shar Dea, right now, you are my prophet and inspirator. Please accept my apologies for being an ignorant leader."

"You're not an ignorant leader, but simply a soul like everyone else, seeking a dream, and being tempted on your journey," responded Shar Dea with a maternal kindness. "There are so many responsibilities placed on your head, Mr. President, that to talk about a vision simply doesn't rank as a 'must do priority'—and that's where we all fail. It is a priority, and in my heart, I know that you see eye-to-eye with me."

"I'm beginning to see . . . see what really is happening," he commented with emotion. He then sighed. "You know, Shar Dea," he proclaimed, "I can't remember the last time I got up and gave a speech from my heart, and shouted with conviction and determination, to speak and to feel the spirit within me reach out and grasp the souls of all those desperate people who wait hopelessly for a vision. I am so taken by your presence. I feel good. I feel young in heart. I feel alive!"

"I believe in you, Mr. President."

"Well, you've certainly said a lot there, my little Empress." He paused for a moment, then asked, "What are we to do next?"

Shar Dea offered encouragement, "You are the leader of a great nation. Your priority in life is to inspire Americans, politicians, and the rest of humanity to strive for and bring peace back to their everyday thoughts. That's the essence of it all, Mr. President."

"To think Peace," he repeated.

"Yes! Mr. President."

# CHAPTER 33

# THE DIALECTIC DIALOGUE

*"Love, it is a wild, free-moving essence that edifies our beings, that glorifies our beings and gives credence to our beings, that brings back the youth in our beings; and if shared with another, truly love, Entity, it is the deepest intimate thing that any two humans can share with one another, that exalts them beyond time and space . . ."*
—Ramtha

Shar Dea's second Christmas season had passed and the period of transitioning was well underway. Spring had arrived and brought with it a scent of change. Both Michael and Donna were recognized internationally as leaders in the peace movement. They were extremely busy traveling to all four corners of the world advocating peace and speaking to local governments and Heads of State. Shar Dea was nominated for the Nobel Peace Prize and many world leaders were fully supportive of her peace effort, which was so dramatically embracing the world's populations. It was a time of change—an event long past due.

The Pope's quest for peace surged world wide like a storm. He wasted no time in keeping his commitments and mission. The role of the Pope definitely prompted world leaders to look inwardly and investigate their ambitions. At first, many political factions did not believe in the Pope's proclamation. However, when a nation expressed doubt or hesitation, the Pope and his envoys appeared at that nation's doorstep. The Pope along with thousands, and in some cases millions of supporters, petitioned for collaboration. Many government representatives were being forced to change their viewpoints.

It was working. The Catholic Church took precedence, and began establishing educational centers throughout Third World countries to set forth good will and programming. As each day passed, the Church became less and less bureaucratic. It poured millions of dollars into relief and education for the poor.

Religious populations, whether Catholic, Islamic, Hindu, Buddhist, or Hebrew, and so forth, united under the enthusiasm and commitment of the Pontiff. Religious rivalry was on the decline. Instead, cooperation and mutual trust seemed to be flourishing.

Unbeknown to most people, the negative elements on the planet were diminishing. Natural disasters were few and minimal in destruction and fatalities. Active volcanos, such as Mt. Etna in Sicily, showed tendencies of becoming less active and dormant. Meteorological patterns were becoming less extreme and more predictable. One of the greatest changes that was occurring was the sharp increase in marine life. This complimented the noticeable increase in migratory bird life throughout the world.

Scientists among the more advanced countries reaffirmed signs of improvement and balance in the biosphere. Prior to these efforts, the biosphere was in a very precarious state which was showing progressive worsening trends. Now, thanks to the international scientific communities' unanimous agreement, supported by most industrial nations, the need for ecological stability of the planet had been finally recognized. Deforestation and expansion into the remaining rain forests was being halted; now awaiting sponsorship from the governing institutions to protect the timberlands of the world.

Statistics were beginning to verify that productivity rates, world wide, were up. This was indicating consistent gains for many industries in most countries. Thus, one could surmise that workers were regaining self-respect and a sense of worth. Another result from this was that world food production was beginning to increase and, in the long term would help to reduce the threat of famine.

The political arena was one of the most visible areas of change. Terrorism had reached an all time low, and political solutions to many of the crises in the Middle East were well underway. Equally, if not more unprecedented, the Great City of the Omnipotent, Jerusalem, had unlocked its doors of secular segregation, and formal communication between the proprietor of the major religions was rigorously established.

Russia and the United States had recently opened up an educational and cultural exchange program for college students. Plans were also being developed to include two million children between ages ten through seventeen within this program. The basis for this agreement was to foster a relationship of trust between these two superpowers.

Chinese, Indian, Russian, American and French scientists had recently negotiated and been granted the opportunity to establish an International Scientific Lyceum. Its main function was to cultivate the sciences, advocating survival and protecting against the misuse of scientific research.

In the United States, the President set forth tremendous energies to rally the minds and souls of the American Spirit.

Opposition was present, and big business buckled down with descent and greed. But like a raging flood which seeks only one destination, and like a storm which carves its own path in the skies, the cries within the hearts of most peace loving Americans were being heard.

The Russian people were more successful. Ironically, in a country where religions do not flourish and God is not worshipped, people for the first time in Russian history, stood openly for peace. The energy behind the Russian people was so great that the Socialist government announced in the United Nation's General Assembly that it soon planned to tear down the symbolic divider of two worlds: the Berlin wall. The commitment and enthusiasm displayed by the Russians was profound. Needless to say, it was somewhat embarrassing for the American movement, which showed more doubt and hesitation.

All in all, within an eighteen-month period since Shar Dea first arrived on the shores of South Carolina, peace had finally caught on in the minds of mankind. Time was one of the most important elements. It was not a time for 'red tape' or arguments, rather a time for man to stand behind his heart and set forth the ingredients for his existence.

* * *

It was May 1st, and the warm fresh air once again recaptured the harshness of winter. Shar Dea and Michael were taking some time off to relax and be together. It had been extremely hectic for them during the past several months and they were both showing signs of strain and edginess.

That morning, while they watched the early morning news, something very pleasing was witnessed on TV. Most of the Communist Countries' celebrations of May Day showed a new appeal. The media picked up on the Communists' efforts to demonstrate their support for world peace. Michael was elated. Back in March, he had spoken to the Prime Minister of China, who shared with Michael the way he wished to advocate peace during the May Day celebrations.

"He did it, Shar Dea!" shouted Michael. "That's great! Do you know what this means, darling?"

Shar Dea was happy to see her man so excited about the parades on TV. "Please tell me what the Prime Minister said, Michael?"

"When I spoke to the Prime Minister back then, he told me that: 'If all Communist countries would unite under one theme for peace, then the attainment of peace would be inevitable in the near future'."

"Now I see it! Look! All the parades that have been

167

broadcasted from each Communist country began the same way—each with exactly 1,000 children evenly split between girls and boys in procession. Each child was wearing a white suite or dress and affixed upon the child's heart, a red rose. It's amazing! He made an effort to communicate with other communist leaders and accomplished his vision," exclaimed Michael.

"You're right, sweetheart! The peace movement is truly becoming more visible. I hope that it continues and steadily grows."

"It will! I feel it in my blood," affirmed Michael.

"That's good," she said. "It's all in the hands of nature now. There is so much taking place on this planet in the unseen world that a psychic would be shocked, literally speaking," giggled Shar Dea.

Shar Dea leaned back and rested her head on the sofa. She had on her favorite rainbow smock and looked quite seductive for such an early hour. As Michael passed her, his eyes firmly glanced her, and he humored her in the manner of an English gentleman: "Tea . . . or . . . me?"

Her reply was more realistic: "I'll take you kind sir. And, if you please, hold the 'eggs benedict'. Thank you!"

Michael extended his hands outward for her; they caressed and ascended to their scenic bedroom which overlooked the ocean. As they lowered their minds into the vision of passion, the brilliant sounds of the Sun radiated over the eastern horizon and echoed throughout their souls.

* * *

At 9:00 A.M. in San Francisco, Tony Yera picked up the phone, and dialed the East Coast. "Hello, Shar Dea?" he said. "I hope I didn't wake you. Isn't it noon back there?"

Shar Dea greeted him, "Good morning, Tony. How are things going?"

"Everything is fantastic here and running smoothly." "Great!"

Tony was very excited. "I got an update for you folks, and it's quite an accomplishment. According to my records, the combined releases from all our publishers, totals over fifty million copies of your little book World Peace. Now that's amazing!"

"Yow!" blurted Shar Dea. Tony continued with his report. "Say what you want. But the best part is that the book is now being printed in twenty-three languages. . . . Well how's that?"

"Tony, you're great!" complimented Shar Dea. "Not once since we had our meeting over a year ago did I have to worry or tell you about running the business."

168

Tony felt honored. "Thank you for your kind words, Sister Shar Dea."

"Tony, are the proceeds going into the Peace Movement Relief Fund?"

"Yes, we are very careful with our tracking and keeping accurate accounting of that money. After expenses, the average balance of the fund is nineteen million dollars. Total revenue generated from book sales was close to forty-one million dollars. As more books are being released, the return will increase. This will give us the freedom to broaden our educational network tremendously, and permit us to reach the impoverished countries at absolute minimum cost to the people."

"You really have things worked out, Tony. May The Almighty Father bless your heart."

"I hope to see you soon," petitioned the former priest.

"Well, Donna, Michael, and I might just be coming out your way in a couple of months."

"Really."

"Yes, we will," she said.

"For a vacation?"

"Aha! Maybe you would like to join us? We've been planning on renting a schooner for a month's cruise around the Southern Pacific."

Tony's response didn't favor the opportunity.

Shar Dea exclaimed, "No? Sailing's not your style . . . How about if we build a small chapel on board for you?"

Tony stood his ground.

"No, again uh? Well you're always welcomed in our hearts."

Tony said his 'goodbye's, and concluded with: "May God always be with you."

"Thanks millions. Chao!"

Shar Dea gently hung up the phone, and contemplated for a minute, absorbing the information that Tony Yera presented. Michael passed nearby, and Shar Dea perked from her thoughts and said to her man, "What a character Tony is." Then she nudged over to Michael, as would a little girl ready to bribe her father, and hinted, "Well, Michael, what's for lunch. I'm hungry."

"How about a nice long walk on the beach to Chuck's Seafood House?" suggested Michael.

"That's five miles from here! Are you crazy?"

"Oh, come on! We'll be back before nightfall," insisted Michael.

Then after a moment of hesitation, Shar Dea let go a big smile, shrugged her shoulders, and said: "Ay! Why not? I'll grab something to nibble on now, so as to hold me over for a while."

The sojourn into thought was soon to begin. She gathered up

a few things: sandles, a towel, and an extra beach shirt. The door shut tight; the house slowly disappeared behind them. The sand was cool, the breeze gentle, and the sun warm. Michael felt vivacious and presented his masculinity well. Seagulls and sandpipers circled overhead and offered refreshing chatters of life.

"Nature is so beautiful," said Shar Dea. "When I look into the ocean, my eyes see its rhythmic flow. When I raise my eyes toward the sky, my mind drifts like the sea. It's beyond me. So much to know and explore. Humans should be more occupied in this pursuit; that's what nature is—a pursuit of true knowledge."

"True, my Empress," commented Michael, "but man is preoccupied with ego and greed. He is so contaminated with it that the innocent children of this planet find themselves victimized by the same disease before they reach their fifth birthday."

"The innocence of a child is most sacred and beautiful," voiced Shar Dea.

"Speaking of children, Shar Dea, when I first met you, we had a discussion about your age. Using today's standards of time, what is your relative age?"

"About fourteen. I'm still a child, and see the world as most sensible children do. That's one of the reasons why many leaders have listened to me. They all see me as a intellectual adult. However, I speak as a child in an adult body—simply innocent."

Michael's mind became instantly naughty. "Well then," he opinionated, "Can you explain some of your adult proficiencies?"

"What do you mean?"

"You sure know how to make love," he stated comically.

His 'aft' received a wack for that. "Thank you," he said. "I deserved that."

As they walked, the beach became completely deserted and mysteriously quiet, offering a feeling that something unusual was going to happen. Shar Dea stopped and stood very still. She turned towards the ocean, and it too was very still. Nothing moved. "Michael," she said, "it's been exactly two years since you rescued me on the beach, the morning I woke up from the electrical storm. Since that time we've grown extremely close. We are now one."

Sincerely Michael looked into her eyes and said, "Yes, that's true."

"Michael, in this sensation of oneness, I feel a mystique surrounding us. Please let me know what you see: Is the ocean perfectly still in your eyes?"

"No. I can see some gentle waves about," he replied.

They walked a few more steps; then she said to him, "Now, in my eyes, I see an ocean in the sky, the heavens below me. I see all: rich in color, sound, and movement. I see myself standing alone. I feel the celestial breeze, and my hair is gently fluffing in front of my face."

All was quiet. All was still.

Then Michael tenderly spoke. "My dear, I also see the ocean perfectly still. I see myself alone, garbed in a white robe. My hands are extending downwards, and a silver light is emanating from them, and into the darkened cosmos."

All became white and great clouds began to appear about them. Soon they disappeared in the transparent mountains of the skies.

"Shar Dea, my Empress, does this mean that we are to part and sojourn separately?"

"No," she said softly. "It means that we have seen the future tense of our lives. We are to find different destinies, with others, and for others."

Michael softly spoke, "But we are one."

"Yes, she said, "and we always have been one."

"I understand," said Michael.

Shar Dea replied, "Michael, I see you with . . ." But Michael interrupted, and said, "Shar Dea, those visions are within me. I know who I'll share my next life with and I am grateful."

"You have learned to retain secrets well, Michael," inspired Shar Dea.

"Shar Dea, the water is now still, perfectly still."

"Good. We are on the same chord." The perfect white sky turned pastel pink, as the celestial breeze quickened. A tint of earthly blue sky beckoned in to remind Shar Dea and Michael of their time and place.

The Earth's air once again filtered through their bodies; they embraced and resumed their walk along the beach. They held hands, splashed and danced in the water. In their hearts a new life had been offered. They accepted it with faith and belief in the infinite.

"How do you feel about your life?" asked Shar Dea.

"Completely changed and free," he replied. "Right from the first time I saw you, I believed in you, though, I resisted it for a long, long time. Now, today, I am here. I stand alone. I stand with you. I feel totally at peace with myself, and yet, one with you also."

"It's amazing how we learn to be more than ourselves without ever losing the feeling of inward oneness," she said.

"I see myself differently, too" he said. "Like the yin and the yang, so to speak. Inwardly, it is the freedom of expression. I say what I feel, and what I know. Outwardly, I say what I envision. Whatever my inner eye can see in the universe in front of me is mine to enjoy and share, for those are my visions. Inward or outward, I feel like a God, but don't understand the God in me. That keeps me going. It's so simple, Shar Dea, we are what we are forever. Perfect stillness is outside of our souls. It's for us to enjoy and not possess."

"What do you mean by 'perfect stillness', Michael?"

"It's just my way of expressing the outside universe, seen or unseen, and how it relates to us. You see, our souls are forever changing. The greater the soul, the greater its knowledge of ALL THAT EXISTS. I see no end in life, Shar Dea. It's infinite."

"You mean that there's no such thing as death?"

"There sure is death! And, may I add—no guarantee on life, either," replied Michael.

"You're getting knowledgeable, my masculinity. When I first saw your eyes, they were truly those of a child. Now, I see wisdom in your heart of a child. Changed you are, as well as silly. I love you for that, Michael. You have grown so much in such a short time."

"I love you for choosing me as your masculinity," Michael said romantically.

"Well, you chose me for my femininity, too!"

"I guess we chose each other simultaneously," responded Michael.

"What about death?" asked Shar Dea.

"Death is simply the choice not to seek eternal peace. We can change for the worst and still find knowledge. However, if you find that your search for knowledge leads you back to what you have already learned, then not much has been accomplished—a prelude for death."

Shar Dea paused for a minute and uttered not a word. They took a few steps, then she knelt down on the sand and said, "God, every soul on this planet today has migrated here from Lemuria, Atlantis, and from someplace in the past. Why?"

Then Michael bowed his head and said, "In order to escape death and find peace."

Holding Michael's hand, she looked up at the sky, and with a tear in her eye, said, "This time, Ara E Hum, will they find Peace?"

* * *

Dusk was nearly complete by the time Michael and Shar Dea arrived at the beach house. Both exhausted and somewhat dehydrated, they made their way into the kitchen for a cool thirst quencher.

"I'm going to take a nice hot bath," said Shar Dea.

Michael watched her lovely body slowly move its way up the stairs and into their bedroom. He soon followed and took a

172

shower in the guest bathroom.

About a half-hour later, Michael was in the bedroom taking a pair of shorts out of the dresser drawer. Shar Dea came up behind him, and said, "I feel a touch of melancholy. Please hold me."

Michael held her tightly. His lips proceeded to tantalize her neck as he spoke of his love for her. Naked and loving, the children of peace left their thoughts and shared the moment in love.

Michael awoke only to find his love in a gentle dream, as she lay beside him. He quietly got out of bed, and as he did, noticed that the moon was beginning to surface on the ocean's horizon. Enthused, he went downstairs to the den to retrieve his camera. He wanted to capture the moon in its glory.

Up and stretching, Shar Dea saw the upper section of the golden moon peeking out above the horizon. "Magnificant," she uttered. She wanted to see it ascend.

The noises Michael made while setting up his tripod on the deck signalled his where abouts. Shar Dea brought two glasses of red wine to toast a wonderous and victorious day.

The moon's color delicately changed to the purist white as it gently ascended upwards. To add to the beauty of the night's environment, a small, but entertaining electrical storm was racing in from the south. At one point, Michael was snapping pictures of the moon and the storm in the same scene. Soon the mid-night thunder shower squeezed out the moon and darkened the skies, except for the sporadic lightening it emanated.

"Shar Dea, this little rain cloud is moving extremely fast. I'm going to bring my camera gear inside."

"Go ahead, sweetheart. I'm going to stay outside until I feel the rain."

"Suit yourself, love," said Michael.

About ten minutes had passed and the sounds of thunder were upon the beach house. Michael was in the den packing his camera equipment, when suddenly the whole house lit up from the storm's lightning. In the next moment, a tremendous, piercing sound shook the house. Michael stiffened. "Shar Dea!" he screamed. He ran out to the deck. His eyes were mortified. He looked, but could not believe what had happened. He stood still, not knowing what to do or what to say.

Then she said in a soft and curious voice, "So you are Michael."

**PEACE**

173

# About the Author

Robert Vincent Gerard received degrees in engineering, social-psychology, a masters in management, and is pursuing a Ph.D. He finds his niche somewhere between an educator and a humanitarian. Improving the condition of American workers and their relationship with management is his current focus.

Most of his work is influenced by the teachings of Jung, Fromm, Krishnamurti, and Christ. He feels that they presented many truths, and as we experience these truths, we find ourselves and others around us becoming more self-knowing and peaceful.

"To see the unseen, as well as touch it, is simply growth," he says. "To give full attention to what you perceive is knowledge in the purest sense." To share these things is his journey. To inspire others to understand that happiness is love emanating from within, is but his life's work.

The author now finds San Francisco, California, to be his new home: "It's people oriented; it's where the old folks are just as curious as the young people, just a tad bit slower. There's more to life and nature out here than anywhere else I've lived."